PRAISE FOR

THE
THIRTEENTH
FAIRY

★ "This series debut has something for most readers—a complex female heroine, middle school angst, plenty of action, and magic—which will leave them eagerly turning the pages."

—*School Library Journal*, starred review

"Equal parts whimsical and adventure-packed . . . A refreshing twist on well-known fairy tales."

—*Kirkus Reviews*

"A fast-paced fantasy that Land of Stories fans will enjoy."

—*Publishers Weekly*

"Fans of fantasy and fairy tales of all kinds will delight in catching all the references to classics."

—*Booklist*

THE
STOLEN
SLIPPERS

ALSO BY MELISSA DE LA CRUZ

THE CHRONICLES OF NEVER AFTER

The Thirteenth Fairy

THE DESCENDANTS SERIES

The Isle of the Lost

Return to the Isle of the Lost

Rise of the Isle of the Lost

Escape from the Isle of the Lost

Because I Was a Girl: True Stories for Girls of All Ages
(Edited by Melissa de la Cruz)

THE
STOLEN
SLIPPERS

MELISSA DE LA CRUZ

ROARING BROOK PRESS
New York

Published by Roaring Brook Press
Roaring Brook Press is a division of Holtzbrinck Publishing Holdings Limited Partnership
120 Broadway, New York, NY 10271 • mackids.com

Our books may be purchased in bulk for promotional, educational, or business use.
Please contact your local bookseller or the Macmillan Corporate and Premium
Sales Department at (800) 221-7945 ext. 5442 or by email at
MacmillanSpecialMarkets@macmillan.com.

Library of Congress Cataloging-in-Publication Data
Names: De la Cruz, Melissa, 1971– author.
Title: The stolen slipper / Melissa De la Cruz. Other titles: At head of title: Never after
Description: First edition. | New York : Roaring Brook Press, 2021. |
Series: Never After ; [2] | Audience: Ages 10 to 14. | Audience: Grades 4–6. |
Summary: Filomena Jefferson-Cho and her friends Jack Stalker, Alistair, and Gretel
are once again in Never After, to help Gretel fulfill a promise to her father to recover
the glass slipper he made for her cousin Hortense, which was stolen by the cunning
and manipulative Cinderella, who is determined to become Princess of Eastphalia—
to do that, the friends will have to infiltrate the castle, and, of course,
avoid being eaten by monsters.
Identifiers: LCCN 2021012395 | ISBN 9781250311238 (hardcover)
Subjects: LCSH: Cinderella (Tale)—Adaptations. | Characters and characteristics in
literature—Juvenile fiction. | Princesses—Juvenile fiction. | Magic—Juvenile fiction. |
Friendship—Juvenile fiction. | Adventure stories. | Fairy tales. | CYAC: Fairy tales—
Fiction. | Characters in literature--Fiction. | Princesses—Fiction. | Friendship—Fiction. |
Adventure and adventurers—Fiction. | Racially mixed people—Fiction. | LCGFT:
Action and adventure fiction. | Fairy tales.
Classification: LCC PZ7.D36967 St 2021 | DDC 813.6 [Fic]—dc23
LC record available at https://lccn.loc.gov/2021012395

First edition, 2022
Series design by Aurora Parlagreco
Printed in the United States of America by LSC Communications, Harrisonburg, Virginia

ISBN 978-1-250-31123-8 (hardcover)
1   3   5   7   9   10   8   6   4   2

For Mike and Mattie
My heroes

Contents

THE
STOLEN
SLIPPERS

OF SISTERS AND SLIPPERS

Once upon a time in Eastphalia,
there lived a girl, beautiful and sweet,
who had very small feet
and was always discreet.
Her father had died,
her mother was tired,
her sister was just as petite.
She met her Prince Charming,
who was very disarming
and made her life complete.

But then came the Beauty,
with eyes like braziers
and a voice of snakes and sandpaper,
who stole the prince at a ball.
Cinderella stole everything,
including the glass slippers—
leaving our sweet girl nothing at all.
For this tale is about
Hortense and Beatrice,
two sisters
not wicked in the least—
more like betrayed,
for the glass slippers were Hori's!
As was the prince!
And the happily ever after!
So this is the story of their friends—
Clever Filomena,
Dashing Jack,
Adorable Alistair,
and Glamorous Gretel—
and how they get it all back.

PART ONE

Wherein . . .

Filomena and her friends return to
Never After.

They discover a house made of candy.

And they meet the wickedly fun
sisters of Rosewood.

CHAPTER ONE

A SLIPPER-Y SLOPE, PUN DEFINITELY INTENDED

"Anyone care to enlighten me on what's happening with this Cinderella scandal, or is this going to be another one of those things I have to discover on my own?" Filomena asks the gang when, after crossing the Bridge to Nowhere high in the mountains above Los Angeles, they arrive back in Never After. After paying the toll to the disgruntled billy goat, Mr. Gruff, they land somewhere on the eastern border of Westphalia, a place that, until very recently, twelve-year-old Filomena thought only existed in her favorite books—and her imagination.

She still can't quite believe she's actually walking through a dark and dangerous forest beside the ever-so-dashing Jack the Giant Stalker and his lovable sidekick, Alistair.

"Sure, happy to enlighten," says Gretel, who has stopped briefly to adjust her bespoke travel cloak. The Cobbler's fashionable daughter has quickly become one of Filomena's closest friends and never misses an opportunity to shed light on Never After's particulars and peculiarities. Gretel explains that they're back in Never After to get the glass slippers from Cinderella, who is apparently a spoiled brat and not at all an innocent pawn of nefarious stepmother schemes.

"Slippers? I thought it was just the one," Filomena says.

Gretel waves her hand. "That's just another fairy tale fallacy. Both glass slippers were stolen. Stolen *Slippers*, with an *S*. You can't wear just one shoe!"

"But didn't Cinderella *own* the glass slippers?" Filomena asks.

Gretel looks horrified. "Lies! All lies! They were never hers!"

Filomena knows Gretel is telling the truth, but it's still hard to believe at times. Despite being a true Nevie at heart (a *super* superfan of the Never After books, duh—also called a *stan* by those who spend too much time on the internet), there are things even *Filomena* doesn't know.

Filomena remains a little unclear as to which stories are

"true" and which are made up. Because, judging from the Never After books, it appears the stories everyone grew up hearing are completely wrong. For instance, the famously evil "thirteenth fairy," Carabosse—the one who cursed Sleeping Beauty—isn't evil at all. She is none other than Filomena's loving aunt. Which makes Filomena . . . Sleeping Beauty? Since Filomena is in sixth grade and hates going to sleep, it's hard to believe she could grow up to experience the terrible fate Carabosse foresaw for her (ogres, bloodshed, tragedy; see book one of this series, ha!).

And now, apparently Cinderella is not some sweet orphan forced to escape the wickedness of her stepsisters, but rather some kind of thief?

This is what Filomena is pondering as she ducks under vines and branches, making her way through a land that still feels strange, like a half-forgotten dream. It's not a place where she feels at home quite yet.

Of course, Westphalia has seen better days. The thorn-covered kingdom finally woke from an enchanted sleep once Filomena and her friends broke the spell holding them captive by chasing away Queen Olga of Orgdale (seriously, go read book one!), but there's still a long way to go before it returns to its former glory. The once-bustling village square is empty and abandoned, and the fields are barren and fallow after seasons of neglect. Filomena's not sure how much time has passed in Never After since she went home to North Pasadena. To her it was only a few weeks, but time works differently on this side of the portal. In the time she's been away, a regent has been installed in the castle, but also the villagers are hoping King Vladimir's heir will return.

King Vladimir's heir . . . That would be *Sleeping Beauty*, right? Meaning one Filomena Jefferson-Cho of North Pasadena, who also happens to be Princess Eliana of Westphalia? *She is the princess of the very kingdom through which they are traveling!* And yes, she still has that glowing scar on her forehead . . . but you can only see it if you say the spell just right. She's a princess. But she doesn't feel like a princess.

Anyhoo . . . are we getting ahead of ourselves? Let's rewind, shall we?

(Cue traipsing backward through the woods, across the bridge, and to Filomena's house in North Pasadena, California; back to her doorstep, where Jack, Alistair, and Gretel showed up; back to the dinner table where Filomena sat with her paranoid parents.

Heck, let's rewind even further than that!)

In her Hollywood studio, Gretel warns the Cobbler's elves that she's going away on a little vacay and asks them to screen all her calls. She, of course, packs her bag as if she's going to Paris—only the highest of high fashion allowed. Never mind that Olga of Orgdale is still out there, plotting her revenge with her terrifying ogre minions. Danger schmanger! Chunky wedges, rhinestone-covered jumpsuits, and cool ripped jeans—check, check, check! She is ready for the next adventure!

Meanwhile, Alistair is grumbling on and on about hunting

for cheeseburgers as he and Jack Stalker prepare to embark on yet another life-threatening, world-saving escapade. Ever the reliable one, Jack promises they'll stop for a quick meal of those so-called "cheeseburgers" once they collect Filomena.

Over in North Pasadena, Filomena's parents are getting ready to say goodbye to their one precious child, rattling off a checklist of items for her to remember before leaving the house: safety whistle, foghorn, headlamp, and the latest tracking app so they can watch her every footstep while she plunges deep into another world.

"It goes like this, on your face," says Filomena's mother helpfully as she straps the headlamp around her daughter's forehead.

"It's the best kind; it illuminates up to fifty feet!" adds her dad, who's rocking on his heels in pride.

"Uhhhh, thanks, guys," says their dutiful daughter (who will remove it as soon as she is able). Both of her parents are practically beaming—pun definitely intended—with pride.

"Remember," says her mom. "You are braver than you know."

Filomena packed all the Never After books she thought she might need for the trip, as well as her trusty Dragon's Tooth sword that was gifted by the Dragons of the Deep. She may not have asked for the responsibility of setting the stories straight and telling the tales true, and writing the thirteenth book, but now that the job's hers, it's one she's taking very seriously. As seriously as she can, anyway, without knowing exactly what she's doing. It seems the books are writing themselves, even if she's somehow helping to complete them by simply surviving the adventures and obstacles that come her way. And sure, she may be a good student and an avid reader to boot, but she's also still learning her role as the embodiment of the thirteenth fairy's powers and duties.

Once the gang is all assembled, Filomena follows her friends through the forest, ruminating on Cinderella and what may be the truth behind the one we all *think* we know so well.

"Do Cinderella's—I mean, do the Stolen Slippers have anything to do with the prophecy?" she asks, leaves crunching underfoot. She's so deep in thought, and the others are so intent on getting to where they're going, that no one seems to notice the shadowy, stealthy presence that has noticed *them*. And is following them.

"You mean *the* Prophecy?" says Gretel with a grimace.

Alistair's face turns pale, and even Jack looks uncomfortable. "No one likes to talk about it," Jack says quietly.

"Because no one wants it to be true," says Alistair.

Filomena nods. She doesn't want to think about it, either. Because if the Prophecy is true, then the worst is yet to come. Jack warned them that even if Olga has indeed returned to Orgdale, her ogres still patrol the edges of Westphalia and keep everyone on their toes. Only a few places in Never After are free from the witch queen's reign of terror. And though

Filomena knows there may be danger lurking nearby, she can't stay quiet—she has too many questions.

"You guys, Aladdin's Lamp and Cinderella's glass slippers are somehow connected to the Prophecy, right?" she asks.

Before anyone can reply, a thunderbolt cracks. A loud boom echoes overhead, rumbling through the sky and making the ground shake beneath their feet. Filomena steadies herself before she can topple over, but just as she gains her footing again, lightning strikes down around her and mocking laughter fills the air—the signature sound of an Ogre's Wrath.

Whatever was tracking them stealthily is now tracking them not so stealthily.

With all the heroism he can muster, Alistair tackles her to the ground just as another thunderbolt hits and screams, "Look out!"

Or not, she thinks as she slams into the forest floor. Though she's appreciative of her friend trying to protect her, swan diving face-first into the dirt was not what she had in mind when she imagined returning to this place. Or, at the very least, it's not what she hoped for.

She certainly can't say she's missed *this* part in particular. The ogre attacks. The imminent danger that seems to follow them at every turn. The near-death experiences. THE HORROR!

Gretel screams, which makes Alistair scream even louder in response.

Filomena winces, seeing as Alistair is still deadweight on top of her. "Hello, still down here!" she grumbles over her ringing ears.

But Alistair can't seem to hear her. Probably because his heart is trying to pound right out of his chest.

The group looks over at the Cobbler's daughter. "Gretel! Are you okay?" asks Jack as he rushes to check on her.

"I'm fine!" Gretel shrieks. "But my white jeans—they're ruined!"

The others let out one combined sigh. Whether it's due to relief or irritation, no one can be sure.

Filomena would roll her eyes if all this dirt weren't stuck between her eyelashes. She spits out a mouthful of mud pie. "Hey, G? Next time, can you try to scream only if you're in trouble? We've talked about this."

"Yeah, we thought you were hurt," agrees Jack.

Alistair nods. "That *is* usually why people scream, Gretel."

Jack shakes his head with a wry smile.

"You guys try getting mud stains out of white denim," cries Gretel. "Why am I even here?!"

"You're the one who insisted that we have to get your friend's shoes back!" argues Jack.

"First of all, they are high-end, one-of-a-kind custom glass slippers with magical properties. Second of all, Hortense is my cousin! Third of all, Filomena's right, the Prophecy—"

Another thunderbolt cracks, and this time the lightning zaps Gretel's hairpins and, subsequently, her carefully styled hair. Her eyes bulge as each strand of hair stands at wicked attention. The rest of the crew waits until the last of the hair spray sizzles out.

Jack pats at the tiny sparks and embers on Gretel's head. He tries not to laugh as Gretel stares at him in disbelief. Then he chuckles nervously, saying, "It looks fine to me."

Gretel swats his hand away. "I can't believe my father is relaxing in Boca while I'm here, getting electrocuted and stalked by giant ogres." She lets out an exaggerated groan.

Filomena, still on the ground, blinks at her friends. "Hey, guys, um, what happened to the sun?"

"Speaking of giant ogres . . . ," Alistair starts. He clears his throat and points to the gargantuan beast of an ogre that's now directly behind Gretel, towering over her.

Gretel looks up and says, "I told you!"

A silent moment passes while everyone holds their breath and stares at the giant beast. Then, Gretel screams again. This time the sound is bloodcurdling.

Alistair pops up at once and holds a hand out to Filomena, an apologetic smile on his face. "At least this time she has a reason to scream, am I right?"

Filomena takes his hand, and he yanks her to her feet. She grins back. "You've got a point there!"

The vines on Jack's arms, which he can release and lengthen at will, are busy wrapping around the ogre as he tries to take down the oversized oaf. "Little help, guys?" he calls.

"Oh, right," says Alistair as he and Filomena unsheathe

their Dragon's Tooth swords. They're just about to charge the ogre when its face contorts. Its eyes pop open in shock. A loud throaty grunt escapes its mouth, causing the ground to tremble. It starts to sway like it's about to fall.

Another scream is heard, yet again belonging to Gretel, which is shocking to no one. What *is* shocking, however, is her incredible rage.

With the fury of, well, a Fury, she stabs the ogre repeatedly—with the pair of heavy-duty fabric scissors that she never travels without. "That's for my white jeans!" A few quick stabs. The ogre tilts some more. "That's for my hair!" The ogre drops to its knees, nearly crushing Jack in the process (who just barely leapt out of the way). Another fury of stabs from Gretel. "And that's for almost squashing my friend!"

The ogre backs away, trips on a branch, and crashes to the ground.

"Okay, Gretel," says Alistair cautiously, holding his hands out. "I think you got him. Do you mind putting those away?"

"Sorry. Phew, that was like therapy." Gretel wipes the blades clean of the ogre's green blood with her hankie. "Oh man, do you think I killed him?" she asks as she sheathes the hot-pink scissors. They slide seamlessly into the tailor-made pocket in her coat, designed solely for situations like this.

Jack shakes his head. "No. Probably just gave him a few cuts. Ogre skin is almost impenetrable. He's lucky you didn't use your Dragon's Tooth sword! But we should disappear before he wakes up!"

"Have you ever looked into anger management?" Filomena teases Gretel as they back away from the fallen ogre. The Cobbler's daughter works with such demanding clientele in a customer-service setting; Filomena has no idea how she gets through each day without ever cutting anyone with those rhinestone-covered fabric scissors.

Gretel laughs. "No, but I have started journaling recently. It's a great outlet. Same with salt baths and—"

Another thunderbolt strikes, interrupting her. It's followed by the sound of massive, booming footsteps that seem to be getting closer and closer.

Alistair cuts in with "Okay, everyone. Can we talk about self-care later? We've got a little bit of an *ogre-pocalypse* here—" A bolt of lightning narrowly misses him as he jumps out of the way. In the same moment, a mighty roar is heard, followed by that all-too-familiar menacing laughter.

A troop of ogres appears, arms swinging as they hack through the dense foliage. Branches and leaves hit the ground just before giant ogre feet stomp over them, crushing them to smithereens. Filomena briefly thinks the ogres are taking the phrase "crisp autumn leaves" to the next level and bets her writer parents would appreciate the imagery. Although they certainly wouldn't appreciate the irony—or the danger that has found their precious daughter once again.

Filomena and her friends take off running then, with Jack Stalker guarding the rear. He pauses to unleash vines from his arms, tripping the ogres and slowing them down.

"That never gets old, dude," shouts Alistair with a grin, looking back at Jack.

Filomena smiles. Despite the mud and screaming, the ogres and the near-death experience, she can't help but think to herself how good it is to be back with her friends. And to be fighting alongside Jack Stalker, the handsome hero of the Never After books. They could always count on Jack, master of those wild vines, to set them free.

ßTEPSISTERS AND ßLIPPERS

Once Filomena and her friends manage to find safety, they settle in an open clearing, sprawling out on the grass to catch their breath. With Jack's help they outran the ogres, who soon gave up the chase. The monstrous beasts rumbled through the forest, headed the other way, deciding that a group of kids wasn't worth derailing their original mission.

"Good. They're back to their regular patrols," says Jack, watching the ogres retreat through his Seeing Eye, a handy device that works like a powerful telescope, capable of seeing anything or anyone. "I think they've given up."

Filomena exhales as her heart slows to its regular beat. She's conveniently forgotten how much cardio is required in Never After. "Gretel, you were saying? About the slippers?"

Gretel sits up, leaning on one elbow. "Okay, it's kind of a long story," she begins. "Anyway, a long, long time ago, my dad made some . . . magic shoes. Like, *insane* magic shoes. And not just any old shoes; these are glass slippers that don't crack when you wear them and that reveal and greatly enhance the true beauty of the wearer. They have other secret powers as well."

"Secret powers?" asks Alistair. "Like what?"

Gretel rolls her eyes. "I don't know! That's why they're called secret, duh!"

"But they're *not* Cinderella's?" Filomena asks, double-checking.

"No. Like I told you, Cinderella's story is a lie," says Gretel. "It's strange, because in the mortal world, you guys think everything's already happened. But in Never After, it hasn't. There's still time to make sure the wrong thing doesn't take place."

"So if the glass slippers aren't Cinderella's, whose are they?"

"Well, that's the thing," replies the Cobbler's daughter. "My dad made them years and years ago for his sister."

Filomena wrinkles her nose. She's so sure of Cinderella's

story . . . at least, the way it's been told, over and over, in countless books and movies in the mortal world: Cinderella, a young lady of means, was the daughter of a widowed father who remarried to a horrid, greedy hag with two awful daughters of her own. When her father died, Cinderella was turned into a servant in her own house. Next, salvation: a fairy godmother, a makeover of fantastic proportions with those famous glass slippers, a royal ball, a marriage to a prince, and a happily ever after.

Gretel continues, "When my aunt passed away, my cousins, Hortense and Beatrice, inherited the slippers. Anyway, a while ago my cousins wrote that something terrible had happened: The glass slippers were missing! They were heartbroken because those shoes were one of the last of their mother's belongings they owned."

Filomena nods, thinking how she might feel if something special to her own mother was taken from her.

"Those slippers have very strong magic in them, and if they fall into the wrong hands, well . . . you guys know the Prophecy," says Gretel.

Filomena solemnly recites the verses out loud.

Thirteen fairies to this world were born.
Thirteen fairies of ogres' scorn.
Thirteen blessings the fairies gave;
All the gifts that ogres crave.
If fairies' gifts fall into ogres' hands . . .

Filomena can't bear to speak the final lines of the Prophecy.

The three of them nod gravely.

Gretel leans back on the grass again, crossing her arms under her head like a pillow. "Dad would have come himself, but he's not as strong as he used to be. He said it's up to me to get them back. For some reason, he chose to trust me with this over Hansel. Probably because Hansel isn't as detail oriented as I am."

Alistair nods. "Well, Hansel *is* an artist."

"So am I!" says Gretel. "Couture is as much of an art as baking cakes!"

Alistair's cheeks redden, an unspoken apology clear on his face.

Gretel's tone softens. "Anyway, if I hadn't met you guys, I wouldn't have even known how to get back here." She smiles bashfully. "We've got to find the Stolen Slippers and return them to their rightful owner as soon as possible. Especially since, according to the Prophecy, we don't have much time . . ."

Jack chimes in then. "As soon as Gretel told us the story of the sisters and their shady stepsister, Alistair and I knew right away: Cinderella is the culprit."

"So Cinderella is your cousins' stepsister?" asks Filomena.

Gretel nods emphatically. "Yes, and she's definitely the only one who had the opportunity. She lived in their house.

And talk about motive. She was always jealous of my cousins. She's always resented them for some reason."

Filomena nods thoughtfully. "But are you guys *sure* Cinderella would steal them? I'm just saying, in my world—our world, Gretel, you know as well as I do how the story goes."

"And how outrageously untrue it is, yes!" Gretel insists. "Trust me on this. The Cobbler is my *father*. Hori and Bea are my cousins, and they've been slandered by this fairy tale! They aren't evil at all! They cared for Cinderella! They took her in when no one else would! And this is how she repays them, by stealing the most precious heirlooms they own!"

"And how does this all relate to the Prophecy?" asks Filomena.

"I'm not quite sure, but I know it's important," says Gretel. "Dad wouldn't have sent me back here otherwise. He's really worried. We've got to get those slippers back from Cinderella, stat!"

"And if we don't?"

"Well, if the Prophecy's anything to go by, I'm pretty sure the fate of Never After rests on it," says Gretel, turning to Jack for support. "Dad kind of hinted as much."

Jack nods. "Right." He doesn't say any more. No one likes to think about the Prophecy too much.

"The fate of our world, in jeopardy? What are we waiting for, then?" Alistair chides, jumping to his feet.

"Exactly! Step one, we have to find my cousins. They can

help us track down Cinderella. There's just one problem," says Gretel. "I have no idea how to get to Rosewood Manor."

"Hmm, that is a problem," says Filomena. "But maybe there's a way to figure it out." She sits up, shrugs off her backpack, and locates what she's looking for. *Bingo.* Book three in the series.

Filomena's friends are used to this by now. Filomena's quiet introspection, her encyclopedic recall of the "fictional" Never After books. At this point, they don't even question it. They just give her a few moments to find whatever it is she's looking for.

She thumbs through the pages, seeking out the right passage. "Aha!" she says. "Thought so. A pair of wicked stepsisters are mentioned in the third book of the Never After series. That has to be them, right? Says right here Rosewood Manor's in Eastphalia." She squints at the horizon. "Which is not far from where we are, right?"

Jack nods, and Filomena knows that's why he brought them here. He's always one step ahead of everyone.

"Stop calling them wicked!" says Gretel, peering over Filomena's shoulder. "Does the book actually call them that?"

Filomena squints at the page, turning it oh-so-subtly away from Gretel's prying eyes. "Hmm, it says 'wickedly *fun* stepsisters.' My eyes must have skipped over the *fun* part since everyone always calls them the wicked stepsisters."

Gretel raises an eyebrow. "Also, how long ago was this written? Can we even be sure they're still there?"

"Yeah, what if they moved?" Alistair asks. "Maybe they're biportal, like you guys," he says, looking at Filomena and Gretel.

Filomena tucks the book back in her pack, zips it up, and stands. She brushes the last bits of dirt from her jeans and shrugs. Her curly hair is a bit of a mess since Alistair pushed her down, and she attempts to smooth it. "Then we find out."

"You say it like it's so simple," says Jack Stalker, a hint of amusement in his eyes. Or was that admiration?

Gretel is busy picking apart a dandelion when Filomena snaps her fingers, getting her attention. "Well? What are you guys waiting for? We have a pair of Stolen Slippers to find!"

CHAPTER THREE

THE WEEPING TREE

Alas, Filomena forgot how vast the kingdom of West-phalia is, or perhaps she never understood how much land it covered. It's one thing to study a map in the pages of a book, and it's quite another thing to walk it. It felt like they'd already trekked for days, but the sun has just started to sink into the horizon when Jack tells them there's still more to go. Dusk falls, and with it their spirits. Filomena, who's never been the kind of kid who gets picked first at dodgeball, is walking more and more slowly.

"My feet hurt," Gretel complains with a frown.

"Why in Never After did you choose to wear *those* things, anyway?" Alistair asks, pointing to her chunky heeled shoes.

"You think I'd ever sacrifice style for comfort?" she retorts. "Plus I haven't seen my cousins in years. I wanted to look presentable."

"Soon your feet are going to look as bad as your hair," replies Alistair. Jack rewards him with an elbow to the ribs and a frown that warns him to keep his mouth shut.

Filomena loops her arm through Gretel's. "Your hair doesn't look bad," she offers, eyeing the frizzy 'do. "You can say it's the new trend back in Hollywood."

"They'll never buy that. I'm the Cobbler's daughter, for goodness' sake. I have a reputation to uphold." Gretel sniffs.

Filomena scans Gretel up and down, checking out her latest outfit. "You look awesome, promise." Tailored white jeans (albeit now with brown stains at the knees), a black-and-white-striped shirt, and a blue blazer with gold buttons, along with accentuating gold bangles and jewelry. Filomena thinks, *I could never pull off an outfit that cool or cute.*

Filomena wouldn't know fashion—not the way Gretel does—if it bit her in the butt. Plus she doubts her parents would even recognize her if she tried to walk out of the house in something like that. Not to mention they'd probably think any sort of interesting outfit will only draw more (unnecessary) attention. Her parents have an unnerving obsession with all matters regarding safety. For Filomena's own good, it's better that she *never* stand out.

Comes with the territory of being evil-queen bait, she muses, thinking of Queen Olga and her compulsion with finding the princess—which was, um, Filomena.

She shudders, then looks down at her own outfit: faded jeans, her favorite hoodie, and worn-in purple combat boots (any combat entered is unintentional) now covered with specks of mud. She couldn't look more different from Gretel if she tried. But it's okay to be different from other people, even your own friends.

Back home, Filomena prefers to be different from the people around her. Especially the mean kids at school. Those Fettucine Alfredos thought they were so cool. Filomena almost laughs remembering when their true natures were revealed at last (ahem—remember the first Never After book, *The Thirteenth Fairy?* If you haven't read it yet, you really should . . .). She wonders if anyone at school has even noticed she's gone. For now, she's glad to be away from all the sixth-grade drama. Even if Never After adventures do come with ogre attacks.

"How much farther?" Alistair whines. "I wish we had cheeseburgers."

"Aren't you sick of those yet?" Filomena asks him.

"Never ever or even after," he says, a wistful look on his face.

She shakes her head. "Jack, are we getting any closer?"

Jack stops walking, then fiddles around in his pocket. Once again he pulls out his Seeing Eye, looks through the instrument, and peers around. Then he puts it down, squinting off into the distance. "Not quite sure. The darker it gets, the harder it is to tell. I don't see any swoop holes we could use to get there faster."

Filomena nods. From the books, she knows swoop holes are miniportals that can transport travelers around Never After much faster than walking.

Filomena's never been truly afraid of the dark, but as she looks around, she starts to feel unease. They're out of the forest now and walking on the outskirts of a village. They haven't bumped into many fellow travelers, and the few they have come across displayed a nervousness that's unsettling. A ginger cat in huge boots had hurriedly stomped by without even meowing a hello, and a troupe of boys with donkey ears galloped away before Filomena and her friends could ask for directions.

The moonlight plays off branches and hanging vines, splattering dark, ominous shadows across the ground and the tree trunks. A high-pitched screech comes from a creature nearby, startling them.

Filomena jumps a little, but not as much as Alistair. At least Gretel didn't scream this time.

"Wh-what was that?" Alistair stutters, gazing around.

"Probably just a chippermunk," replies Jack coolly. His voice doesn't waver. There's a reason he's the dashing hero of the Never After books. His fear is rare and even more rarely noticed by others even when it is there. Only Filomena notices. In truth, she feels a little too keenly aware of Jack at times, attuned like a compass to his moods and his reactions.

There's another screech, and finally they come across fellow travelers. Sure enough—Jack is right—it's a pair of chippermunks. Except Filomena finds they're nothing like the happy little critters described in the books; these creatures are downright downtrodden. They're slightly larger than squirrels, and instead of ties and tailcoats (according to the author of the Never After series, chippermunks are always ready for a party), they wear shabby rags.

The chippermunks scream almost as loud as Gretel when they notice Filomena and her friends on the road.

"It's okay, we're not ogres," says Alistair soothingly. "We're not about to kidnap you or take you to Queen Olga."

The chippermunks look slightly relieved. "You're too short to be an ogre," squeaks one.

"Well, excuse me," says Alistair with a laugh.

"Are you guys from around here?" asks Gretel. "Would you know the way to Rosewood Manor?"

"What's it to you?" one chippermunk asks suspiciously.

"The girls who live there are my cousins."

"No, no, we don't know anything or anyone," says the other chippermunk, shaking its little head forcefully and tugging on its companion's sleeve. "Please leave us alone."

"We're just hoping to—"

"LEAVE US ALONE!" screeches the chippermunk. And with that, they scurry off into the night.

"What's wrong with them?" says Filomena. "They acted like we were . . . I don't know, trolls or something."

Jack sighs. "It's like this everywhere in Never After now. Olga has too many spies, and no one trusts anyone else. Once upon a time, chippermunks were more than happy to chat and maybe even share a glass of acorn tea. But times have changed."

"How awful," whispers Gretel.

Alistair's shoulders slump.

"Come on, let's keep going," Jack urges gently.

They keep walking in the growing darkness. Filomena's ears are perked for any other strange noises; she doesn't want to be caught unawares by an ogre ambush again. She can't shake the feeling that they're being watched somehow, that the night has a thousand eyes on them. Something howls in the distance, long and low, and she feels it in her bones now: abject animal fear. Being in Never After is nothing like living in sleepy, bucolic North Pasadena, where the worst that can happen is a neighbor enthusiastically overdecorating their front yard, resulting in a letter from the town committee that their gargantuan trellis is an eyesore and must be taken down immediately.

A twig snaps under Filomena's foot then, and she clutches Gretel's shirt.

"Filomena, please! The last thing I need right now are wrinkles in my top," Gretel says, shrugging out of Filomena's grip.

Jack appears next to Filomena and clears his throat. "You can hold on to my arm if you'd like," he says softly.

Filomena blushes, now unnerved by his very nearness. She's always harbored a secret little crush on the Jack Stalker of the books, and the Jack Stalker in real life is even more handsome and dashing than described. Her heart flutters in her chest and she's too shy to accept. "No, it's fine. I'm okay. I was just spooked by the sound, is all." She remembers her parents' encouraging words: *You are braver than you know.* But it's hard to be brave when you're walking around in pitch black.

"It's okay to be frightened of what you cannot see," whispers Jack. He holds out his arm.

This time Filomena takes it without saying a word. Aside from the chippermunks, the road is empty, and every cottage they pass is dark. Not one candle is lit in any window.

"Where is everyone?" Gretel asks, rubbing her arms as though she's felt a sudden chill.

"Ever since the fairy tribes went underground, people have been left to live without magic and without hope. The lights went out all over Never After," Jack says quietly. "Since then the ogres patrol the villages at random, at any hour, and they're worse at night. Sometimes they'll grab someone off the street for nothing. The ogres will say they're breaking the rules and then start breaking their bones. So if anyone *is* here, they're probably hiding."

Filomena doesn't miss the hint of sadness in Jack's tone,

the way his eyes wander somewhere she cannot place. She knows instinctively that he must be thinking of his own family. The way they, too, had to hide from unforeseen threats that arrived in the night without warning. The way hiding didn't save them from the ogres or the fires.

She trembles at the thought of how horrifying that must have been for Jack—watching his home, his family, burn. How their screams must still haunt him. The smell of burnt rubble, the ashes where once they all had laughed together and lived as a family. She grips Jack's arm a little tighter, giving him a reassuring squeeze. He offers a small smile in response.

Then his face straightens; he's back to being the cool and composed Jack Stalker. "If my calculations are correct, we should be arriving in Eastphalia soon enough. It should be just through these woods and around the bend. We'll know we're on the main road when we see the Weeping Tree."

"Oh wow, you mean the site of the Last Battle?" Filomena asks excitedly. She'd read all about it in the Never After series. The Weeping Tree—which used to be known as the Tree of Life—was once home to many of the Summer Court's thirteen fairy tribes.

"Yes," Jack affirms a little curtly, and Filomena is chastened. To her it's only a story about an epic battle, but Jack *lived* it.

"There it is," says Alistair, pointing just ahead, to a large, looming figure.

Jack pulls out his Seeing Eye, which shines brightly in the darkness. "Still standing," he says, more to himself than to any of the others.

Filomena looks ahead, and then up, up, up her gaze drifts. She tilts her head as far back as she can manage without breaking her neck. The Weeping Tree is enormous, reaching straight up to the sky. There is no ladder tall enough in the mortal world that can reach its topmost boughs.

She feels the ground beneath her shake, and she hears what sounds like a distant sob. A muffled cry. The kind of cry a person might try to hold in because they're scared someone will hear and make them cry harder.

The group walks closer and closer to the tree, and finally they are close enough for Filomena to walk right up to it. She reaches out a hand, but another hand stops her.

It's Jack's. "Don't," he whispers.

Only then does she look away from the tree. In Jack's eyes, she recognizes sadness again. The same kind she suddenly feels, here, in close proximity to the abandoned fairy abode.

She turns her sights back to the bark, eyes traveling over the seemingly numberless grooves, which look like trails of tears. "Are these—"

"Tearstains," says Jack with a solemn nod.

Alistair approaches the tree, hesitation in his steps. He looks up at the sky. "I remember when this thing would light up almost all of Never After."

Gretel approaches next. "All of it? But how?"

Jack looks down, lightly kicking at nothing in particular. "There were so many fairies here. On any given day you'd find huge festivals up in the branches, as well as all around the base. The entire kingdom of Eastphalia would attend the parties most nights. Of course, that was when there was nothing to fear. Before the lights were dimmed."

"Or taken," mumbles Alistair. "It's not fair."

Jack rests his hand on Alistair's shoulder. "I know. It isn't."

"We have a saying in my world," interjects Filomena, "that life isn't fair."

Jack turns to her. "But it's supposed to be." He looks pained.

"It's meant to be," Alistair adds with conviction.

Filomena can't quite understand how they believe this so strongly. Where she's from, people basically expect things to be unfair. It's just . . . normal. Filomena was picked on because she was different—too smart and too sensitive. Her parents' former accountant once stole a lot of money from their family, and they weren't able to recover it. Her mom lost a prize she should have won for her writing if it hadn't been for a technicality. Life isn't fair. That's what Filomena had learned early and often.

In her world, not only do people expect things not to be fair; they accept it. Most of the time without question. Maybe that's part of the problem with her world.

"Well, of course, it *should* be fair," she argues. "Some things, though, maybe even most things, are out of your control. You can't change everything."

"No? But you can certainly change some things," Jack retorts. There's a defensiveness in his tone that Filomena knows is not because of her.

"Hey, I didn't turn the lights off on this tree. I'm only saying—"

"That it's easier to accept bad things than it is to try to change them?" Jack says, that edge to his voice growing stronger.

"Guys," Gretel cuts in. "We're here to fix things. Remember? To get the slippers back? And hopefully to make sure the Prophecy doesn't come true? To change things for the better?"

Filomena nods. "For the better."

"For the better," Jack repeats, although he doesn't sound very sure of himself, which Filomena notices is very unlike him. He's Jack! The dashing hero of the Never After books! He's a hero—to her, at least. This is worrying. Very worrying, indeed.

"Maybe we shouldn't have come," Gretel says. She sighs, then sits down on a nearby stump. "I probably won't be able to find the slippers anyway. I can't even find my cousins! Who was I kidding? There's nothing we can do. The ogres are going to win."

Filomena frowns at Gretel's disheartened spirit. Melancholy is thick in the air around them. Even Alistair's sunny personality has dimmed. They're not even walking anymore; they're all sitting by the tree—or slumped by the tree, more like.

Filomena feels a heaviness in her heart, but she fights it. That's when it clicks. "Wait, Jack, didn't you say that since the fairy tribes have gone underground, people here have been without not only magic but also hope?"

A confused look crosses Jack's face. "Yeah . . ."

"Well, maybe it's contagious. The lack of hope. I know it can kind of feel that way, even where I'm from. It's like one person freaks out, and they freak out the next person, and the next thing you know, everyone thinks it's just gloom and doom and the sky is falling—especially if they're just staring at screens and reading bad news all day," she says, thinking of her parents with a pang. She's seen it enough times to know— the way one person's anxiety and fear feeds off another's.

"But what does it matter? What's the point of anything?" moans Alistair, who sounds as if he's about to sob.

"Hmm, I think maybe we need to get away from this tree," Filomena suggests.

"Huh?" asks Jack as Filomena pulls on his elbow.

"Come on," she says. "I think we need to get away from here. The tree's making us all too sad and depressed and like we can't do anything about it."

Filomena's words seem to bring Jack back to himself, and his eyes clear. "Right. We should head on anyway. Hortense and Beatrice's house can't be that far from here."

It takes some cajoling, but Filomena and Jack finally convince Alistair and Gretel to keep walking past the tree as well. Their forlorn faces soften the farther away they get.

Once they're safely away from the Weeping Tree, Alistair begins to complain about being hungry again instead of being sad. Gretel remembers she has a great stain-removal trick. Jack is back to his calm and capable self.

As they make their way around the bend, Filomena takes one last look at the tree. She can still hear it softly weeping.

For the thousands of fairies who used to call me home . . .
For the thirteen born to the Fairy King and Queen . . .
Esmeralda, Antonia, Isabella, Philippa, Yvette, and Claudine,
Josefa, Amelia, Colette, and Sabine.
Beautiful Rosanna, who married the King,
Clever Scheherazade, who spun a thousand and one dreams.
And the kindest of them all, Carabosse, who was the thir-
  teenth.
My branches knew them well, kept their secrets and kept them
  safe,
But they are gone, and the time grows late.
Now I am alone, withered and old, the last of my kind, the
  last of their soul.

For a moment, the tree's sorrow sweeps through Filomena; she can feel the intensity of its loss. She wipes a tear from her eye and whispers, "I'm so sorry. I didn't even know them at all, but I miss them, too."

She wants to tell the tree that there is hope yet. The missing princess of Westphalia has been found—and lives!

Aladdin's Lamp did not fall into Olga's hands. But the glass slippers are still missing. And two fairies are dead—maybe more. Where are the rest of her aunts? How many of the fairy tribes survived? How many of the thirteen fairies are left?

Filomena ruminates on all this and feels a cold shock sweep over her body. Then the grim last lines of the Prophecy come back to her.

If fairies' gifts fall into ogres' hands . . .
Death and destruction shall befall this land.
Thirteen fairies born to the Fairy King and Queen;
When none live, so shall Never After die with them.
And that is the End of the Story.

Chapter Four

Stranger in a Strange Land

Even after they are past the contagious grief of the Weeping Tree, the atmosphere in the rest of the kingdom of Eastphalia isn't that much better. Filomena thinks it looks like a ghost town, the kind of place she's only read about or seen in movies, where the wind makes doors open on creaky hinges and tumbleweeds roll down empty streets. Except she feels less like she's in a fairy tale and more like she's in a postapocalyptic dystopia, the kind of book her parents might write—if they ever get tired of romance novels (Mum) or mysteries (Dad)—just to show her the dangers of those kinds of places and why Filomena must never, never go to them. Of course, she would never *deliberately* choose to wander around a postapocalyptic world, but try telling her parents that.

If Westphalia is a kingdom that is slowly waking up, Eastphalia is a kingdom that has given in to slumber. The darkness is foreboding, as is the quiet, and the pace of their footsteps is the only sound for miles.

Except Filomena can't shake the feeling that something—or someone—is following them. She'd assumed at first that it was ogres, but the feeling has remained long after the ogres had gone. She takes out her headlamp (which she can't bear to actually strap to her forehead like her parents insisted) and swings it wide, behind and in front of them. Just as her dad promised, it illuminates fifty feet, shining its bright light into the enveloping darkness.

But there's nothing. No one. There's definitely no one around. Maybe she's just imagining things. Maybe that creepy-crawly feeling on her skin is just because they're walking in the dark, and hungry—Mum's spaghetti dinner and Alistair's cheeseburger but dim memories by now.

"Does anything look familiar at all?" Jack asks Gretel.

Gretel sighs. "I was just a kid. But I sort of remember it was at the edge of the village, at the start of the woods. And it was covered with beautiful yellow and pink roses; my aunt planted them for both her girls."

"Are we just going to keep walking in the dark?" Filomena asks softly. "Alistair's almost sleepwalking."

It's true: While Alistair's feet are moving, his head dips from side to side. At any moment now, he might just collapse and fall asleep on the ground.

Jack catches Alistair before he trips on his own feet. "Come on, bud, let's keep going," Jack tells him.

Alistair rubs his eyes and yawns. "Okay, okay." Soon he's stumbling once more.

"We need to rest," says Filomena.

Jack nods. "You're right, we should find some kind of shelter for the night, but not here. Another ogre patrol could come through at any time. Let's keep walking for just a little longer."

So they trudge ahead in silence for a long while. After walking for the good part of another hour, Filomena hears a rustle in a nearby shrub. Her friends stop and turn, their eyes following as she shines the light on it.

Blue and indigo fruits dangle from the bush like ornaments.

"Don't, they're bumbleberries," warns Jack.

Filomena nods even as her mouth waters at the sight of the plump, juicy fruit. She's read about bumbleberries. They explode painfully when eaten; villagers plant them by gates to dissuade trespassers or thieves from coming any closer.

"I bet one wouldn't hurt too bad . . . ," Alistair says, perking up and reaching out to pluck one particularly delicious-looking berry.

Jack swats it from his hand. "You know better," he scolds.

Alistair groans. "I can't take it! I'm hungry! My belly's rumbling so loud, it sounds like an Ogre's Wrath in there!"

"Still, better than being *inside* an ogre, am I right?" Jack teases. He places an arm around his pal to cheer him up.

Filomena and Gretel chuckle, and Alistair eventually laughs along, too. Even though he's pretty *hangry* right now, joking about it somehow takes the edge off. And remembering how he was almost ogre dinner makes Alistair lose just a wee bit of his appetite.

"Too soon," replies Alistair, making the other kids laugh even harder. He reminds them of how he once found himself in ogre soup. The way the giant's limbs had suddenly rubbered like a toy snake. The sinking flesh his friends had to pull him from, like gross quicksand.

Alistair is neck-deep in bad memories when they hear a noise like someone stumbling.

Filomena whips around with her headlamp and illuminates a figure crouched behind them.

"Sorry! Sorry! Didn't see you folks there!" There's a boy on the path, and he looks just as surprised to see them as they are to see him. He's tall and gangly, wears a cap and suspenders, and carries a worn sack on his shoulder.

"Hail, fellow, fairly met," says Jack, using the standard Vineland greeting.

"Hail Vineland," the boy responds a little too eagerly, catching sight of Jack's green-and-brown garb.

Jack nods. "What are you doing out so late at night, stranger?" He asks the question genially, but there's an edge to his voice.

"Apologies, I was just making my way home," the strange boy says. "And you, my friends? Travelers, are you? You don't look like you're from here." He stares at Gretel's gold-buttoned blazer and Filomena's purple combat boots.

Jack doesn't respond, and Filomena doesn't have to be a Nevie to understand why. Even in her world, you do *not* talk to strangers. Especially ones who suddenly appear behind you, in the dark, in the middle of the night. *Hello, stranger danger!* her parents would scream. *Stalker! Kidnapper! Robber! Mugger! Murderer!* This could be literally any (or maybe all) of the numerous dangers her folks warned her about. Also, could this boy possibly be the stealthy presence she'd been feeling all evening?

"And where is your home?" asks Jack. His vines slip down to his fingers in readiness.

"Not far," says the tall boy. He shuffles on his feet nervously. "Just getting out of work, I am." He stares at the vines twining on Jack's wrists.

"And where's that?"

The boy shrugs. "I work over at the fort, up by the river." He squares his shoulders defensively. "It's the only job left in these parts." He looks shyly at them. "Where, pray tell, are you folks headed?"

Jack shakes his head at the group, indicating not to answer.

"It's all right, I understand," the boy says. "But if you guys want a place to rest, I don't live too far. It's right dangerous to stay out on this road too late. Ogres come by this way, and they'll be hungry, or bored. Best to get indoors before the midnight moon."

Gretel elbows Jack and makes frantic eyes at him.

"Oh, and, by the by, does anyone fancy a candy apple? I have a few left," the boy offers, opening his sack to reveal a glimmering bushel of candy apples that shine in the moonlight.

Again, Jack shakes his head even as Alistair strains to see what's in the bag.

The boy shrugs, takes an apple from his sack, and starts to eat it. It's coated in a deep red glaze and makes a satisfying crunch when he bites into it.

Alistair moans beside Filomena. *Candy apples,* he mouths.

"Sure you don't want one?" the boy asks. "I've got plenty." He takes another bite and then tosses the apple aside. It makes a distant *thump* as it hits the ground, the noise interrupting the dead quiet surrounding them.

Alistair's eyes follow the noise. He appears offended that this dude just got rid of a perfectly wonderful candy apple— one that *he* could have eaten, no less!

"Very kind," says Jack coolly. "But we're just fine, really. I know my way around these parts. Just looking to get where we're going quickly. The fewer interruptions, the better," he hints.

"Not at all," the boy says, licking his fingers. "Hope you guys get to where you're going. In one piece, that is."

Filomena thinks that sounds like a hint of his own.

The boy cocks his head to the side as he considers them. "A little advice: Stay off the main road if you can. Since the Weeping, lights've been dimmed around here, and it's not safe. When you get to the fork, there's an inn on the left. Not too bad. The owner's a decent chap and will feed you bread and meat."

"How far?" asks Alistair eagerly.

"Oh, not far, only twenty miles as the crow flies."

The kids exchange nervous glances, uncertainty taking over each one's face. That sounds like quite a ways away. Twenty miles? That's practically a marathon. They can't walk that far. Not in the dark.

"Sure I can't help you?" the boy asks. "I know my way around *these parts*."

If Jack is offended, he doesn't show it. They're all exhausted.

Gretel offers an apologetic shrug to her friends before she responds, "All right. I'm looking for my cousins, Beatrice and Hortense. They live at Rosewood Manor. Do you know where we might find them?"

"Ah, yes! The twin Roses of Rosewood Manor!" the boy says, his face lighting up. "I don't know exactly where they are, but I know someone who will. They've moved around a bit since the Weeping. Come, come with me. In the morning

I'll take you straight to someone who can help you find them."

The four kids eye one another. He sounds so friendly and appears so helpful, but as much as they want to believe him, they're rightfully wary of the situation.

"Truly, I'm not far from here. My house isn't grand like Rosewood Manor, but it's comfortable, and you can fill your bellies before making your way in the morning."

The four look at each other again and then at the boy. No one speaks.

At last the boy shrugs and shoulders his pack. "Have it your way." He begins to walk down the path. "Good luck!"

"Wait!" cries Gretel. She gives Jack a look that silences whatever he's about to say. Jack sighs. It's clear he can't·stop her.

The boy looks over his shoulder and stops walking, letting the group catch up to him. "Changed your minds, have you?" he asks with a smile. "Awful dark out here tonight."

"Hold on. First things first, we don't even know your name," Filomena says, crossing her arms. If he's a character, he's one she doesn't recognize from any of the books. And she has read all twelve! Many times. Rereading the Never After series is her favorite hobby.

"The name's Rory," he says with a bow. "Rory Hexson. At your service!"

Filomena doesn't recognize his moniker, either. None of them do—it's apparent by the looks on their faces. It doesn't ring any bells. They keep their own names to themselves for now.

"Well?" he asks. "Are you coming with me or not? I don't have all night."

It's so tempting. Shelter and food. A place to sleep. Something to eat. They've been walking in the dark for what has surely been hours. And it'll be midnight soon, and as Filomena's parents often remind her, nothing good ever happens after midnight.

But what if this guy is the type who has a basement dungeon . . . with chains . . . the kind her parents have warned her about. Her parents would absolutely freak if she wound up in a BASEMENT DUNGEON. She's seen enough scary movies to know that certain situations must be avoided at all costs, especially since you might not be able to escape once you're trapped in a BASEMENT DUNGEON!

"Listen, I don't think this is a good idea," Jack whispers, his eyes on the older boy.

Gretel hesitates. "I don't know . . ."

Jack turns to his loyal friend. "Alistair?"

"He says it's not far . . . and he'll help us out in the morning . . . which means, um, breakfast, too," says Alistair hopefully.

"Filomena?" asks Jack.

"Uhhh," says Filomena. On the one hand, she desperately wants a place to sleep and something to eat. On the other hand, can they really trust this stranger?

Jack squares his shoulders. He looks around. At the empty path. The nearly black sky. The dark houses, the shuttered windows. The absence of sound and soul. They will find no shelter here. Filomena knows he's considering the dangers of the road against the dangers of Rory's home.

It's up to Jack to keep them safe. That's how the stories are written, anyway. Jack is nimble, Jack is quick. Jack can get them out of any trick. Filomena is glad that kind of pressure isn't on her. She wouldn't know how to handle it. Then again, if the books have taught her anything, it's that sometimes you can't predict how you'll deal with something—until you do. Sometimes you can even surprise yourself with your own courage and strength. A few lessons she's learned from Jack himself.

Jack motions for the four of them to move closer together. "I'd rather keep walking. I think that's the safest way," he tells them. "Let's go."

"I'd rather not?" whines Alistair. "Keep walking, I mean."

"Oof, I'm not sure I can walk any farther, either," says Gretel. "Sorry, Jack."

"Filomena?" Jack asks.

Filomena shrugs helplessly. Jack and the others accept her silence for what it is; there's a mutual understanding among them. It seems to be settled. Alistair and Gretel don't look like they will budge another inch down this dark road, and keeping off the main path seems like an even more treacherous decision.

"All right," Jack says reluctantly, turning back to Rory, who's still waiting for an answer. "We'll go with you."

"I promise you won't regret it," says Rory. "*Now* will you each have an apple, my friends?"

Alistair looks to his friends, cheeks flushing. "I'll take one."

Jack looks like he isn't sure about this at all, but it's too late—Alistair is already eating one, and soon Gretel and Filomena each have one, too.

Alistair is almost rapturous. Gretel looks dreamy as she licks hers. But Jack shakes his head. He turns to the strange boy with a tight smile. "Lead the way . . . *friend.*"

Rory nods, his big smile stretching even wider. "Wonderful! Right this way!" He holds his arm out toward the vast expanse of the woods.

The group looks into the dark, eerie forest. With silent agreement, they each take a first step toward it. Filomena takes a bite of the candy apple.

It's the sweetest thing she's ever tasted.

Chapter Five

Candy Land

Filomena had no idea how hungry she was until she ate the apple—which she not just ate but devoured until it was only a skinny core on a stick. The others made just as quick work of theirs. Instead of satisfying Filomena's hunger, however, the candy apple seems to have made her feel much hungrier and emptier, as if her appetite can never be sated.

Of course, Alistair feels the same way. "I could eat a thousand more of these," he proclaims.

"You're in luck then," says Rory with a smile. "I've got many more waiting for you back home."

"Any chance you might have some cheeseburgers as well?" Alistair asks.

"Sure," says Rory.

But Filomena doubts Rory even knows what cheese-burgers are. This guy doesn't strike her as the type to have buns, *hun*. Or to know anything about Sir Mix-a-Lot, unlike Filomena's dad, who plays a lot of early-nineties pop music. (And grills amazing cheeseburgers. Maybe he'll grill some for Alistair one day.)

The forest is quiet save for the sound of twigs snapping underfoot and small creatures skittering around nearby. Every so often Filomena hears a rustle of leaves, tiny foot-steps tapping the ground, the hooting of owls, and the wind whistling through branches. They keep walking deeper and deeper into the forest.

Filomena feels as if she's in a trance. If she stopped to think, she might wonder why they're following a veritable stranger and where exactly he's taking them. She would con-sider how Jack wanted to keep walking on the main road, and question why they didn't follow his advice. Because Jack always knows what to do. But those aren't the thoughts she is having right now.

Rory's voice echoes deep and warm in the darkness, like honey cake. "Almost there, my friends. Just a few more steps. Follow me . . ."

Alistair lets out a relieved breath. "Oh, thank Sunflower Suns. I'm starving."

"We don't want that, now," says Rory.

If Filomena were thinking straight, she'd notice the suspicious tone in Rory's voice—the way he's so eagerly doling out such extravagant treats.

Except right at that moment, she's so hungry, she can't think straight. Can she have another candy apple please? Now? Maybe two candy apples? Three?

Just as she's about to ask if she can have another apple, they arrive at their destination at last. "Here we are," the overly tall and gawky boy says proudly, pointing to a dwelling ahead that's half-hidden by a copse of trees.

Filomena blinks a few times, wondering if she's suffering from some sort of delirium or a hallucination. Is that a mirage? Is that—can it be? Is it? Oh my! Goodness! Is it really? Oh wow! It's . . .

"Hold on, hold on," cautions Jack, attempting to come between his friends and the—

"Gingerbread house!" Alistair exclaims gleefully, jumping straight up in the air and dodging Jack's outstretched arms. "I haven't seen one of these in ages! I thought the ogres ate them all!" He barrels past Jack, straight toward the candy-covered cottage.

Filomena gasps. Of course she's read about Never After's infamous gingerbread houses, but she never thought she would actually see one, much less stay in one. Or eat one this big.

Gretel claps her hands, waving her fourth candy apple in the air. "Gingerbread! My favorite!"

"Wait! You guys!" warns Jack. "If you guys can just wait before you . . ." But no one listens. The gingerbread house is a beacon, a temptation that cannot be denied.

Rory tips his cap with a flourish. "Don't be shy! Go ahead! It's all yours! *¡Mi casa es su casa!*"

He doesn't have to tell Alistair twice. *A house made of candy!* Alistair takes off running, followed closely by Gretel and Filomena. *A HOUSE MADE OF CANDDDYYYY!*

Just like in Filomena's wildest, sweetest, most fanciful dreams, the house is indeed made completely from sweets. Peppermint candies frame the windows, the red and green kinds, both swirling with white. Thick white sugar frosting traces the roof and the chimney and the door. Other candies are stuck to the icing, a rainbow's worth of lollipops and gummy bears, as well as various delicious chocolates and peanut butter treats. There are so many kinds of candy, including fat squishy mochi balls in a rainbow of pastel colors, and a dazzling array of milk mints like the ones Filomena and her Korean dad like to snack on. Oh my, there are even—are those?—can it be?—yes! *British* Kit Kats! Smaller and yet more chocolaty than the American kind!

Filomena has never felt hungrier in her life. She licks her lips. She can almost taste the chocolate bars from here. The scent of sugar dances in the wind as a light breeze blows her way. Those British Kit Kats are calling her name.

Candy!

When's the last time they've eaten? She tries to think. It

was so long ago she can't remember. Feels that way, anyway. Is there any reason for her existence other than to eat all this delicious . . .

CANDY!

The chimney blows whipped cream for smoke. A ladder leaning against the little house reaches up to the tip-top of the chimney, which means if she can climb the ladder, she can gobble up all that whipped cream!

Alistair takes a handful of sugar-dusted toffee almonds and chocolate snowcaps and stuffs it in his mouth. Gretel is daintily munching on peach hearts, in between trying a variety of marshmallow puffs.

SO MUCH CAAAAANDY!

"Try the door!" Alistair calls, his mouth full of frosting as he greedily pockets butterscotch candies, his hands already stained from the blue, pink, and green jellies. The colors are all around his mouth as well. He hasn't taken it easy on the candy house, that's for sure. Filomena's surprised it's still standing at this point.

They don't notice that Jack hasn't followed them. And what's that noise from behind? It sounds like . . . some kind of yelling? Someone saying, "Don't eat it"?

But why in Never After would Filomena not eat candy? That's so silly! The whole point of candy is to eat it! She doesn't turn around to investigate the commotion, and neither do Gretel and Alistair.

Filomena's mouth waters at the assortment of delicacies,

the dizzying array of treats. She takes Alistair's advice and goes to the door first, wiping her finger along the nearest edge. When she tastes it, she closes her eyes. This icing is beyond incredible: vanilla mixed with sunshine and happiness.

One bite turns into many. Soon, she's busy stuffing her own face just as freely as Alistair, her own hands stained and sticky with sugar.

"Not like the gingerbread houses back home, huh?" says Gretel.

"Nope!" agrees Filomena, who's always been proud of the gingerbread houses she and her parents would assemble every Christmas. Her mom would buy a kit from the supermarket, and they would spend an afternoon frosting and decorating. Filomena was never allowed to actually eat the house, though; it was primarily for show. She's pretty certain their gingerbread creations wouldn't taste nearly as good as this one.

"This is heaven!" says Gretel, munching on almond-flavored flowers.

If the group was suspicious of their new friend at first, they aren't anymore. Instead a hazy sugar high has replaced all thought in Filomena's brain and, it appears, in her friends' brains as well. But the more they eat, the hungrier they become.

"All right, all right," Rory says, chuckling at the sight of them with frosting-covered lips and sugar-dusted hair. He looks strangely rumpled; he's lost his cap, there are scratches on his arms, and his sleeve is torn. *Strange. When did that happen?* But instead of asking, Filomena reaches to grab more candy—

Except Rory stops her. "That's quite enough for one go, don't you think?"

The three of them pause their chomping and stare at Rory, bewildered. Enough? No amount of candy is ever enough! Doesn't he know that?

Filomena blinks at the tall boy. They just walked approximately one bazillion miles—behind a STRANGER who STALKED them. Oh yes, he was the stealthy figure she had noticed following them earlier, wasn't he?! In the far reaches of Filomena's brain, an alarm bell starts to ring—*This boy is a* stranger, *someone we never should have spoken to on a dark road . . . and now he has the absolute gall to limit our candy intake?*

Excuse me?!

Who is this guy?! And by the way—hey, wait a minute . . . Where's Jaaa . . .

Just as she's about to ask, Rory walks past her and says, "Because I wouldn't want you to get too full now. There are much better treats inside the house than outside of it."

Say what?

More candy? Better candy? Inside?

MORE CANDY INSIDE THE HOUSE?

Instantly she forgives him.

But, oh . . . What was she wondering before? What happened to . . . you know . . . the other person who was with them . . . what was his name?

Before she can remember, Rory is brushing past them to get to the door. Reaching for the knob, he says, "After you," and opens it.

There's that voice again, the one coming from far away that's telling her to *stop—wait—don't* . . .

She brushes the thought aside like it's a fly. Because now she can smell an entirely different, heavenly aroma. Pastries, cakes, and desserts of the utmost delicacy. Ooooh . . . are those pancakes on the counter? Sure enough, the scent of sunflower syrup wafts over and wiggles up their noses. There are trays of doughnuts and assorted cakes and pies heaped with elderberries, razzlemangoes, and plumquats. There are several chocolate fountains—white, dark, and a Never After specialty: hazelmilk. There are chocolate-covered strawberries, cream pies, and warm beignets. The middle of the room is set with bowls of cookie-dough bites, towers of cupcakes, and vats of pudding in every flavor.

The scent of honey and vanilla fills the air like a wonderful warm embrace.

Inside the house, confectioners' sugar drifts in the air like little snowflakes. It's . . . magical. Enchanting. Filomena sticks her tongue out to catch some powder and smiles.

Alistair's mouth is watering, too. He's got his eye on a towering stack of flower-shaped white-and-yellow suckers:

Sunflower Suns. The tower is so high, it's leaning. "Look, guys, it's practically like these Sunflower Suns want to fall directly into my mouth and down into my stomach!" He reaches for the closest sucker, which looks like it might tumble, when—

Rory clears his throat. "All this is yours to enjoy, my friends. But first we have to agree on how you're going to pay for it."

Alistair's hand stops mid-reach, and he frowns. "Pay? What do you mean, *pay*?"

"Well, you can't expect to eat your fill of my home without compensating me for it, can you?" Rory asks reasonably.

With that, he kicks the door shut behind them—and locks it.

The lock, Filomena notices, even through her growing sugar haze, is not made of candy at all, but of solid steel.

CHAPTER SIX

HITTING A SOUR PATCH

Filomena and her friends freeze at the sound of the door closing them in. Even with all these tasty treats around, no one wants to be locked inside a gingerbread house with no way out.

Ha! Just kidding. Of course they do!

CANDDYYYY! PASTRIESSSS!!! CAAAAAAKE!!!! MORE CANNNNDY!!!!

Who *doesn't* want to be locked inside a giant house built out of candy, gingerbread, and frosting and chock-full of desserts as far as the eye can see? Heck, at this point, you'd probably have to drag them out of the place. And they'd probably go kicking and screaming, rather than agree to go at all.

So whatever this Rory Hexson wants, they'll pay it. *What does he want? Do we even have any money? What is money?*

Their minds are hazy and sluggish, and no one seems able to think past eating as much sugar as they can manage. All thoughts of missing glass slippers, of finding Hortense and Beatrice, of the dangers of the prophecy coming true—all that is forgotten. If you were to ask Filomena why she's in Never After, she would tell you it's to eat candy and to live inside the gingerbread house forever.

"As for the matter of payment, I happen to have drawn up a contract that outlines the trade of sugary-treat consumption in exchange for the execution of a handful of chores around the house, along with similarly equitable compensation," their host informs them.

Alistair shrugs. "Sure. Fine with me. I'll sign anything. Right, guys? A few chores can't hurt. And nothing's free in life." He turns to his friends, checking for their input on the subject. It's clear by his expression that he hopes they won't screw this up.

Filomena understands his anxiety. When will they ever get this chance again? To live in a real-life gingerbread house? For as long as they want? And to eat as much candy as they want? And they don't have to pay rent! *Sweet!* (Literally!) Well, um, it looks like they will have to pay somehow . . .

"Yeah, of course. Wouldn't be fair not to keep it tidy if we're going to eat so much of it," says Gretel. She sounds fairly neutral, even as she hungrily eyes a tulip cake resting on a windowsill. She leans close to Filomena's ear and whispers fiercely, "I'm not sure about you, but if I don't get a bite of that soon, I don't know what I'll do. The purple-and-yellow frosting is calling to me so loudly, it's singing. I want to answer back."

Filomena agrees with Gretel's reasoning. She's got her own eye on a few choice slices of a luscious chocolate cake with a mirror glaze. Can they just hurry up and make the deal already?

None of them have noticed that Jack is nowhere to be found and not in the house with them. Who's Jack? All they care about is getting more candy.

"So where do we sign?" Alistair asks.

Rory walks over to the kitchen counter and starts opening drawers.

"Is this made of gingerbread, too?" asks Gretel, drumming her fingers on the table.

"Of course."

"A little predictable and cliché, don't you think? You couldn't even mix surfaces? Who was the interior designer in charge here?" says Gretel. "I would have gone with a chocolate marble cake, maybe."

Rory ignores Gretel and pulls open another drawer, causing the items inside to *tink* as they clatter around. "Where's that contract?" he mutters. More items clanging. More papers shuffling. After digging around for a few more moments, he finally finds it. "Aha, here we go. The contract."

He holds a scroll in his fist and shakes it open, unrolling a very, very, very, very long document. It stretches across the floor, all the way to where Alistair is standing. (This is important to note, because Alistair is currently on the opposite side of the room. Like, way across the room.)

Looking down at it, Alistair chuckles nervously. "That's quite a contract."

Filomena is starting to get impatient. Will they ever get to eat more candy and move on to cake or pie? And she's just noticed there's ice cream for dessert. She bends down to examine the part of the contract closest to Alistair's toes and starts reading aloud. *Dust the invisible fairy dust.* She looks up at Rory. "Is this a joke?"

"It most certainly isn't," he replies sternly.

"How can you even dust something that's invisible?" she argues.

"You dust it until it's even more invisible," he replies.

Did he just say that like it makes total sense? Filomena sighs. The only things longer than this list are their long faces. This is ridiculous! They'll be here for eternity if they have to read the entire thing! And there's so much candy to eat. They really should be focusing on eating more candy and not on haggling over some silly contract.

"Does this contract list every piece of candy in this

house?" Alistair asks, catching sight of a few items on the scroll.

"Of course," says Rory with a smile. "For you will have to pay for every bit of candy you eat. As you can see, my house has myriad variations of every kind of sweet, and each one must be accounted for correctly."

Filomena nods. Of course, of course. That made complete sense. So much candy! So much glorious, delicious candy!

Gretel picks up the part of the contract that's nearest to her and frowns. Her eyes squint at the tiny spidery handwriting. "I can see a list of chores, but there's something here at the end about 'equitable compensation'? What does that mean?"

Their host claps his hands. "All it means is payment must be equitable to what has been consumed! No need to worry, my friends! All is well. Don't you want to start eating candy? And dessert? And pudding? And I believe we have the Cobbler's special over by the stove." He winks.

"Come on, let's sign it," says Alistair. "If we sign it, we can get back to eating candy. I'm ready, and I'm still hungry."

"Me too," says Filomena, consumed by an overwhelming urge to eat this candy for the rest of her entire life.

"Hmm," murmurs Gretel. She looks like she's trying to remember something but then gets distracted by the sight of the tulip cake, not to mention the Cobbler's special, which looks like the biggest mound of chocolate mousse anyone has ever seen.

While they're hesitating, Filomena has a flash of memory. Shouldn't there be four of them? Aren't they missing someone? But for the life of her she can't remember if that's right or who is missing.

"Excellent," says Rory, handing them each a pen.

Filomena is about to sign when she hears something very faint, like a voice from very far away. It sounds like someone is trying to warn her about something—she shakes her head. "Do you hear that?"

"Hear what?" asks Gretel.

"Nothing," says Filomena, whose stomach is grumbling loudly. Whatever it was, it's gone now. She doesn't hear anything.

And so, just like that, they sign their names—their real names—on the dotted line. And it's done. For the privilege of eating as much candy and dessert in the gingerbread house as they want, they've promised that Rory Hexson will receive equitable compensation from them until the debt is fully paid.

It's been days. Months, maybe. Entire lifetimes. No one knows for certain. All they know is they wake up, do their chores, eat the house and everything inside it, then go to sleep, wake up, and do it all over again. This is their lives now.

Every other day or so, they remember to wash themselves and their clothes. They take them outside to wash in a bucket—a bucket! As if they live in medieval times, which is also the name of a restaurant in Van Nuys where you can eat big turkey legs while watching middle-aged men who are accountants in real life pretend they're knights and joust. But of course Filomena can't expect a house made of candy to have something like a washing machine, now can she? They wash their clothes in a bucket, and afterward they wring out and air-dry them on a clothesline out back. The only thing that makes this okay is that the clothesline is made of licorice. So they snack on it while they wait for their things to dry.

One morning, after a breakfast of lemony cloud pancakes with honey-flower syrup, Gretel screams in the bathroom.

Alistair almost drops his mop. Filomena, who was eating icing from Rory's latest sugary creation, runs to her. "What's wrong?" she asks a white-faced Gretel.

"I can't button my jeans," Gretel mutters. "It's fine. They must have shrunk in the wash."

"Oh," says Filomena. "That happened to me ages ago." She lifts her shirt to show how she's been keeping her pants up with a piece of string since the button won't button and the zipper won't zip.

"Me too," says Alistair. "Rory was nice enough to measure me for some new pants the other day."

Filomena raises an eyebrow. "Really?"

"Yeah, he promised he would get me new clothes . . ." Alistair looks confused. "Of course, that was weeks ago . . ."

Gretel's eyes clear for a moment, like she's coming out of a daze. She looks around at the chocolate wafer walls. "You guys, where are we?"

Filomena laughs nervously. "What do you mean?"

"I mean, what are we doing here?" Gretel demands, frantically looking around their sugary surroundings. "How long have we been here?"

"We're in the gingerbread house," says Filomena matter-of-factly. She doesn't understand why Gretel is so confused. Duh, they're living the dream. They live inside a house made of delectable desserts!

"But why?" Gretel won't stop asking. "Weren't we supposed to go somewhere and do something?"

"Were we?" wonders Filomena.

"Sunflower Sun?" asks Alistair, taking one from a vase on the dining table and holding it up.

"Oh!" says Gretel, who can never turn one down. "Don't mind if I do."

"What were you saying?" asks Filomena, also taking a sucker. Yum. Pearberry.

Gretel shrugs. "I don't remember. Alistair, do you mind passing me another Sunflower Sun?"

If Filomena was in her right mind, she would have noticed that they were becoming more like zombies than people. Mindless drooling zombies who worked on cleaning the house even as they inserted more and more candy into their mouths—sometimes simultaneously. Clean and candy. Clean and candy. The daily routine.

"Gretel?" Alistair asks one afternoon. "Are you eating candy off the floor?"

Gretel looks up from the floor, where she has been eating candy. "Am I?"

Alistair nods. "You are."

"Oh." She shows him what she's eating: chocolate–peanut butter dust.

Alistair shrugs, kneels, and joins her. Soon he, too, is eating candy off the floor.

Filomena wants to say something about this, but something's flickering in her mind. Gretel had mentioned something a little while ago, something about how they were supposed to go somewhere and do something. Something important. Why can't Filomena remember? She strains to remember . . . It had something to do with Gretel's cousins . . . and . . . glass . . . glass . . . slip . . .

"Cherry cheesecake?" Rory asks, appearing in the doorway. He's holding a plate with yet another creamy concoction.

"Oooh, my favorite!" says Filomena, and she completely forgets whatever she was just about to remember once more.

CHAPTER SEVEN

OBSERVATIONS AND OBSTRUCTIONS

The days slide past one another like fruit rolls on Alistair's tongue. Filomena is on the roof picking at whipped-cream clouds, while Alistair and Gretel lounge beside her. They are content and peaceful, even though Filomena's starting to feel ill from eating so much cream. But she's ignored it before, and she'll ignore it again. To be honest, she has been feeling nauseated for so long now that she's almost used to it.

"Don't you think it's strange?" Alistair muses.

"What's strange?" asks Filomena between bites.

"Rory never eats any of the candy or dessert in the house. We never see him eating it."

"Huh, you're right. He never does," says Gretel. "That *is* strange."

"What does he eat, then?" Filomena wonders.

Alistair laughs. "Who knows? More for us!"

Filomena joins in the laughter, but she's wondering if she heard correctly. Was the answer to what Rory eats actually "more *of* us" rather than "more *for* us"? Curious . . .

Whether it's because her stomach is bothering her or for some other reason, Filomena is determined to discover the answer to the question Alistair posed. When she climbs off the roof, she finds their host where he always is: in the kitchen, looking up dessert recipes.

"Rory," she says, "can I ask you something?"

"Sure," he says genially. He shows her the page he was perusing. "Look at this coconut cake. Isn't it a beauty?"

"That does look scrumptilicious," agrees Filomena.

"Gretel and Alistair will like it, too, don't you think?"

"Sure," says Filomena. She's trying to hold on to the thought in her head. What was she going to ask him? Something about . . .

"Oh!" She smacks her forehead. "Rory, we noticed you never eat the candy or any of the desserts you make for the house."

"I don't?"

She shakes her head. "No, you never do."

Rory places his feet up on the desk in the kitchen and puts his hands behind his head, considering her question. His legs really are quite long, Filomena notices. Almost too long for a person. "Well, after a while, once you make so much of it and live in it, it gets old," he admits.

"So what do you eat, then? You do eat, don't you?" asks Filomena, who's suddenly feeling nervous.

Rory swings his feet back down and looks at her with a smile. "Oh, don't worry. I eat." His smile widens.

Filomena stares at him. Are those . . . ? Is she seeing things, or are his teeth pointy? Are those . . . fangs? She blinks, unsure of what she just saw.

Rory's smile vanishes, and the fangs—if that's what they were—disappear. "I haven't eaten in a while, but I'm going to eat very soon. A veritable feast!" Then he laughs, a hollow cackle that fills the room and sends a shiver up Filomena's spine.

"Really? More than this?" Filomena asks, motioning to the bountiful spreads in the kitchen and the dining room.

"Oh yes. Much more." Rory winks. "Don't worry, you're all invited."

More days pass. Now Filomena, Alistair, and Gretel are outside on a bright, sunny afternoon. Today's chores are gardening tasks. This includes scrubbing the dew off the grass. Turning on the white chocolate sprinkler. Planting more tulips for tulip cakes. Sugaring the garden with brown sugar and cinnamon.

Filomena stops what she's doing and stares at something in the distance. "You guys?"

"Yeah?" asks Alistair, who's pruning the gummy-bear bush.

Gretel looks up from planting more sugar trees.

Filomena points to something she finds odd. It's just beyond the gumdrop garden. "What's that?"

They follow her pointed finger. It's some sort of box with bars all around it.

"What do you think it's for?" Filomena asks, standing up. She wipes her sticky hands on a rag, then licks the sugar remnants off her fingers. She momentarily forgets what she just pointed out. But it comes into view again, and it's so different from everything in the candy-covered garden that she can't help but stare.

Gretel spits out the last bit of licorice in her mouth, suddenly losing her appetite. "I don't know why, but it's giving me the creeps."

Filomena stares at it. She's seen it before . . . in some kind of book? She used to read, didn't she? She used to know things. She used to do things other than just eat candy and do chores around the gingerbread house. Or did she? Why can't she remember?

The two girls walk over to the strange object with Alistair alongside them. They begin to inspect it. Gretel runs a hand over the steel bars. "Is it for making candy?"

"That's quite the contraption," Alistair says.

"Do you think Rory uses it?" asks Gretel.

"And where is Rory anyway? He was supposed to bring us more cupcakes. When was that? I've been craving them forever," says Filomena.

Alistair pauses to think, tapping a finger on his chin. "You know, I can't quite recall. But he did say not to leave the house or the garden."

"How long have we been here?" Filomena asks.

Gretel shrugs.

Had it been one day? Two, maybe? Weeks? Months? Years? How many sunsets had passed since they entered the gingerbread house, and why can't any of them remember?

Filomena glances around. "Wait a second . . . Weren't there . . . four of us? Where's . . . where's . . . what's his name?" She gasps. "Where's Jack?!" She turns to her friends, her face ghostly pale and drained of all color.

"Jack! Oh my fairies!" cries Alistair. "Where's Jack?!"

"Jack!" echoes Gretel.

What happened to Jack?! And how is it that none of them even noticed he was missing until right now?

"When was the last time we saw him?" Filomena demands. "THINK!"

"We were walking in the dark," says Gretel, "and we met

this guy who said . . . who said it was dangerous on the road. That was Rory." Her forehead scrunches with the effort it takes to remember.

"And he offered us candy apples," says Alistair. "I remember!"

"And we were walking in the forest, and we saw the gingerbread house," says Filomena, her mind racing. "And Jack said—"

"Jack said to STOP!" cries Alistair. "Jack said not to go!"

Gretel gasps, horrified. "He yelled at us not to eat the candy!"

Filomena can't believe it. Memories are flooding back to her now. She remembers . . . some kind of altercation. Screaming. And then . . . it all goes blank.

"He was trying to stop us! And then something happened . . . What if Rory . . . ?" She can't finish the sentence; she's too terrified.

Was their friend being murdered by their all-too-genial sugar-pushing host while they were busy eating candy? How could they not notice? What is wrong with them?!

Gretel looks like she's going to scream again.

So she does.

Filomena joins her. "JACK! WHAT HAPPENED TO JACK?!"

"Calm down," says Alistair. "Calm down!" Of course, this only makes the girls more panicked. Because when does telling someone to calm down ever actually help to calm them?

"Are you telling us to calm down because we're girls?" says Gretel huffily.

"No, I don't think it has anything to do with that," says Alistair. "Anyone can get upset. Duh. It's just that you're screaming so loud, and if Rory hears . . ."

"Rory, who owns this cage, which is big enough to fit all of us!" Gretel screeches.

A cage. That's what the strange thing is in the backyard. *It's a cage.*

Filomena wants to throw up.

Something is very, very wrong. How could she not have noticed until now? She thought she was living a dream, but she's woken up to a nightmare.

CHAPTER EIGHT

THE GINGERBREAD MAN?

Filomena is hyperventilating into a cotton candy bag. Alistair is patting her back. Gretel is pacing. They each are crashing from their sugar high.

Filomena tries to think of any advice her parents might offer to calm her down. But she can think only of advice that tends to freak her out even more, such as "Stay calm and don't panic!" Even though her parents themselves are, in fact, in a constant state of panic.

She tries to think of situations back at school in North Pasadena, where nothing ever happens. Correction: where nothing ever *used* to happen. She remembers being chased up a tree by the Fettucine Alfredos. Jack helped her get away . . .

Jack! Where's Jack? What happened to him? And what's that cage for? Why does it look big enough . . . for a person? For three people, even?

Filomena realizes something else. In the last hour or so, since they noticed Jack is missing, they haven't eaten any candy, and she can actually *think* for once. They all can.

Gretel wheels around in her chunky wedges, which are now coated in chocolate and marshmallow fluff. "You guys, it's hot out here. Does anyone have any water?"

Water! When was the last time they had water? No one was ever too concerned with hydration. But why? Oh, right. Because they're surrounded by a limitless amount of candy! Who needs water, or anything of substance, when you can have more candy?

What exactly is in all this candy? Filomena wonders how she could have been so hopped up on sugar that nothing else mattered.

"Gretel, stop pacing. You're making me nervous," says Alistair. "Here, have a candy apple."

Gretel screams again. "A candy apple! That's the last thing I need! I think my teeth are falling out!" She puts her fingers inside her mouth to check.

Alistair gasps. "Now that you mention it, I think my teeth are rotting, too."

Filomena stops panting into the empty cotton candy bag

and pulls it away from her face. She fingers her own molars; they definitely hurt. At Filomena's last dental appointment, the dentist told her to lay off the sweets, and here she's been stuffing her face full of them. She might not remember everything yet, but she knows if her parents have to pay for a root canal, she's really going to be in serious trouble.

Filomena looks out into the sunny afternoon, no longer blinded by the allure of candy. "Wait a minute," she says. "I think I know where we are." One good long look at the gingerbread house has her wheels turning. Her mind starts racing as she tries to think back to the Never After books. It must be in the books, but why can't she remember? At first, it's difficult, but as Filomena's mind continues to clear, she's finally able to concentrate.

She starts to remember. Words, stories, books. Her parents write books. Her parents have read her books. Fairy tales, when she was little. Fairy tales from the Never After series, her favorite books.

Okay, okay. Gingerbread, she thinks. *What books or stories or fairy tales include gingerbread houses? There are so many, aren't there? They're a staple of the fairy-tale genre.*

"Gingerbread house. Who lives in a gingerbread house?" Filomena asks.

"Um, we do?" says Alistair.

"I mean, who else?" says Filomena.

"What are you getting at?" asks Gretel.

"I feel like we're missing something obvious here. But I

don't know what, or how." Filomena sighs. *Think, Filomena, think. Think of the fairy tales you grew up hearing and reading.*

Finally, it hits her. Her eyes go wide with realization. *"Run, run as fast you can. You can't catch me, I'm the Gingerbread Man!"*

Gretel lifts an eyebrow. "Wait. You think Rory is the *Gingerbread Man?"*

Alistair laughs. "The Gingerbread Man!"

But Filomena is adamant. "His name is Rory . . . which means 'red-headed' in Gaelic . . . you know, ginger! He's a ginger! The Gingerbread Man!"

Gretel shakes her head firmly. "The Gingerbread Man is a friend of my dad's. He's a baker and he's *nice.* That creepy candy dude is *not* the Gingerbread Man."

"Do you have any other ideas, then?" Filomena asks. She's out of ideas herself.

"Well, I know he isn't *that,*" Gretel says.

"But who else could he be?"

"Okay, wait," says Gretel. She stands from her resting spot and starts slowly walking around the property. She touches various things as she goes: the bubblegum bushes, the candy apple trees, the lemon-drop patch. Then she turns to the cage. "I think . . . I think I know where we are!" She turns around. "It feels like it's on the tip of my tongue. Except my tongue is coated with so many layers of sugar that I can't concentrate, and my brain has turned into blue-and-pink cotton candy fluff!"

"You can do it," says Filomena.

"We believe in you!" cheers Alistair. He reaches for a watermelon-candy slice, and Filomena slaps it out of his hand.

"No more candy!" she says.

Alistair pouts. "Just a little nibble?"

Gretel ignores their bickering. "Why does it feel like something's missing from my mind? There was something there that isn't now. Like it just went *poof* and disappeared. But the *memory of the memory* . . . it lingers."

Gretel makes her way to the front of the house. She traces her hand around part of the front door. The frosting gets stuck between her fingers. Her fingertips catch on peppermints and gummies. She purposely avoids her favorite: the almond treats. Too tempting. She looks at the cage again.

Is it a cage? No . . . There are wheels on the bottom. Why is that? It's because . . . it's not just a cage; it's a cage on an oven rack.

It hits her then, like a chocolate train barreling around a Christmas tree.

"No! It can't be!" Gretel shakes her head, backing away from the cage in horror. "No!" she yells, louder.

"What is it?" asks Alistair.

"Oh noooo," Gretel cries. "I . . . I can't . . ." She flings herself into Filomena's arms and sobs against her shoulder. "All this time . . . I'm so sorry! I should have known! I blocked it from my memory! I've been here before! This is where Hansel learned to bake . . . This is where . . ."

Filomena hugs Gretel tight, finally beginning to understand. The candy. The cage. "Of course," Filomena says. "We're being fattened up on purpose, aren't we?"

Oh, don't worry. I eat, Rory had said. *I'm going to eat very soon. A veritable feast . . . You're all invited.*

The Cobbler's daughter sniffles. "This is the witch's house!"

Now it's Alistair's turn to hyperventilate. "But where's the witch?" he asks, eyes wide with fright.

"Rory," says Filomena. "Our host . . . He's the witch's son." Her mind's working quickly now. "He told us his name when we met him, remember? Rory Hexson. It was right there in his name. *Hexe* is German for witch—my mom's part German so she taught me a few words. 'Witch son.' Hexson. Rory the witch's son. And he told us he works up at the fort! The ogre fort! He told us the truth but he was very careful about it. His name is Rory Hexson, he's the witch's son, and he's an ogre! That's why he's so tall!" Filomena shudders.

"Well, well, well," says an all-too-familiar voice.

The three jump at the sound.

Their all-too-genial host is decidedly not his jolly self. Rory smiles and deliberately shows off his fangs, which drip with drool.

"You're right about who and what I am. My mother was

the Witch of the Forest." Rory looms over them, no longer slumped, no longer hiding his extraordinary height. "Now, come on," he commands, pointing at the cage. "In you go. I don't think I can wait any longer. I've been very, very patient. But I think it's time for me to feast. As it says in the contract, I am owed *equitable compensation,* and I believe you three have *eaten your weight in candy.*"

"No!" cries Filomena. Gretel hides behind her.

"No?" echoes Rory. He shrugs. "Okay." He looks so reasonable that for a moment Filomena almost believes him.

"Okay?" she asks. Is it really that easy? That doesn't seem right.

It isn't.

With a snap of the witch son's fingers, a few murmured incantations, and a burst of magic, into the cage they go.

He leaves them to marinate in their failure—and in a tasty garlic-butter sauce.

CHAPTER NINE

OUT OF THE OVEN AND INTO THE WOODS

"Jack will save us," says Alistair. "He always does."

Filomena hopes fervently that Alistair is right. She has no desire to be this cannibal witch son's dinner. Plus, the butter is making her skin itchy. Gretel is fretting about what it's done to her hair. "I thought my white jeans getting dirty was the worst of it, but this really takes the cake," she tells them. "Also, I wish we could have some cake right now."

"I don't think I can ever eat dessert again," Filomena laments. Would Jack be able to save them? Where was he, anyway? Would he just show up out of the blue? In the books he always appears right in the nick of time.

But those are just stories.

And stories aren't real, right?

Except Never After *is* real. When they first met, Jack told her. *Why don't you think stories are real? They're the only truth we have.* And so she closes her eyes and believes. Jack is coming to save them. Jack will appear in the nick of time. She doesn't realize she's said this out loud until Gretel replies.

"I don't doubt it," says Gretel, her teeth chattering from cold or fear. "But I wish he would hurry up with the rescuing."

Meanwhile, Rory returns and begins wheeling the cage out of the garden and into the woods toward an altogether different-looking cottage.

This one isn't made of gingerbread; this one is a run-down disheveled shack. This is where the witch really lives. The gingerbread house is like a chicken coop, where beasts are fed and watered before the slaughter. Filomena's skin crawls once more.

"You're a witch and an ogre," Gretel accuses. "Where's your mother?"

"Oh, you know exactly what happened to her," says Rory grimly, a vengeful edge to his voice.

"Oh, I'll push you in the oven, too, don't you worry," Gretel threatens.

"I'd like to see you try," says Rory cheerfully. He whistles a happy tune; Filomena smacks herself for not noticing earlier how skinny he is. He looks to be practically starving, with sunken eyes and hollow cheeks. This creature had been waiting a long, long time to eat. They'd thought he was a boy, maybe a little older than Gretel, but he's much, much older, almost ancient. An ancient monster waiting to feed . . .

Inside the ramshackle cottage, Rory opens a hatch in the floor and wheels the cage down a ramp . . . into what else but . . . a BASEMENT DUNGEON!

Filomena was right! Her first instinct was correct! He's a creeper with a BASEMENT DUNGEON! Oh, her poor parents. They would be terrified if they knew her current whereabouts. Filomena laughs hysterically.

"What's so funny?" Rory sneers. Alistair and Gretel look concerned.

"Nothing—nothing," says Filomena, who's trying not to panic.

The basement dungeon holds one of the largest ovens Filomena has ever seen; it fills almost the entire basement. Rory pulls on its iron handle, and a blast of heat and smoke billow through the room.

The witch's son turns his attention to the knobs, muttering to himself. "Hmm, I think a nice slow roast, under three hundred degrees. Or should I broil them first to get them crispy? I do like the crunch . . ."

Filomena looks desperately around the cage for anything they can use to open it—but there's nothing. Alistair is trying to pick the lock, but it's useless. Gretel's face is shocked. She's been here before. She's frozen and mute.

Rory sets the oven temperature and starts wheeling them inside.

Alistair moans in fright. Gretel is too scared to scream. Filomena rattles the bars of the cage. "You won't get away with this!" she threatens. "Stop, stop this now!" She yells, hoping that somehow, someway, Jack can hear them.

"Why? Who's going to make me?" Rory laughs.

"Me," says a familiar voice. Vines suddenly appear, wrapping around the bars of the cage and pulling it out of the heat of the oven.

Vines?

And there standing at the foot of the ramp is none other than their dear friend, the ever dashing, ever patient Jack Stalker, come to save them out of the blue and right in the nick of time! Just like in the books!

Rory turns around, enraged, just as an arrow pierces him right in the chest. He falls to the ground with a thump. "What the . . . ?" He gasps as another arrow pins his arms to the ground, and then again as yet another—and another!—finds its mark.

"See, I told you guys," says Alistair smugly as Jack's vines make quick work of the steel bars, ripping the cage door open with a flourish.

"Miss me?" Jack asks with a smile.

"What took you so long?" Alistair chides.

"I had to wait until you were out of the gingerbread house and the enchanted garden," says Jack, huffing and pulling the vines. "The witch's magic was too strong to fight when you were in it."

A strikingly pretty girl with long, straight black hair appears next to Jack. She looks about sixteen, with a bow and a quiver of arrows slung over her shoulder. Filomena thinks she looks a little like her cousins on her Korean dad's side. "Hurry. The arrows are only going to slow him down," the girl says. "We've got to move!"

"Hortense?" says Gretel as she steps out of the cage.

"Gretel?" the girl stares at Gretel.

Gretel stares at the girl.

"It really is you!" Gretel shrieks.

"And you!" cries Hortense.

They run to each other, both squealing with delight. Gretel holds her cousin in front of her, one hand on each shoulder. "My goodness, look at you! It's been ages!"

"It really has!" Hortense replies. "What did you do to your hair? You're blond! And, um . . . curly?" she says diplomatically, eyeing Gretel's frizzy ends.

Gretel rolls her eyes. "It's a *long* story."

Filomena gasps. "Hold on! You're one of the wicked step-sisters!"

The girl's mouth drops open, and she looks terribly offended. "I most certainly am not! Tell her, Gretel!"

Gretel sighs. "I told you, Filomena. Those fairy tales are all lies. My cousins are not wicked in the least! They're not even the slightest bit malicious! Cinderella, on the other hand—"

"Explanations later; we really need to get out of here," says Jack, interrupting. "If he casts a spell, we're all toast."

"Toast!" says Alistair as he runs out of the cage. "I could use some hot buttered toast!"

Filomena is about to follow her friends up the ramp when she thinks of something they've forgotten. "Gretel!" she calls. "Help me!" She starts trying to roll the body of the fallen witch's son closer to the open oven door.

Gretel runs back, and Alistair joins as well. With Jack's and Hortense's help, too, the five of them roll Rory into the cage and push him into the oven.

The witch's son opens his eyes just in time to see his former victims claim their victory.

"Give your mom my regards!" yells Gretel as she heaves the oven door closed. The thick iron door muffles the screams, but Gretel still shudders.

"Savage," Filomena says approvingly. Together they run

up the ramp. Filomena's parents are wrong after all; there *are* ways to escape a BASEMENT DUNGEON. You just need a little help from your friends.

Before they take their final leave of the gingerbread house, they collect their luggage—Filomena's backpack full of books and Gretel's designer suitcase. Jack leads them out of the forest, and they run to keep up. It's only when they're a good distance away that Jack lets them stop to catch their breath. Alistair, looking wretched, suddenly bends over and vomits multicolored swirls of candy all over the place, and dangerously close to where Gretel is standing.

"My shoes!" Gretel gags just before she turns away. She looks like she might join him in the candy purge.

Alistair is crimson with embarrassment. "Oh dear! Sorry about that. I guess candy and doughnuts don't fare well with running for our lives."

"More like dough*nots*, am I right?" Filomena offers her best dad joke, courtesy of her own dad, to make Alistair feel better, even as she bends down and clutches her own stomach.

Alistair gives them a weak smile. "Good one."

"Anyway, this is all my fault. I should have known better," says Gretel, who's looking pretty wretched herself. "I'm so sorry!"

Alistair shakes his head frantically. "You have nothing to be sorry about. I was first to eat the candy, and I *live* in Never After. I should've known better."

"Yeah, that's true," Gretel allows. "Plus you puked all over my shoes, so I'd say we're even."

Filomena smiles at her friends and realizes they haven't even addressed the most pressing subject. "What happened to you?" she asks Jack. "Where did you go?"

Jack takes a deep breath. "I tried to stop you guys."

"Yeah, we sort of remember that now."

"I thought there might be something in the candy apples," says Jack. "Nothing is ever given away for free here. There's always a catch."

Filomena nods.

"But when we got to the gingerbread house, I knew we were in real trouble. I tried to use my vines to stop you, but the witch's son was too quick, and then when you guys were inside the house, it was too late. I couldn't even come close to it; the magic was too strong. So I knew I just had to wait it out. I figured he wouldn't, um . . . roast you guys for a while. Witches are patient, and they like their prey to have a little meat on their bones. So I kept going, thinking I would find someone to help"—Jack motions to Hortense—"and thankfully I bumped into Gretel's cousin."

"Hortense Rose," she says. "Nice to meet you. Call me Hori; everyone does."

"Nice to meet you, Hori. Alistair Bartholomew Barnaby, at your service," says Alistair with a bow. "Thank you for your assistance in our escape."

"My pleasure," says Hortense. "Can't let the witches win!"

"I'm Filomena Jefferson-Cho of North Pasadena," Filomena says next, extending her hand.

"That's quite the title," Hortense says with a smile. "It's a pleasure to meet you. I hope you don't still think I'm wicked."

Filomena blushes. "My bad."

"It's all right. Apparently Cinderella's been trashing my reputation all over the place," Hortense says dryly.

Filomena looks uncomfortable and changes the subject. "How long were we in there?" she asks.

"Not long," says Jack. "A few days."

"It felt like years," says Gretel as she tugs up the waistband to her pants.

"Magic warps time and sense," says Jack.

"Oh right," says Gretel, tucking her shirt into her pants and attempting to smooth down her hair. "I must look a wreck!"

"I tried to stop you," says Jack, "but none of you would listen to me. It was like you couldn't even hear me." He shakes his head. "The candy really got to you."

"Thanks for coming back for us," says Filomena shyly.

Now it's Jack's turn to look shy. "Couldn't let my friends be witch supper, could I?"

Alistair chuckles. "No way. I'd never be witch supper. I

might not be as nimble as some"—he winks at Jack—"but I'm not that slow!" Alistair considers what he just said. "But I also knew you were going to get us out of there."

"Group hug!" cheers Filomena, and the four embrace happily. Gretel pulls in her cousin as well. For an all-too-brief moment, they enjoy the safety found in a circle of friendship.

Afterward, the cousins walk with arms linked, chatting and gossiping as they lead the way out of the forest. The others are reduced to mere eavesdropping.

En route, they overhear Hortense tell Gretel about an upcoming royal ball and how excited she is to attend with her boyfriend, Prince Charming.

Filomena wonders if she's heard this correctly. "I'm sorry, did you just say you're dating Prince Charming? As in . . . *the* Prince Charming?"

Hortense turns around and gives her a quizzical look. "Yes, why? Do you know him? We've been exclusive since we started seeing each other. If he's been talking to other girls, I swear I'll—"

Filomena shakes her head, thinking she's only twelve and way too young to date Prince Charming. Besides, Filomena has already decided she's never going to marry any kind of stuck-up prince, no matter what. "Nope, don't know him. I only know *of* him."

Hortense exhales a sigh of relief and turns her attention back to Gretel.

"You know, I could really go for some candy right now," Alistair laments.

"Oh, you," says Gretel while Jack and Hortense laugh.

After a second, Filomena joins them, too.

But they all sober up when Filomena reminds them why they're here. They have to recover the Stolen Slippers, lest they lead to the destruction of Never After and The End of the Story. Quickly now, they follow Cinderella's supposedly wicked but in truth pretty awesome stepsister as she leads them out of the woods.

Introducing Cinderella

Once upon a time in Eastphalia,

A widower married a widow

And counted their daughters three—

Hortense, Beatrice, and Cinderella—

Happy as can be.

Hortense and Beatrice's mother was an angel

Who loved her three daughters true.

But when her new husband tragically expired,

her stepdaughter, Cinderella, suddenly ran wild.

Cinderella demanded everything; she ran up the bills.

Harangued the servants till they made for the hills.

Her stepmother tried to placate her, tried to make do,

Worked day and night to please this terrible shrew.

Until one day, her heart gave out.

She'd given Cinderella everything

Until there was nothing left to give.

But Cinderella wanted more.

Cinderella told everyone her stepsisters were wicked,

That their mother was a brute,

That she was victimized and persecuted

When that was furthest from the truth!

One fine day, Cinderella disappeared

Without leaving even a note, except to gloat

That her godmother had been informed of her dire situation

And insisted on providing immediate reparation!

So off she went, in a poof, in a flash—

Hortense and Beatrice left in peace at last!

Except, they discovered, she'd taken their treasure,

Their mother's glass slippers, at her leisure.

The girls wailed, they cried,

They gnashed their teeth and swallowed their pride.

They wrote messages and entreaties asking for the slippers,

But Cinderella said, "No, never, they're mine.

Come for them if you want them."

And so they did.

PART TWO

Wherein . . .

Filomena learns the true meaning of the phrase "a Cinderella story."

The gang infiltrates Wonderland in disguise with one rule: Don't blow their cover.

They blow their cover.

CHAPTER TEN

THE TWIN ROSES OF ROSEWOOD MANOR

J ack and Hortense lead the group out of the forest and onto a meandering path that ends in an intimidating row of bumbleberry hedges. The growth clusters between and behind black iron gates that stand twenty feet high. "There's a house back there?" asks Filomena doubtfully.

"Hidden, but I assure you it's there," says Hortense. "Best that you can't see it from the road. Mustn't draw any ogre attention, now, must we?" She removes a large iron key from her pocket and unlocks the entrance gate.

Filomena watches approvingly. Her house in North Pasadena has many locks and alarms to keep her family safe from the ogres of their world as well.

Hortense walks them up a pathway to a grand manor house. Just as Gretel said, the house is covered in yellow and pink roses that twine around its soaring columns. "Wow," says Gretel. "It's so much bigger than I remember."

"Mom renovated a few times. You were here when it was just a cottage," says Hortense.

Filomena thinks the house wouldn't look too out of place in the fancy neighborhoods back in her hometown. It has that kind of regal grandeur that immediately intimidates. She hesitates a little and finds Alistair is staring at the building as well. "What's wrong?" she whispers, wondering if he's maybe a little shy because of its magnificence.

"Nothing." Alistair sighs as he stares at the manor with genuine despair.

Filomena and Jack share a look. They know their friend all too well. Alistair is deeply disappointed that the house is not made of gingerbread nor stuffed with candy. "Come on," Jack urges. "At least we can be sure there's no witch in there."

Hortense rings the bell, and a butler with a forbidding look opens the door. "Welcome back, Miss Rose," he says in greeting. He ignores the rest of them.

"Thanks, Archibald," says Hortense, handing him her hooded coat, bow, and quiver of arrows.

"Good hunting today?" asks Archibald.

"You could say that." She smiles. "Is dinner ready? My friends are famished."

"Just about," replies the loyal servant. He regards the raggedy group with a sniff of disdain. "And shall Mistress require the formal service for supper?"

"Yes, please," says Hortense. "And these are my friends. They can wear whatever they like to dinner."

"As you wish," says the butler, stepping from the doorway as if he has no choice.

Gretel follows her cousin inside, marveling at all the changes made to the place. "I love the chandelier!" she squeals, looking at the foyer's crystal centerpiece.

But Alistair, still standing outside, is hesitating once again. Jack and Filomena wait, too, not wanting to enter without their friend.

"What now?" asks Jack a little impatiently.

Alistair grimaces. "I don't know if this is a good idea."

Gretel overhears and comes back to the doorway to glare at him. "Why not?"

He frowns and puts his hands on his hips. "Oh, I don't know. Maybe because the last time we stepped foot in a stranger's house, we nearly ended up as his dinner!"

"I really doubt Hori has any plans to eat us," Filomena whispers.

"What was that?" Hortense asks.

Filomena winces. She hates being rude to her hosts. "Nothing!"

Gretel crosses her arms and glares at the three of them. "If you guys think for even a second that my cousins aren't pure of heart, I don't know what to tell you."

"I guess she did help rescue us from that creepy candy dude, and she's kind enough to invite us in . . . ," Alistair starts. Then his face crinkles. "Even if there's no candy here."

Jack flicks him on the forehead. "That's a good thing, you big lollipop."

Alistair rubs his head. "Oi! Violence! I thought we talked about this!"

"Right," Gretel concedes. "If you fools want to stay out here and risk being found by ogres again, be my guest. I'm going inside." With that, she storms out of sight.

The butler watches all this with a raised eyebrow.

Filomena begins to follow Gretel inside, but at the doorway she turns and faces the boys. "Well? In or out?"

Jack puts a hand on Alistair's shoulder. "I've been here before, you know. It's perfectly safe. But listen, if you don't want to come in, I'll stay out here with you. Friends stick together. You know that."

"You'd do that for me?" Alistair asks.

"Yeah," says Jack, as if it's not a big deal at all. As if a night in the shrubs is comparable to staying in a comfortable manor house.

"I guess I would, too," Filomena admits.

"And me," says Gretel, who's come back to collect them once more. "But come on, my cousins live here. If they're witches, then so am I."

"Now that you mention it . . . ," jokes Alistair.

"Don't even go there," warns Gretel, wagging a finger. "Remember my past!"

"Okay, okay," agrees Alistair as he falls in step with Jack and enters at last. If he is worried about being locked inside when the butler closes the door behind them, he gives no indication.

The house is even more impressive inside, with its various sitting rooms and visiting rooms and reception rooms. It looks like the kind of glamorous mansion you'd see in an "Eastphalia's Greatest Homes" feature for a magazine or a television show. It's practically a palace, with legions of staff running around; valets and footmen and lady's maids rush to make them comfortable, offering drinks and plumping cushions. Hortense, their kind and gracious host, bids them to join her in the main salon, which features a picture window with a view of the grounds below.

Filomena takes it all in. So if Cinderella didn't have to

cook, clean, or manage the chimney . . . then what was that all about?

"Cinderella lived here?" she asks.

Hortense nods. "Yes. She had the biggest bedroom, upstairs. We insisted she take it because she needed the biggest closet for all her gowns."

"She didn't live in the attic?" asks Filomena.

"The attic? Why on earth would she live in the attic?" says Hortense, shaking her head. "It's dusty up there, and there are probably mice!"

"Where do the servants live?" Filomena wants to know; maybe there's a hole in the story somewhere and she can find it.

"They have their own homes on the estate," Hortense replies, motioning to a row of tidy cottages that they can see out the picture window. "But Cinderella wasn't a servant," she says, her tone mystified. "She was our sister."

Gretel looks meaningfully at Filomena as if to say, *I told you so.* "Give us a tour, Hori," she requests, and her cousin obliges.

Hortense shows them a music room with a grand piano, a sewing room, multiple ballrooms, and a formal dining room with a table that could easily seat twenty.

The kitchen boasts not just a skylight but an entire ceiling that's made of glass, so transparent it seems nothing is there at all. With darkness falling now, they can see the entire night sky above them, and through the floor-to-ceiling windows, the silhouette of the Weeping Tree in the distance.

"Wow," Filomena says aloud, stopped in her tracks at the awe-inspiring view.

Jack, who's standing beside her, looks over as well. "When the fairies still lived in the tree, you could probably see the lights from here," he says softly. "It must have been a beautiful view."

Filomena nods. Their reverie is broken by the sound of quickly approaching footsteps on the curving staircase. There's a screech, and the kitchen door opens with a bang. A striking girl with long black hair appears. "Gretel?! Is it really you?" She tackles Gretel in a big hug. "It *is* you!" the girl says.

She looks exactly like Hortense, from her honey-colored skin and deep dark eyes down to her button nose and the freckles across her cheeks.

When Gretel and the girl release their embrace, Gretel turns to her friends proudly. "This is Beatrice, my other cousin."

"And my twin sister," adds Hortense. "Can you tell?"

Filomena, Jack, and Alistair nod and laugh.

"Except we're not identical, actually," says Beatrice. "We're fraternal twins."

"We just look alike because we're sisters," says Hortense, wiggling her nose.

"Obviously Hori's prettier," says Beatrice shyly, giving her sister's arm a playful squeeze.

"Nonsense," says Hortense, who's not having it. "You are."

"No, you are," says Beatrice.

The twins giggle. It's clear they're each other's biggest supporter. "Okay fine, Gretel is prettiest," says Beatrice at last.

It's only then that Filomena notices Gretel's artfully golden hair is exactly that—artful. Otherwise Gretel has the same dark eyes and spray of freckles on her rosy golden cheeks.

When Gretel notices Filomena looking at the three of them with interest, she catches Filomena's stare and explains. "Forgot to tell you guys: My dad's only half Eastphalian," says Gretel. "He told us his mother was from Seoul."

"Uncle is well?" asks Beatrice.

Gretel nods. "Golfing every day, and he's a big fan of Cuban food." She turns back to her friends. "Where are my manners? Bea, these are my friends."

"We've already met Jack," says Beatrice. "He's been really worried about you three."

Jack looks a bit sheepish.

Beatrice turns to Filomena. "You must be Filomena, the girl from the other world. Jack said you're really smart and very pretty."

Now it's Filomena's turn to look embarrassed. Jack thinks she's pretty? No one's ever called her pretty before, other than her parents. She blushes. "I guess that's me?"

"And you're Alistair, of course," says Beatrice.

"Of course," says Alistair, standing a little taller. "What did Jack say about me?"

Beatrice and Hortense giggle again.

"All good things, I assure you," Beatrice says warmly. "That you're the best friend any guy could ever have."

Alistair wipes his brow in mock relief. "Oh good. Usually he just says I'm short and loud."

"That too," says Beatrice.

Alistair's shoulders slump a little.

"She's kidding!" Hortense assures him.

Beatrice turns to her sister. "Hori, Archibald says your arrows are bloody! Don't tell me you put yourself in danger again," she says with a worried look on her face.

"I had to! They were captured by that horrible ogre," Hortense replies defensively. "You know, the creepy one who works as a cook at the fort."

Beatrice shudders. "Well, I'm glad none of you were hurt."

"Ogres are so clumsy and slow," Hortense says dismissively. "They're just big brutes. Bullies, the lot of them."

"Please don't go hunting again. You promised Charlie you wouldn't anymore," Beatrice says, admonishing her spirited sister.

"Charlie? You mean Prince Charming?" asks Filomena.

"Prince Charming is just what *Palace Weekly* calls him," explains Hortense with a laugh. "It's not his real name."

"Prince Charming, the most eligible bachelor in all of Never After!" teases Beatrice. "But he's not so eligible anymore, is he, sis?"

"His real name is Prince Charlemagne, but he goes by Charlie," says Hortense affectionately. "I can't wait for you guys to meet him."

"Oh, before I forget—this came for you today. I think he sent you a message," says Bea, rooting around in a wicker basket on the counter. "Here it is." She hands her sister a large envelope made of the finest parchment. It's stamped with the royal seal of Eastphalia.

Hortense opens the envelope and reads the note inside. "Huh. He says he can't come to dinner, as he's needed out of town. He'll just meet me at the royal ball next week." Her face changes as she puts it away.

Gretel puts an arm around her cousin's shoulders. "What's wrong?"

"The Queen of Hearts is holding a royal ball in Wonderland in his honor," Beatrice tells them. "It's practically an open secret that Charlie's supposed to announce his engagement to Hortense at the big event. That's the whole point of the ball." She motions to a stack of glossy magazines and tabloids whose covers display multiple photos of a handsome prince and Hortense holding hands. "Is She the One?" blares the *Never After Post*. "Hori and Charming—Meant to Be?" demands the *Palace Inquirer*. "Royal Ball and Royal Announcement Imminent!" screams the *Daily Crown*.

"Except," says Hortense, who now looks deeply worried, "he hasn't asked me to marry him yet."

"And she's been waiting for an invitation to the royal ball for weeks now," says Beatrice, her face mirroring her sister's worry.

"It didn't come today?" asks Hortense.

Beatrice shook her head. "Nothing."

"I guess I'm not going," says Hortense, worriedly re-arranging the already perfectly arranged flowers on the nearest counter.

"No way! Prince Charming is your boyfriend! You have to attend!" Beatrice is obviously incensed at the very thought.

"But what if I *can't* attend?" Hortense says unhappily, leaving the flowers alone.

The other kids are confused as they try to follow the conversation. "What do you mean, if you 'can't' attend the ball?" asks Jack.

Hortense sighs, her cheeks going pink. "As you can see, I kinda sorta haven't been invited yet . . ."

Alistair chuckles nervously. "Well, that's awkward."

Beatrice throws her hands up in the air in frustration. "Can you imagine? Not being invited to your own boyfriend's party!"

Alistair, still nervous, shakes his head. "I . . . I don't know. I don't have a boyfriend."

They all ignore him. "I can't go without an invitation," says Hortense, biting her lip.

"Nonsense! You're definitely invited!" says Beatrice hotly.

"If I was, the invitation would have come by now," says Hortense. "I don't think I'm getting one. He must have changed his mind about me."

With those words, Hortense bursts into sobs that could break anyone's heart.

CHAPTER ELEVEN

LIES AND ASHES

Gretel and Beatrice gather around Hortense to comfort her. "There, there, there's no need to cry, it can't be as bad as all that," says Gretel. There are murmurings and hugs as they try to make Hortense feel better, and Filomena wishes she could say or do something, but she feels helpless. Romantic drama isn't something Filomena is familiar with, even though her mother is a successful author of bodice-ripping romance novels. Filomena is decidedly not allowed to read them; she's only twelve years old after all.

Filomena is about to tell Hortense the plot of one of her

mother's books (Filomena's not being allowed to read them has never stopped her from doing exactly that) when the snooty butler enters and announces that dinner is served in the main dining room.

"Of course, of course. Please, you guys must be starving. Let's eat," says Beatrice, ushering the crew out of the kitchen.

The dining table is laid out with all manner of delicacies. A lazy Susan in the middle of the table groans under the weight of the veritable feast. There are little bowls filled with pickled vegetables, potato salad, dried fish, vibrant red kimchi, slippery cuttlefish, tofu skin, braised lotus roots, platters of barbecued meat, and a tureen of tofu soup.

"So much *banchan!*" says Filomena happily, taking a seat and picking up the chopsticks set next to her plate.

"Ooh," says Alistair. "What is all this?"

"They're like little appetizers," Filomena explains. "We eat this almost every weekend at my house." She feels homesick for a moment, thinking of Mum and Dad eating their Korean barbecue alone.

"Granny's old recipes and a few Eastphalian dishes as well," says Beatrice. "That's also heart of caulichoke and savory pomfrey cakes. Please, eat."

Filomena, Jack, Gretel, and Alistair dig in lustily, even as Filomena can't help but feel guilty for eating at a time like this, when it's clear the Rose twins have no appetite.

"First Mom's glass slippers are gone, and now this," says Hortense between sniffs.

"Cinderella has to be behind this, too," Beatrice declares, rapping her chopsticks on the table.

Hortense dabs at her eyes with Gretel's hankie. "You think so?"

"Who else? She must have made sure you weren't invited to the ball." Beatrice passes dishes around while she talks to her sister. "Cinderella must have overheard us talking about Mom's vision for your future."

"Auntie had a vision?" asks Gretel, looking up from her *soondubu*.

"Yes. She said she saw a vision of Prince Charlemagne dancing with Hortense at his engagement party. At least, we think it was Hortense because Mom said the girl was wearing glass slippers. And Hori's the only one who owns a pair. Mom gave them to both of us, but they're Hori's. They fit her better. Not my style." Beatrice shrugs.

"But crystal goes with everything," murmurs Gretel to no one in particular.

Beatrice doesn't hear. "Our mom was a seer," she tells the group. "When we were little, she would tell us this story of a royal ball and a prince who marries a girl in glass slippers. And she would always end it with 'And that girl is you, Hortense.'"

Hortense smiles through her tears. "Except I swore I would never marry any kind of prince." She places a few slices of *galbi* on her plate but only moves them around and doesn't take a bite.

"But then you met Charlie," Beatrice says with a fond smile.

"I didn't know he was a prince. He was just Charlie from my alchemistry class." Hortense laughs. "He pretended not to understand magical particle physics."

"Because he's been in love with you since day one," says Beatrice.

"Well, I fell in love with him, too," says Hortense. "And I told Bea, 'Maybe Mom was right.' I wore the glass slippers on our first date." She looks wistful. "He said, 'Hey, did you know I'm supposed to marry a girl who wears glass slippers?'" Hortense sighs at the memory. "I told him I'd heard the story but didn't believe it. We make our own fate."

"You might not have believed in the fairy tale, but *someone* believed it," says Gretel. "Someone who was living in your own house." She passes a bowl of sticky white rice to Alistair, who heaps his plate with a mountain of it.

"Our stepdad was so sweet. He'd lost his wife and doted on our mother. He and Mom bonded because they had both lost their spouses. But Cinderella was nothing like him. She's always been so bitter." Beatrice frowns. "Our stepsister, Cinderella. She acts so sweet and kind, but she's not. There's something wrong with that girl. She's always playing the victim."

"Once Mom asked her to help sweep the fireplace after she made herself some s'mores. It's all we heard about for weeks!" says Hortense. "And she didn't even offer us any of those s'mores!"

"She acted like Mom turned her into a servant!" Beatrice adds.

"Just another Cinderella story," says Hortense, huffing.

Seeing the confused look on Filomena's face, Beatrice quickly explains. "In our house, whenever anyone plays the victim and whines that they've been mistreated, even when they totally have not, we call it a 'Cinderella story.'"

"Oh," says Filomena. She thinks it's best not to share that in her world, a Cinderella story is the rags-to-riches tale of a plucky and lovable heroine who overcomes obstacles like, er . . . two wicked stepsisters.

"The worst part is I lent her the slippers; that's why they were so easy for her to steal," says Hortense. "She acted so pitiful. She said that unlike us, she'd never owned any-thing beautiful, which is a total lie—Mom bought her all the clothes and jewels she wanted. She almost bankrupted us."

Beatrice agrees, and Gretel shakes her head, wagging a piece of amaranth-flavored zucchonion with her chopsticks. "That miserable little—"

Hortense places her hand over Gretel's. "I know. I know. But name-calling won't do us any good. Trust me, I've had my moments."

"Cinderella has always had a huge crush on Charlie," Beatrice says. "But he never noticed her or gave her the time of day. I doubt he even remembers what she looks like."

"You really think she stole Mom's glass slippers because she thinks whoever wears them at that royal ball is going to marry him?" asks Hortense.

"Absolutely. Your happily ever after is what she's after," says Beatrice. "She was always so jealous of you."

The sisters are so alike, Filomena observes, but Beatrice is thoughtful, while Hortense is livelier. Hortense is prone to strong outbursts of emotion, while Beatrice is a little more reserved. But it's clear they are both distressed by this turn of events. Filomena pauses to take it all in. She can't help but wonder . . . Why does her world know an incorrect version of the story of Cinderella and her stepsisters? The tales as the world knows them are wrong. Who wrote them? Who told them? Who lied to her world? And . . . why?

"We've got to get those slippers back. That's why we're here," says Gretel. "Dad said it was *mucho* important."

"The Prophecy," says Hortense, shuddering. "We know. I wish I'd never lent them to her. Although, even though Cinderella is spoiled rotten, it's not like she's an ogre . . ."

"But remember, whoever Charlie marries becomes queen of Eastphalia," says Beatrice. She looks pointedly at her sister. "You've got to be at that ball. We can't let Cinderella win."

"But what if Charlie's changed his mind about me?" asks

Hortense. "Maybe he's chosen someone else and that's why I didn't receive an invitation."

Beatrice purses her lips. "Do you really believe that? The guy took alchemistry *twice* so he could sit next to you."

"Plus he sent you a message saying he'd see you at the ball," reminds Gretel. "That doesn't sound like a guy who's changed his mind."

"I guess he's just assuming I'll be there. Which I can't be without an invitation," says Hortense. "The kingdom of Wonderland is pretty strict about these things. Their queen is pretty scary as it is."

"Can't we get a message to Charlie?" asks Gretel. "Can't he just bring you as his plus-one?"

"It's not his party; it's just thrown in his honor. And what's a plus-one?" asks Hortense. "Besides, I'm not going to beg." She stares off into the distance. "You really think Cinderella has something to do with me not receiving an invite?"

"One hundred percent," says Beatrice.

"Where is Cinderella now?" Filomena asks aloud.

"She went to live with her godmother, who just happens to be the Queen of Hearts and the ruler of Wonderland," Beatrice tells them.

Filomena raises her eyebrows. "And when is the ball? Next week?"

Beatrice nods.

"So we have time," says Filomena, thinking quickly.

"Time for what? There's no time. The ball's practically around the corner. It's hopeless." Hortense sighs. "The glass slippers are gone, and Cinderella's going to wear them to the ball, and somehow Charlie will choose her as his bride. Isn't that how the story goes in your world? Gretel told me a little about it. And somehow if that happens, it will trigger the end of Never After, too."

"Do you think the magic of the slippers will overcome his love for you?" asks Filomena.

"Oh, I—I don't know. I mean, we haven't said we love each other yet," Hortense answers, looking miserable. "I mean, I think he loves me, but I don't know for sure."

Filomena thinks it's so silly not to tell someone you love them, but then blushes when she realizes how deeply she's buried her crush for Jack, too. So, as the kids say, she gets it.

"Fairy magic is powerful! It's hopeless!" cries Hortense.

Filomena thinks of the Weeping Tree, the dimming of lights, and the despair that's spread throughout Never After since the fairies went underground. She adamantly shakes her head. "No. Nothing is ever hopeless. There's got to be a way to get those slippers back." She pauses a moment. "The stories as we know them in the mortal world are wrong. That's why I loved reading the Never After books!" She stands up and paces the room for a moment, thinking. "I know! We'll go to the queen's palace, and we'll steal the glass slippers right back! And get you an invitation to that party!"

"We're doing what now?" asks Alistair.

"Stealing back the slippers," says Jack. "It's what we came here for, isn't it?"

"But Wonderland is guarded by Chessmen, Never After's most elite military force. We'll never get inside," says Hortense.

"Yes, we can," Filomena says triumphantly. She puffs with pride and pushes her curly hair from her face. "This might be hard to believe, knowing how cool you guys think I am. But I'm *awesome* at chess."

CHAPTER TWELVE

THE QUEEN'S GAMBIT?

The next morning, after a good night's rest, they gather around the table for a quick breakfast before saying their goodbyes. They decided the night before that only Jack, Filomena, Alistair, and Gretel would venture to Wonderland to execute the first initiative in Operation Stolen Slippers: scoping out the Chessmen's security forces around the palace. Meanwhile, the Rose sisters will travel to Charmingham Castle to see if they can get a hold of Charlie and set the matter straight. Hortense figures there is no harm in asking her boyfriend what his actual plans are for the royal ball; they are a couple after all. Filomena privately thinks this would all be settled much faster if Charlie and Hortense had smartphones and could text each other. But this is Never After; all that's available are talking mirrors, and unfortunately the ogres control most of those. The only accessible talking mirror left is in Snow Country, which is miles away.

"Good luck and be careful," Beatrice calls, waving from the manor doorway.

"The Queen of Hearts is a tyrant, so make sure you don't get in trouble, or you'll lose your heads," adds Hortense.

"Oh dear, I forgot all about that," says Alistair, taking two steps backward. "I'd like to keep mine on, please."

"We'll be fine," says Filomena, pushing him forward. "Keep walking."

"I guess it can't be any worse than almost being eaten by an ogre," says Alistair.

The Rose sisters outfitted their friends with horses for the journey, which the footmen bring them out from the stables. Jack's already on a magnificent chestnut stallion and helps Filomena climb up behind him. "You all right?" Jack asks.

"I used to ride the ponies in Griffith Park," she tells him, hanging on for dear life. "This can't be that different, right? I mean, other than the fact that we're not going around in a circle at a slow canter."

Jack tugs on the reins and laughs. "Just try to hold on."

Gretel, who has Alistair behind her, clucks her tongue. "Let's go. I need to get back in time to do a face peel. All this running around is making me break out!"

It's a few leagues to Wonderland, and the path is quiet. No ogres for once, although Filomena keeps her ears perked for any sign of thunderbolts or booming rumbles, no matter how distant.

"So, any idea what we're going to do when we get there?" asks Alistair.

Jack shakes his head. "Nope. But I reckon we'll figure it out like we always do."

Filomena agrees. "Sounds like a good plan to me."

"No plan is a plan in itself," says Jack.

"But no stopping at gingerbread houses," says Alistair sternly.

"Seriously," Gretel adds. "My teeth still hurt."

"So does my stomach," Alistair says. "If I never have another Sunflower Sun, it'll be too soon."

"Never thought I'd hear you say that," Filomena teases.

She gazes ahead at the empty path, then looks down at her combat boots. They're still caked in cake and covered with grime. She's glad to have durable footwear as she glances at Gretel's shoes. Her friend's chunky wedges have been swapped for a pair of rubber rain boots.

Gretel, noticing Filomena noticing, looks down at her feet as well. "Oh, yeah. Hori let me borrow these."

"Why rain boots?" asks Filomena.

"Wonderland is a bit swampy, apparently," Gretel replies. "At least, that's what they told me."

"It is," Jack confirms. "That's what Wonderland is. One big swamp."

Alistair adds, "Before it was called Wonderland, it was the kingdom of Leastphalia. Their motto was 'Last but not least,' except they sort of were. Although now that I think about it, maybe it was 'Last and not east.'"

"You're joking," says Filomena.

Alistair just laughs.

Jack shakes his head. "Actually, a long time ago, Wonderland was supposed to be that—a real wonderland. It was the most beautiful of all the kingdoms of Never After. But something changed a few years back. Since then the kingdom has massively deteriorated and its queen—she was called the Queen of Hearts because she was lovely inside and out—became a despot. Everyone avoids it now, so the royal ball in honor of Eastphalia's prince must be the queen's way of trying to become popular again."

They ride until midday, trekking along a path that leads to the neighboring kingdom. When they get closer to Wonderland, they feel a distant hum of activity, sounds of life, for the first time on their journey. They hush one another, moving carefully now to avoid being discovered.

Even from this distance they can see the spires of Wonderland's castle come into view. The walls around the kingdom are black and white like chess pieces; for a moment Filomena thinks the walls are moving, then she realizes the movement is actually soldiers. So these are the famous Chessmen of Wonderland. Some are pawns wearing berets; some are knights on horseback. A few wear pointy bishop hats, with a few rooks standing in between them.

"Chessmen," whispers Jack.

"I see that," says Filomena. "They're using zone defense."

Jack looks over his shoulder at her with an admiring smile. "How do you know?"

"I told you guys—I'm great at chess. I beat my dad all the time. See them?" she says, pointing to the pawns. "They can only move forward one square at a time. That's why they move slowly. The bishops can only move sideways. Knights can move in the shape of an L. Rooks can move longitudinally or laterally."

Filomena jumps off the horse when they get closer. "Here's a plan: I'll distract them while you guys see if there are any other entrances to this place. Who knows? Maybe I'll even get inside!"

"Keep an eye out for those bishops," warns Jack. "They can hit you with their staffs."

She nods.

"Wait a minute! What are you doing?" Alistair cries.

"They're Chessmen! You'll get killed—or worse—checkmated!"

"What happens at checkmate?" asks Filomena.

"They take you to the queen!" wails Alistair. "You don't want to see the queen! You know . . ." He makes a slashing motion at his throat.

"Filomena, be careful!" adds Gretel. "Wonderland is not for the weak!"

"I'll be fine!" Filomena assures her friends. She's not sure why she's acting so brave all of a sudden, but seeing the black-and-white chess pieces makes her think she can engage the Chessmen. Maybe she can lead them away from the front of the castle to give Jack and their crew enough time to scope out another way inside. Filomena's dad is not bad at chess, but she's better.

"Are you sure about this?" Alistair says worriedly.

"Not really," says Filomena, stepping carefully through the tall grass. "But what else can we do?"

As Filomena inches toward the castle gates, she notices that even the lawn in front of the castle is trimmed and colored in black-and-white squares. She steps onto the closest black square only to find the nearest pawn soldier sliding forward.

"Halt!" it commands.

She freezes, realizing what just happened. She took one

step, and the pawn followed suit—just like in a real chess game. Filomena tries to take a step backward, but she can't—it's like she's being blocked by an invisible wall. Filomena groans.

"I'm a pawn!" she grumbles. The pawn is the only piece that *cannot* move backward. It is also the lousiest piece in the game. Why can't she have been a queen? That way she could zoom anywhere on the board.

"Who goes there? What is your intention in Wonderland?" the pawn soldier barks.

"Oh, I, uh—I was just wondering if I could have a meeting with the Queen of Hearts?" Filomena asks.

"Is she expecting you?" the pawn demands.

"Well, um . . . no," Filomena has to admit.

"INTRUDER! You have stepped onto our territory. Win the game or lose your head!"

Fairysticks! Now she's really done it—she's plunged headfirst into engaging the Chessmen, and now if she loses, she will lose her head.

She can't step backward. She has to play.

She scans the board covered with Chessmen. Their defense is pretty tight; most are grouped in a close formation at the back of the board that will be hard to break, surrounding a soldier wearing a wig topped with a crown—that must be the queen's representative. Just as in chess, they are protecting the queen.

Filomena slides into the next square, and a bishop zooms

toward her. It's on a black square while Filomena's on a white one, so there isn't any way for their paths to cross. But Filomena swears he—or maybe it's a she, it's hard to tell—is definitely about to smoosh her. The bishop whizzes past and swings its staff in a quick little motion, just a jerk of the wrist. The staff sails by Filomena's ear as she tumbles out of the way. It missed but was close. Really close, and she guesses that staff would knock her to the ground if it makes contact.

"Cheater," Filomena cries. Weapons aren't part of chess, but then again, this isn't a traditional game of chess. She considers her next move. So far, she's traveled across the board in a straight line. That's what pawns do, but they also move on the diagonal when they attack.

She plants her feet and leaps to the square sitting next to her along the diagonal. It's occupied by another pawn, which her move should capture.

As she lands, the pawn soldier flies out of the square. It tumbles through the sky and crashes somewhere off in the trees. *Yes! Victory!*

At least her plan seems to be working; all the Chessmen are trained on her now. She sneaks a look to see if Jack and the others are having any luck finding another entrance.

Then something tall blocks out the sun—something big and round and towering. No, wait—it isn't towering; it *is* a tower! No, wait—it's just a knight with a tower-shaped hat. The soldier looms above her. It came out of nowhere with that *L*-shaped move. It's now trying to push Filomena and knock her out of the game. She wonders what it might be like if she loses her place and is suddenly tossed into the bushes. At a minimum she'd have the worst headache of her life, or maybe the fall would break both her legs. She hopes she'll never learn the answer. Wait—the pawn did say if she loses the game, she loses her head.

Oops.

She makes her next move, coming close to the Chessmen's zone defense. That's when she sees something interesting: a weak point in their cluster. It's a certain path to victory, and she takes it.

Three moves up, two moves across, and she's almost there. The Chessmen tremble in front of her. Actually they wobble. They make their next move but have no way to block the opening. Filomena leaps into the square and calls, "Checkmate! I win!"

"No one beats the queen," the nearest knight says sternly.

"What? But I won! I won fair and square!" she protests.

"This is Wonderland—nothing's fair here," the knight replies with an evil smile. "Haven't you figured that out yet?"

Filomena doesn't need to hear anything more. She runs out of there as fast as her cardio-loathing legs can take her.

After narrowly escaping the angry legion of Chessmen, Filomena regroups with her friends at the agreed meeting place behind a line of trees. "Did you find another way inside?" she asks, catching her breath as she arrives.

Jack shakes his head. "There's only that one entrance," he says, motioning to the front of the castle. The Chessmen have moved aside to allow a slew of carriages—carrying what look to be decorations and trimmings for the upcoming royal ball—to enter the castle.

"There's no getting in that way," says Filomena. "At least not directly, like I tried to do. Even if you beat them at their own game, you still lose."

"Yeah," says Jack, frowning as he glances at the castle entrance.

"Told you," says Alistair.

"So what's the plan?" asks Gretel. "Now that we're here, don't we need one?"

Jack is still staring at the phalanx of Chessmen arranged in rows around the entrance to the castle. Finally he shakes his head. "I typically wouldn't suggest this, but I'm afraid we have no choice."

The others wait for his answer. At last, he unveils his plan. "We'll have to use deception."

CHAPTER THIRTEEN

OCEAN'S FOUR

The gang is in low spirits when they arrive back at Rosewood Manor, and it appears the sisters didn't have
much luck, either. Everyone gathers in the great room for tea,
which is comforting after a day playing chess and hiding from
soldiers and being turned away from Charmingham Castle.

"You guys go first," says Gretel, leaning back on the couch
cushions in relief after that long horseback ride. "What happened?"

"Charlie wasn't there," Hortense says. "He's already left
for the ball, which means he's already a guest of the Queen

of Hearts and will probably be locked up in Wonderland until the party."

"There was no one who could even help us; the whole royal entourage was gone. And they were wondering why Hortense wasn't in Wonderland with Charlie," says Beatrice, who holds her teacup out for Archibald to fill.

"I should have asked about it earlier," frets Hortense. "But I didn't want to push."

"It's okay," says Beatrice.

Hortense moodily stirs her drink. "Maybe this is what's supposed to happen, especially since everyone in Filomena's world already thinks Cinderella is the hero of this story."

"Don't say that. You can't lose hope," argues Filomena.

"No, you can't," Gretel insists, taking the seat beside Hortense. She grabs her cousin's hand. "Remember what my dad always says? We don't give up in this family."

"Except hope's deserted these lands, just like the fairies." Hortense sighs.

"Hold on! The fairies didn't abandon Never After; they were forced to go underground," says Filomena. "I read all the books. That's what they say!"

Hortense sits up, her eyes blazing. "Didn't they, though? The fairies abandoned us! Of the thirteen, Colette and Sabine are supposedly still alive! But where are they? We haven't seen them in years! They're all gone! And so is everyone else who matters! Gretel, even your dad left! So, I'm very sorry to say it, but maybe we *do* give up in this family!"

There is a shocked silence.

"You don't mean that. You're just angry," says Beatrice soothingly. "She doesn't mean it. Have another macaron."

Hortense doesn't reply.

Beatrice turns to the others, offering the plate of French cookies, which her sister refused. "What happened in Wonderland? I take it you didn't get past the guards."

"No," Jack explains, taking a pistachio-flavored macaron. "Chessmen everywhere."

Alistair huffs. "Pesky little swamp creatures is all."

"But there's no getting past them," says Jack. "Filomena got close, but sometimes a direct approach isn't the best way."

"So what are you saying?" Beatrice asks keenly.

"Indirect approach," Jack adds, waving the half-eaten macaron cookie in the air. He offers Beatrice and Hortense a knowing glance, as if that says it all. "Ahem . . . A little . . . misdirection, perhaps." He pops the cookie in his mouth and smiles.

Their faces crinkle in confusion until understanding begins to settle in.

"You mean we're going to have to lie, like Cinderella does," Beatrice states flatly.

"I won't lie," says Hortense. "I won't stoop to her level."

Jack offers a solemn glance. "I'm sorry, but there's a lot at stake. You know the Prophecy. I don't like it, either. There's more than just your relationship on the line here. We've got to get those glass slippers back. We can't let Cinderella win and cause The End of the Story."

Beatrice slams her fist on the table. "No, we can't!"

Hortense's frustration morphs into sheer determination. "All right," she says, looking up at Jack. "What do we have to do?"

They gather around Jack, some seated, some standing.

"I'll pose as a Chessman," Jack says, talking quickly. "That way I can help protect you guys once we're inside. Alistair . . . you can pretend to be a baker. Hired to bake bread for the ball. Filomena"—he turns to her—"you'll be a page. Cinderella's page, if you can manage. Or close to it. You need to make sure Hortense gets an invitation to the royal ball." He looks at the Cobbler's daughter. "Gretel, maybe we can pass you off as a royal seamstress; I'm sure the queen will want to use your skills. That will allow you access to the royal chambers, where you can look for the slippers."

Gretel nods. "Sounds good to me. I won't have to pretend very much at all. I know what I'm doing." The others nod, and Gretel adds, "Plus I'll have my fabric scissors in case I need to cut a witch."

"Not to toot my own horn, but I can bake a pretty mean loaf of bread if I do say so myself," Alistair offers. He jokingly dusts off his own shoulder for effect.

Filomena doesn't want to break the newly lightened mood, but doubt creeps in when she thinks of her own skills. "Um, what exactly is a page?"

"A messenger of sorts," Hortense tells her. "Sort of like an assistant to the royal family."

"You'll be expected to carry out certain duties," Jack explains. "Just do as they say."

"To a point," says Alistair.

Filomena nods. "Of course. Nothing to hurt our mission."

"Right," Jack says.

"Obviously," Gretel adds. "And whatever we do, we can't blow our cover. Promise?"

She holds her hand out, and the others stack their hands on top of hers, one by one.

"Promise," everyone says in unison.

Jack catches her eye, and Filomena feels electric all over.

Still, she's nervous. She hates lying. And she's not the only one. As she looks around, she sees familiar expressions on her friends' faces. The hesitation is clear as day. But so is the commitment. At least she isn't in this alone.

Jack's face hardens as he looks from Gretel to Filomena. "One of you needs to have eyes on Cinderella at all times."

The girls nod.

"Watch the real evil stepsister," Filomena says. "Got it."

"Let's get to work, then," Beatrice says.

"Yeah." Gretel smiles. "It's time to play dress-up."

With Gretel's, Hortense's, and Beatrice's help, costumes are sewn and procured, and that afternoon the group gathers together once more, now decked out in their new attire. Jack practices standing guard, dressed in the black-and-white checks of a royal Chessman and fully equipped with the royal Wonderland insignia. Filomena's dressed as a royal page, in fitted trousers and a smart jacket in the Queen of Hearts' signature red color, a satchel attached at her midriff with a notepad inside it. Alistair really looks like a baker in his white apron and jacket topped with an authentic baker's toque.

He tips it to them. "How do I look?"

"Like my brother, Hansel," Gretel says. "What about me?" She twirls in a fashionable dress that conveys style while not being so luxurious as to have her mistaken for royalty. She wears a measuring tape draped around her neck, a pencil for measuring is tucked behind her ear, and her sewing kit is in her hand.

"So seamstress-y," Alistair says, nodding enthusiastically. Then he turns to Jack, inspecting his imposter's uniform. "Dude, dapper much?"

Jack smirks, adjusting his collar. "Really? Thanks." When he catches Filomena looking at him and blushing, he blushes, too, and looks away. He clears his throat. "Okay, remember the plan. Everyone know their roles?"

The others nod.

"Take messages. Do what they say. Get Hortense invited to the party," Filomena says, repeating her duties aloud to help remember them later.

"Infiltrate the royal sanctuary," Gretel says. "Figure out where Cinderella's hiding the glass slippers. Hem the ladies' gowns. Stab Cinderella with my pushpins, make her bleed!"

"Wait—no," replies Jack.

Filomena laughs. "Too far. Save that as a last resort."

Jack nods. "We have to blend in. Not stand out."

"The last thing we want to do is get caught," Filomena agrees.

"Yeah, I really don't want to be held hostage again, okay? Let alone by the Queen of Hearts," Alistair shudders.

"And remember . . . ," Gretel starts.

"Don't blow our cover!" they all repeat in unison.

The group turns back to the Rose sisters. Hortense and Beatrice will travel to Wonderland as well, so that Hortense can prepare to attend the ball at a nearby inn. Hortense chimes in then. "Thanks for all your efforts, but I'm going to tell Charlie how I feel about him. Even if I end up the laughingstock of Never After and the *Palace Inquirer* never lets me live it down!"

Beatrice nods her head. "Well, aside from that, Cinderella can't become queen of Eastphalia. Who knows what kind of chaos she could cause with that kind of power."

"Wait—I just realized," says Filomena. "Aladdin's Lamp. The Stolen Slippers. They're gifts from the fairies . . ."

The rest of the group nods like they've known this all along, and perhaps they have. Filomena turns to Hortense.

"You said the fairies abandoned this land, and that your uncle did, too . . ." Filomena's mind is moving quickly, solving puzzles, remembering hints from the books.

"What was your mother's name?" she asks excitedly, thinking she might have cracked something.

"Sheila," Hortense and Beatrice reply.

"Oh," says Filomena. That isn't one of the thirteen names she knows by heart.

"But our grandmother—her name was Yvette!" says Gretel. "Remember? Granny Yvie."

"She told us she was from somewhere else. We always assumed it was Seoul, Korea, because she was also famously biportal. But now I think she also meant the soul of the kingdom. She must have been from a tribe that lived in the Weeping Tree. She was one of the thirteen fairies," says Beatrice. "Anyway, Uncle said she taught him everything he knows, including how to weave magic into everyday objects."

"The glass slippers. The Cobbler made them, but he learned the craft from her. That was her fairy's gift. Her blessing," adds Hortense.

"We've got to get them back," says Alistair. "Ticktock, ticktock."

"We will," Gretel says.

"Soon," adds Jack.

"And we'll tell this story true," Filomena reassures them. "I promise."

Hortense nervously nods her head. "Okay."

Beatrice takes her sister's shaking hands in her own. "I trust them," she says.

"Me too," Hortense says firmly, squeezing back.

"All right, come on then," Gretel says, flashing a wicked grin. "We have a royal event to hijack."

CHAPTER FOURTEEN

Fake It till You Make It

U pon arriving back at the gates of Wonderland, the crew looks one another over for a final inspection. "Are you guys sure I look like a real baker?" Alistair asks. He picks a nonexistent piece of lint off his white top and starts to pace. "I feel like I should smell like freshly baked bread or something."

Jack grabs Alistair by his shoulders and holds him steady. "You're fine. It'll be fine. Take a deep breath. We can do this."

"Yeah, will you chill?" Gretel says. "You look as real as any baker I've seen. Come to think of it, I've never questioned if any baker was real."

Filomena sighs. "Gretel's right. Plus, your anxiety is making me nervous!" She rubs her sweaty palms against her dress, trying to relax.

"Okay, guys," Jack says. "We all just need to stay calm." He lowers his voice. "We won't get past the first guard if we're on edge like this. The only way we're going to fool anyone is if we act like we are *exactly* who we say we are."

"How are we supposed to do that when we know we aren't?" Alistair asks a bit too loudly.

"Shh!" Filomena warns, glancing around. "Jack's right. We need to somehow go beyond pretending here. We need to *believe* we are who we are, or we'll never be convincing enough to get in."

"Yeah. We'll be busted in two seconds," adds Gretel. "And if one of us gets caught, we all will." She peers at her friends, a stern look on her face. "And remember? Don't. Blow. Our. Cover!"

The others nod.

"All right, all right," Alistair says. "I am a baker boy. From . . . um . . ."

"Snow Country," Jack says. "Trained by the dwarves themselves. Remember them?"

"Yeah, okay," replies Alistair, his tone a bit calmer now. "They were a cool bunch of dudes. Incredible at soufflés."

"If anyone asks, I'll say I've been sent from Vineland," Jack says. "Our soldiers are some of the best in all the land. They'd be foolish to turn one of ours away. Besides, I'm already in uniform."

"Yeah they would," Alistair agrees. "That should get you right in without a hitch."

Jack looks at Filomena. "I'll say you were sent with me, that you're one of our finest handmaidens and can assist with any royal wedding duties. Kind gestures and offerings aren't uncommon from Vineland."

"Okay," Filomena says. A handmaiden from Vineland. Seems simple enough.

Even though lying goes against everything her parents ever taught her, right now, she just needs to become a page. Then an idea hits her. "I know," she says. "Let's pretend these are new jobs we've just been hired for. This way it doesn't feel like we're lying."

"Oooh," Gretel says, shaking a finger at her. "Clever! When you look at it that way, it's like we're not lying at all."

"That's true," replies Alistair, one brow lifting as he considers. "If you think about it, we *do* have a job to do . . ."

"So it's not very deceitful at all, then," Jack says. He grins at his friends. There's a newfound confidence in the air around them.

"Our main job is to get Hortense an invitation to the ball, steal back the glass slippers, and stop Prince Charming from marrying Cinderella, because if the wrong version of the story happens for real, then Never After is in terrible danger," Gretel reminds them. "There's no way we can blow this. My father sent me here for a reason. I can't let him down."

Her friends nod in agreement.

"Once we pass through those gates, we don't discuss any of this," Jack warns. "If anyone overhears us—"

"Off with our heads," Alistair finishes.

More nodding. Jack puts out a fist like Filomena taught him, and the three others tap it. "All right. Let's do this."

The kids pass through the gates with a certain cool swagger. Gretel's measuring tape flaps at her neck in the breeze. The first group of Chessmen stand guard just beyond the gate that blocks off the palace grounds. At the sound of approaching footsteps, they turn, inspecting the young troupe with curious gazes.

"Aye, what do we have here?" one muses aloud.

"Not sure. There's no kiddie table set up just yet, is there?" another jests.

While the soldiers laugh at them, Filomena and her friends remain poised, unflinching.

"Chessman Rook Jackson Green reporting for duty," Jack says with a sharp salute, using a common Vineland name as a pseudonym.

"Little young to be a rook, aren't you, boy?"

"We start training young in Vineland," Jack replies, posture straight, shoulders back. "Everybody knows that."

At this the soldiers stop laughing.

"Aye," one says. "Wasn't told of any Chessmen coming from Vineland, though. Who sent you?"

"Came straight from the Queen of Hearts herself. She ordered the two of us to serve at the palace." Jack gestures to Filomena. "This is her new page. As you can see, she's already outfitted as part of the royal staff."

At the mention of the queen, the soldiers hesitate. "Queen is expecting you, is she?"

"Yes, and you know she does not like to wait," Jack says meaningfully. Alistair, standing behind him, makes a slashing gesture across his throat.

"All right, go ahead." The guards have clearly decided it's best not to question the queen's orders.

"Cheerio, I'm a baker," Alistair offers. "My place is only in the kitchen. Snow Country cuisine, best bread in all the land." He tips his hat.

"If you boys will excuse me," Gretel says assertively, stepping between the soldiers. "I've got hemming to do. The ladies' gowns are a priority. Queen's wishes."

The soldiers nod, moving aside to let Gretel pass.

"Come on," Gretel adds, taking hold of Filomena's arm.

Filomena offers a curt smile to the soldiers as she lets the Cobbler's daughter tug her along. The two girls make their way across the lawn to the palace entrance. Their feet sink into the swampy marsh with each step they take.

"This is disgusting," Gretel mumbles.

"You're telling me," replies Filomena. "What happened to their groundskeeper?"

Gretel, who's also from California, knows exactly how important proper lawn upkeep is. She shakes her head. "And they're royalty. Can you imagine?"

Upon entering the palace, the girls are whisked away from each other and sent to see to their tasks. Inside, the palace is harried and frenzied; courtiers arrange furniture, paint the cracked walls, and hurry to and fro with a dozen different tasks. Just like the grounds, the place is kind of a dump. This is Wonderland? Everything is too small or too big, and the haughty Caterpillar—who is apparently the Queen of Hearts' chief of staff and acting majordomo—has no time for any of Filomena's questions.

Unfortunately, in order to deliver messages as a page, Filomena is expected to know where everything and everyone is. But seeing as it's her first time in Wonderland, she doesn't know anything at all.

"What do you mean, you haven't sent this message to the royal minister of accounts?" demands the Caterpillar.

"I tried—the, uh, passage is blocked . . ."

The Caterpillar huffs. "Fine, just . . . clean up the princess's chambers. They're filthy."

"The princess?"

"Cinderella's room," the Caterpillar replies. "You really are new, aren't you?"

Filomena nods, exhilarated at the prospect of cleaning Cinderella's room. She's sure to find the glass slippers there.

The Caterpillar mumbles something under his breath about green girls from the country, but there's no time to be offended.

Of course, Filomena has no idea where Cinderella's room might be in the palace. She's walking around the corridors hoping to find some kind of sign when she overhears two lady's maids chatting as they pass her in the hallway.

"Come on, the princess is waiting," one says.

The other, a brunette, rolls her eyes. "She's the worst."

Filomena, after straightening her face and smoothing down her lapels, rushes to catch up with the pair. "Excuse me?" she asks. "I heard you say you're off to see Cinderella? I've been sent to clean up her room. That's only if you two could use an extra set of hands, of course." She smiles at them warmly. "I wouldn't want to impose."

"Oh! Not at all!" the brunette says. "Come, I'll take you straight to her chambers. I could use a break anyway."

"Me too," the other girl says. She looks older, and she offers Filomena a smile as they lead her to the villain herself.

They weave through the palace, and Filomena takes notice of her surroundings, catching certain landmarks to remember for later—a golden statue here, a unicorn tapestry there. When they reach a large, ornate door marked with a golden crown—*ugh, lame*—Filomena fights back an eye roll of her own. She hasn't even walked through the door yet, but she can already tell that Cinderella is a total diva.

The older lady's maid opens the door, allowing Filomena to enter first. Filomena straightens her posture before she walks in, unsure of what to expect. She glances around the room nonchalantly. No sign of the glass slippers anywhere.

No sign of Cinderella, either.

"Where is she?" the older lady's maid asks a chamber-maid inside the room.

"Doing her hair treatment" is the reply.

"Oh, thank goodness, that'll take a while," says the brunette. She motions to Filomena. "This is the mademoiselle's new helper."

The chambermaid raises an eyebrow. "What did you do to deserve that?"

Filomena is taken aback and has nothing to say in response.

But the chambermaid doesn't seem to notice. "Go on then. It's a mess, as usual." The three maids giggle and leave Filomena to the task.

They weren't kidding; Cinderella's room really is a disaster. There are clothes strewn everywhere, as well as under-garments, shoes, books, and jewelry. There are half-eaten plates of food on the bedside tables and candy wrappers under the bed. It's by far the messiest room Filomena has ever seen. If Filomena's mother saw this, Cinderella would be grounded for *years*.

Now, where could Cinderella have hidden those glass slippers?

Filomena checks the closet first, and though there are shoes scattered all around—from suede kitten heels to riding boots to feathered mules—there's no sign of glass slippers anywhere. She opens the bureau drawers; T-shirts and shorts and leggings and all sorts of undergarments are twisted into piles. Nothing. She looks in the many open trunks, where gowns and furs and cloaks are stored. Nada. She looks under the bed and finds only half-eaten pizza. (Alistair once said he described the treat to several Never After chefs when he returned from the mortal world the first time and caused a trend.) Gross!

Filomena's about to canvass the room one more time when she hears a loud clamor of pots and pans coming from the kitchen.

She crinkles her face. "Alistair!" she mumbles under her breath. She hopes her friend is all right.

CHAPTER FIFTEEN

IF THE SHOE FITS...

Filomena runs toward the noise. When she reaches the entryway to the kitchen, she stops in her tracks. The scene before her would be comical if they weren't undercover—and if Hortense's future and the very existence of Never After didn't depend on them.

Alistair is on the floor in a heap of pots and pans. Flour covers him from head to toe. The other kitchen staff are laughing, cursing at the mess, or shaking their heads at him.

Alistair chuckles nervously, rubbing his side. "Don't worry, guys. This is just part of my process."

Filomena rushes over to help him up. "Absolutely," she agrees. She waves her hand. "He's an artist. Just like Hansel Cobbler. You might have heard of him?"

The head chef points a finger at Alistair. "You better get your act together, kid. I don't want to see another mess like this in my kitchen. The Queen of Hearts doesn't look kindly on this kind of nonsense. She'll have your head for it, she will."

Filomena thinks the Queen of Hearts must be a cold-hearted sovereign indeed. She's a person who cheats at chess, for one. Filomena remembers Jack telling them that, once upon a time, the queen was truly lovely in every way. What happened? Why is the Queen of Hearts now a terrible bully?

Alistair flushes and nods to the red-cheeked chef. "Yes, sir. My apologies. Won't happen again."

Filomena tries to keep a poker face even as her heart thumps in fear. As much as she wants to scold her friend for being so careless, she doesn't want him to lose his head. Or blow their cover.

"He's all right," she tells the chef. "Just a little spill." She offers Alistair a sympathetic smile, then bends down to help him pick up the scattered items.

"You okay?" she asks him softly.

Alistair grabs as many pans as he can at once, stacking them in his arms by size. "Yeah. No use crying over spilled flour," he says, repeating a phrase he's heard Filomena say before.

"It's *milk*," she corrects.

In answer, Alistair swipes a finger through the powdery mess on the floor. Then he holds his finger out to her. "It's flour," he says. "See?"

"Forget it," she says. "Just . . . be careful, okay? We don't want to make any commotion while we're here," she whispers, lowering her voice. "Remember?"

Alistair knows she's right, so he nods in agreement. "Of course I remember," he whisper-shouts back. "You're acting as if I'd intentionally make a fool of myself. You must be tripping," he says, borrowing another one of her world's phrases.

The irony isn't lost on her. "Well, actually, you're the one who—"

"Too soon!" he says, scrambling to his feet.

Filomena shrugs, gathering what's left of the pots and gently shoving them at Alistair. "Here—I have to go check on Jack and Gretel. Just, keep it together. Please! And remember what Gretel said! Don't blow our cover!"

"I won't!" Alistair promises, taking the pots. He places them on the counter. Then he adjusts his baker's hat and tries to wipe some flour off his nose. He only winds up smearing more all over himself in the process. "Now, if you'll excuse me. I have baking to do." He sighs, turning to some large mixing bowls on the counter.

Filomena's about to say something smart back when she catches some of the other cooks staring at her. She responds with a nervous laugh. "And I have, um, page stuff to do," she says. "Bye!"

She darts out of the kitchen before anyone can ask her any questions. Once she lands safely in the hall without any accusations thrown her way, she leans against a wall and breathes a sigh of relief. After taking a few moments to calm herself down, she peeks around to see if it's safe.

No one seems to suspect her of anything unusual. With a casual low whistle, Filomena starts to make her way down a corridor to check on Jack. Sure, Alistair might be the clumsy one of the bunch, but it's Jack who's surrounded by a group of dudes with weapons.

She speed-walks her way to the entrance of the castle and slips past the guards on duty. "Pardon, pardon. Royal page coming through," she says.

"Hey, what do you think you're doing?" one asks. But it's a futile attempt at stopping her.

"Very important things," replies Filomena, skirting past him without missing a beat.

She makes a face to herself once she's outside. *They could really use better guards,* she thinks. What kind of palace is this? And where is this frightening Queen of Hearts she's heard so much about?

So far, Filomena has seen no queen, no Cinderella, and no slippers! Time is ticking away, and of all the notes she's made, she's not crossed a single task off their very important to-do list! She can only hope Gretel's having better luck.

She finds Jack on the training fields. From what she can tell, it doesn't look like Jack's accomplished much. He's mid-shot, aiming a bow and arrow at a target in the distance. Filomena squints, trying to make out what it is.

It's a creature with wings . . . It looks like . . . It can't be! It is! It's a fairy! She gasps. The targets are fake fairies! And there are holes all over them! She can't believe Jack's about to shoot at one. *What is he doing?!* She marches over to him, hand on her hip and notepad in her hand.

Just as Jack releases his arrow, Filomena reaches his side.

He turns to look at her, an amused grin on his face. "Bull's-eye! Did you see that?" he says excitedly.

"Yeah, I saw all right," she replies, narrowing her eyes at him. "Do you see what you're shooting at?"

He does a double take, checking his surroundings. The other Chessmen are busy with their own target practice and duties or have joined in casual conversation while they work.

Jack bends his head down toward her so she can hear him, his voice lowered. "It's heinous, I know. But it's part of my job. And yours, too, now."

He's right of course. With a sigh, she nods. "Okay. I'll be cool."

Jack adjusts his collar, straightening back up. "Cool," he says, repeating the word. "Have you been able to weasel your way into Cinderella's good graces yet?"

Filomena shakes her head. "Not yet. She's been busy

doing some sort of hair mask. The maids say she spends too much time near the fireplace. Dries out her follicles."

"Huh," Jack grunts, aiming another arrow at the target. His face clearly says he has no idea what Filomena is talking about, but he's too polite to comment.

Filomena leans against a nearby tree. "I figured I'd check on everyone in the meantime, see if you found anything."

Jack nods. "Have you seen Alistair?"

She chuckles. "Yeah, he's making a mess in the kitchen. His baker disguise? Totally convincing. His top-chef skills on the other hand? Not so much."

Jack grins. "Figures." He focuses on the target then and shoots another arrow but misses the bull's-eye by a quarter inch. His lips tighten in disappointment. "And the slippers?"

"No sign of them," Filomena replies, crossing her arms. "You?"

He shakes his head. "Nah, I highly doubt they're buried in the dirt out here. I'm afraid I'll be kept out here for the whole day, including the ball. They want the Vineland soldier on the grounds at all times, in case I need to . . . uh . . . shoot anyone."

Filomena turns to inspect the target. Jack's a crack shot. Almost all the arrows have pierced either the bull's-eye or the areas just around it. She shudders. Who might Jack have to shoot? And . . . would he? Where does the pretending stop? Aloud, she asks, "Just how far are we supposed to take this?"

He frowns. "Let's just focus on finding what we need and getting out of here."

Filomena nods, stepping away from the tree. "Yeah, sooner rather than later, I hope."

"Me too. And, Filomena?" Jack says, beckoning her closer. "Don't forget the invitation," he whispers.

"Don't worry," she tells him. "I'm on it."

Inside the palace, Filomena finds Gretel in the ladies' dressing chamber, where a group of ladies-in-waiting and various courtiers are being fitted for their ball gowns. Gretel's on the floor, hemming a lady's dress.

"This color is absolutely striking on you," Gretel says around the pushpins sticking out of her mouth. She grabs one and slides it through the fabric. "Just a few inches and you'll be ready to dance."

The girl claps her hands. "Wonderful! And dance I must. Straight into the arms of the love of my life!" She squeals. "I can't wait to meet Charming!" She looks down at Gretel. "Do you think he'll like it?"

Gretel looks up at her. "The dress?"

The girl nods, a hopeful look in her eye.

"Of course," replies Gretel with a grim look on her face.

Filomena watches Gretel at work. She looks so at ease as she goes from girl to girl, fitting them for their gowns and taking measurements. She hardly has to pretend at all. It's what she does. Not just here but in real life, too.

Eventually, Filomena clears her throat and Gretel notices her presence.

The Cobbler's daughter turns around. "Hi! Have you come to help fit the girls?" Gretel asks.

"Um, yeah!" Filomena says. "Of course. That's my job!" She chuckles, forcing a fake smile as the other girls look over to her.

"Perfect," replies Gretel. "Cinderella will be here shortly, I'm told."

Filomena's just about to reply when the door bursts open.

With the way the other ladies cower, Filomena half expects to see a hideous beast emerge from the doorway, but when Cinderella appears, her beauty is impossibly dazzling. The "wrong" stories at least got that right. She's beyond gorgeous.

Cinderella is a vision with golden hair, bright cornflower-blue eyes, and a perfect button nose. Every feature on her face is symmetrical, elegant, breathtaking. She is slender and long limbed with a swanlike neck and a tiny waist. Her dress is a heavenly vision of beauty—a creamy silver-and-blue confection that matches her eyes and sparkles in the light. In fact, everything about her is the pinnacle of pulchritude and perfection.

That is, until she opens her mouth. "Move!" she snaps,

her rosebud lips curling into a sneer as she pushes a girl out of her way without pausing.

Her ice-blue eyes are as cold as a glacier as she surveys the room. "Are you the seamstress?" she inquires, giving Gretel a cool once-over.

"Yes, I am," replies Gretel.

"You're late," Cinderella sneers, even though it's actually she who is late for the fitting, which is why Gretel started working on the other ladies' gowns. Cinderella walks over to the main fitting stand in the center of the room; the hapless lady who happens to be on it almost trips over her skirts trying to get away.

No wonder that chambermaid asked Filomena what she had done to deserve this gig. Cinderella's a terror. Gretel and Filomena watch in horror, exchanging glances.

"Well, what are you waiting for?" Cinderella barks.

Gretel hurries over and kneels on the floor to start pinning Cinderella's dress. Filomena can tell that what Gretel really wants to do is stab one of those pins right through the fabric and prick Cinderella's skin. But Gretel remains professional. This is probably not the first time she's had to play nice with a nasty client.

Plus if there's any hope of finding those glass slippers, they have to get on Cinderella's good side.

"Your dress is exquisite," Gretel beams, glancing up from where she's kneeling.

"Of course it is," says Cinderella, her nose in the air.

Filomena moves to stand nearby. Close enough to eavesdrop. Far enough to stay out of Cinderella's wrath. She and Gretel both check out Cinderella's footwear. Not made of glass, sadly.

"Are you excited for the ball?" Gretel asks innocently as she pins.

Cinderella peers down at Gretel, eyes narrowed. "Are you excited to have one of those pins jabbed in your eye?" she retorts. "I'm not here to make conversation with the help."

Gretel stands, ready to remove her earrings. She's had it with this girl.

But Filomena places her hand on Gretel's shoulder, stopping her with a look. It's full of warning, begging Gretel not to blow their cover.

Gretel turns back to Cinderella. "Of course not," she soothes, trying to remain calm. "I'm sorry to distract, Your Highness."

A smug smile tugs at the corners of Cinderella's lips. "That's what I thought. You weren't hired to gossip. So keep quiet and make sure this dress catches that prince!"

Well, so much for asking Cinderella which pair of shoes she plans to wear with her dress.

CHAPTER SIXTEEN

LIKE MOTHER, LIKE DAUGHTER?

Filomena watches in silence as Gretel adjusts Cinder-ella's gown. An inch here, an inch there. The pushpins so far have pierced only lace and silk. Gretel appears to have her emotions under control.

Filomena glances around the room at all the court ladies waiting their turns in gowns of varying colors, lengths, and fabrics. Some have trains that trail behind them as they walk. Filomena can only imagine how beautiful they'll look on the dance floor; it will look as if they're floating to the music.

So far, the princess has managed to make two girls in the room cry by making fun of their hairstyles. Just then the chamber door opens once more, interrupting Filomena's thoughts as well as Cinderella's insults.

The woman who enters looks exactly like Cinderella but twenty years older. The same golden hair, the same cut-glass cheekbones, the same slim figure and elegant carriage.

All the ladies gathered in the room drop to their deep-est curtsies, and the nervous chatter dissipates. So this is the infamous Queen of Hearts. She looks like she's definitely broken a few hearts in her day—or squashed them beneath her pointy heel, more like.

"Mom!" Cinderella cries. "I'm not ready! I told you not to come until I was ready!" She stomps her foot, throwing a little tantrum right there in front of everyone.

Mom?

But didn't Beatrice say that Cinderella went to live with her godmother? Wait, the Queen of Hearts is Cinderella's *mother?*

What's going on here?

Didn't Hortense and Beatrice say their mother married a widower? Something's not quite right . . . Filomena wishes she could consult her Never After books, but she left them back at Rosewood. She definitely heard correctly, though. Cinderella called the Queen of Hearts "Mom."

Gretel clears her throat and stands up, explaining that she has to collect more pins for the dress. Filomena leaps at the chance as well. "I'll help you," she tells Gretel. The two of them huddle by a sewing kit across the room.

"Did you hear what she said?" Filomena whispers.

"Calling the queen 'Mom'? I sure did," Gretel replies grimly.

"But didn't your aunt marry a widower?"

"That's what she thought," whispers Gretel. They both turn back to the Queen of Hearts and Cinderella. Both are looking at Cinderella's reflection in the mirror.

The queen clasps her hands to her chest. "My darling! You are a vision!"

"I know." Cinderella smirks. She turns and twirls on the podium, preening and primping while the queen and the ladies of the court ooh and aah.

"The most gorgeous girl in all the kingdoms of Never After!" the queen declares.

"I know I am!" says Cinderella.

"You don't even need those silly magic slippers to catch the prince! One look at you and he'll forget all about that stupid girl!" the queen declares.

At this, Cinderella's face falls. "DON'T MENTION HER!" she shrieks. "MOM! YOU MORON! The glass slippers are a secret!"

Cinderella motions at the rest of the ladies in the room. "OUT!" she screams, and tosses the nearest vase in their direction. It shatters against a mirror, making huge cracks on the surface so that Cinderella looks jagged and distorted in its reflection.

Filomena and Gretel exchange terrified looks.

"Us too?" asks Filomena as quietly as she can.

"NO!" yells Cinderella. "Obviously not! FINISH YOUR WORK!"

"Come on," says Gretel, kneeling at Cinderella's feet again. "Help me," she tells Filomena.

Filomena's thoughts are racing. So Hortense and Beatrice were right—Cinderella *did* steal the glass slippers to steal Prince Charming—er, Prince Charlie. And the Queen of Hearts knows about it. Had they planned this all along?

"Oh, darling, it's all going to be all right," says the queen, falling onto the nearest couch and fanning herself with a red lace fan.

"That's what you said when I had to move into that house with those horrid girls," Cinderella seethes.

"You *had* to live with them, otherwise who would've kept the spell going? Lord Rose had to believe that you were his daughter and that his wife was dead. Even though he never had a wife! Or a daughter!" The queen cackles.

Cinderella snickers. "You know, I actually think that old wench Sheila actually fell in love with him. She fell for his sad story."

"People are so gullible," clucks the queen.

All of a sudden, Cinderella jumps like she's been stabbed.

Because, um, she has. "Ouch!" Cinderella cries. There's a tiny drop of blood on the dress.

"Oh! My apologies!" says Gretel. "My hand slipped."

"MOM! She stabbed me!"

"Who hurt my baby?" cries the queen.

The tension in the room is so thick, you could cut it with Gretel's fabric scissors. Gretel is shaking with fury, so Filomena puts a hand on her arm, trying to communicate with the tightness of her grip. *Don't. Blow. Our. Cover.*

"She didn't mean to! It was an accident!" says Filomena, trying to come between the queen and her friend.

"I'm sorry! I'm sorry!" cries Gretel at last.

The queen worries at Cinderella's hair, even though that's not where she hurts.

"I'm fine," grouses Cinderella, slapping the queen's hand away. "Leave us. She has a job to do." She turns to Gretel. "And remember, it doesn't require talking."

"Of course, Your Highness," replies Gretel through gritted teeth. "I didn't come here to talk."

Next the queen orders Filomena to follow her to her chamber, and not too long after that, Filomena finds herself on the floor beside a bucket of soapy water. She looks at the coarse brush in her hand, unsure. She did not think this was what the queen had in mind when she mentioned honoring Filomena with the highest of royal duties.

"I said scrub!" the queen barks from her chair, holding out her bare foot.

Filomena cannot believe her page duties have landed her here—kneeling at the feet of the Queen of Hearts, of all places! She'd much rather be back in North Pasadena, grounded or doing her Algebra I Honors homework. And she loathes algebra with a passion.

Strangely, the queen's feet are not as beautiful as the rest of her. They're coarse and flaky and almost monstrously rough. Filomena holds her breath as she scrubs the queen's heel. She decides right then that she will never speak of this *to anyone*.

The queen leans back in her seat and lets out a satisfied sigh. "Well, don't be shy. Make it tickle!"

Filomena frowns but does as she's told. She rubs the bristles a bit harder against the queen's foot, grimacing the whole time.

Finally, *finally*, the queen sits up, pulling her foot from Filomena's grasp. "That's enough," she says rudely. "I'm going to bathe."

Filomena can see where Cinderella gets her manners. "What should I do next, Your Majesty?" she asks reluctantly. All she knows is the next task better not involve armpits.

The queen nods to another door across the large room. "Through there is my office. The last of the royal invitations for the royal ball are stacked on my desk. See to it that they get downstairs to the messenger. They need to go out today."

Filomena stands, holding back her excitement. At last, she'll be able to cross one item off her list of very important things to do.

"Yes, Your Majesty," she replies calmly, as if it's just another mundane task.

"Now!" the queen bellows. With that, she retreats into her bathroom and slams the door.

Rude!

The Queen of Hearts could really use a chill pill. Maybe some chamomile tea. But never mind that. Filomena's got some work to do.

She hurries into the queen's office. Bingo. There, teetering on the edge of the desk are multiple stacks of invitations. All are stamped with the royal seal of Wonderland. And the royal seal also happens to be sitting in the middle of the desk.

Filomena opens drawers until she finds what she's looking for: leftover invitations. Victory! She grabs a feather pen from the desk and begins to scrawl Hortense's name in the fanciest cursive she can muster.

There.

Looks legit.

She stamps the envelope with the Queen of Hearts' royal seal of Wonderland, securing it shut.

Fait accompli.

Or is it fete accompli?

CHAPTER SEVENTEEN

THIEVES AND LIARS

Filomena pushes a cart stacked tall with mail down the corridor. It's stuffed to the brim with royal invitations. Her brow crinkles at the sheer amount. She peeks at the names on the envelopes: All the aristocratic and royal families are invited, from Queen Christina of Snow Country to Robin Hood and Maid Marian of Sherwood Forest. The Queen of Hearts is throwing a huge bash of epic proportions. No wonder it's already legendary.

Filomena whistles to herself as she walks down the hall, trying not to be obvious in any way. For in the middle of this stack of invites is one for the very girl whom Cinderella does not want to attend: *Hortense Marie Rose*. The same girl whose life Cinderella is trying to steal.

Jealousy can make people do foolish things. It's nothing Filomena hasn't already seen back in her world. When someone envies another person's life—or, in this case, their magic glass slippers and future royal husband—they won't let anyone or anything stand in their way. Cinderella's spun a story that resonates across the globe, even though almost none of it is true.

Why does Filomena's world know the story that way?

Especially since that version of the story hasn't happened yet?

Filomena had asked the Rose sisters this question before setting off for Wonderland with her friends.

"Somehow whoever told the stories wrong felt that the power of the stories would *force* the wrong thing to happen, as if it were inevitable. You would have been cursed and eaten by ogres, for instance," said Hortense. "And who knows what will happen if Cinderella actually marries Charlie and becomes queen of Eastphalia?"

"We don't know, but it has to be bad," said Beatrice.

"It won't happen," Gretel had assured them. "We'll make sure of it. It's just a story for now."

"But one day someone will have to tell the stories correctly," said Hortense.

"Don't worry, I'm taking notes," promised Filomena.

Now all Filomena really wants to do is roll this cart right over the wannabe bride herself. In truth, she can't see any prince agreeing to marry a girl he doesn't love, so indeed, there's got to be some kind of magic in those glass slippers that Cinderella wants to harness. Cinderella may be gorgeous to look at, but she's ugly at heart. True beauty is on the inside, in one's spirit and character, and that's what Cinderella lacks. It's depressing to think of how much value is placed on appearance when having a lovely character is what makes a person truly arresting and attractive.

Is Cinderella planning on using some kind of spell that will allow her to fool the prince for a little while, like she and the queen probably used to fool Lord Rose? They fooled him all the way to his death. Is that what they want for Prince Charlie? No, that doesn't sound right. Cinderella might have caused the death of Hortense's and Beatrice's stepfather, but she doesn't want to kill Prince Charlie. She wants to marry him.

Filomena is going to make sure it won't reach that point—thanks to the nifty little invite buried in the cart.

Plan one is set: Hortense will be at the royal ball.

Filomena fights back a smile as she nears the entrance to the palace, where the royal messengers are lounging.

"Yeah?" one of them asks with a sneer.

Filomena clears her throat. "The queen needs these royal invitations sent out. At once. Can you see to it, please?" she says. Her tone is polite but firm. This is her job, after all.

He yawns. "Yeah, yeah, we'll get them out."

She smiles at him. "Thank you so much."

Filomena moves aside so he can take hold of the cart. As she watches him wheel it away, she grins. One task done. Next up: finding the stolen glass slippers.

She tiptoes back into Cinderella's room.

They've got to be around here somewhere. Buried in some nook or cranny. A place Cinderella would never expect anyone to look.

Filomena ponders possible hiding spots. Cinderella wouldn't let items so valuable out of her sight. But what if Cinderella hid them so well that no one will ever find them? No. Filomena can't think like that. She holds on to hope with a firm grip and prays the others are doing the same.

Maybe Gretel's had some luck in the glass slippers department. Filomena knows Alistair and Jack aren't going to be much use in finding them; the boys are too busy with their own duties. And Filomena highly doubts Cinderella would hide the glass slippers in the kitchen of all places.

She walks back out to the hallway when a loud commotion ahead startles her, pulling her from her thoughts. It's coming from the foyer near the palace entrance. Courtiers and staffers rush by, blocking her vision. Amidst the frenzy, Filomena stands on her tiptoes to see what's going on. People start yelling, and new voices join in with every passing moment. More guards rush into the palace. The flurry of activity is blinding.

She hears someone yelling louder now. One voice in particular is more distinctive than all the others. "THIEF!" this voice cries.

Filomena freezes. She frowns at the sound of that all-too-familiar voice. She knows that voice.

"THIEF!" the voice yells again.

Oh fairies!

It's Cinderella, and she's furious.

Uh-oh.

Sounds like someone blew their cover!

Filomena squeezes through the growing crowd, rushing toward the chaos. Her heart hammers in her chest, thrumming loudly as she races forward. She's terrified to see which of her friends it is, if it is one of them, and it has to be one of them—who else could it be? She hopes against hope that she's wrong. Once she sees what's happening, her heart plummets to her feet.

The imposter isn't Gretel. Or Jack. Or even Alistair.

It's Beatrice.

She's disguised as a cobbler, with a cap over her dark hair and a shoehorn dangling from her apron. There's a bag over her shoulder, presumably with a shoemaker's tools inside.

Except Beatrice isn't supposed to be here at all! She's supposed to be back at a nearby inn, helping Hortense get ready for the royal ball! Why is she here?

There's a noise by Filomena's elbow, and she turns to see Alistair. As he edges over to her, Filomena notices that he's got flour all over his face, as well as a brown streak on his cheek that she hopes is chocolate. Gretel appears next, push-pins still in her mouth.

"What's Bea doing here?!" Alistair whisper-shouts.

"I was wondering the same thing!" Filomena whisper-shouts back.

They stand there in horror. "She's going to blow our cover!" Alistair says. He palms his forehead.

"She better freaking not," Gretel says. They turn back to watch the commotion.

Cinderella is red with rage. "THIEF! GIVE THEM BACK!" cries Cinderella.

"Give what back?" asks Beatrice.

But before Cinderella can answer, the crowd parts as a stately figure appears in their midst: the Queen of Hearts.

"What in Wonderland is going on here, may I ask?" the queen demands, surveying the situation.

"Mom!" cries Cinderella.

Mom? mouths Beatrice, catching Filomena's face in the crowd.

Filomena shrugs.

"What is the matter?" asks the queen.

"I caught her red-handed!" says Cinderella.

"I don't know what you're talking about!" cries Beatrice.

Cinderella pulls on the bag over Beatrice's shoulder. Beatrice pulls back, and in the tug-of-war, a pair of glass slippers tumbles out.

"See! I knew it! There they are! I checked the chimney and they were gone!" cries Cinderella.

Up the chimney! Of course that's where Cinderella would hide them! Why didn't Filomena think of that? The glass slippers sparkle on the floor, luminescent and translucent and filled with an air of magic.

"I have no idea how they got there!" says Beatrice. "This is a mistake!"

The queen narrows her eyes at Beatrice but doesn't seem to recognize her. "Pardon?" she hisses. The word is short, blunt, and it reeks of *Liar, liar, pants on fire.* "Chessmen!" the queen calls.

A group of guards appear, faces grim. They're holding pointy staffs. "Yes, Your Majesty?"

"Arrest this thief!" The Queen of Hearts points a sharp red-manicured finger in Beatrice's direction.

"What do we do?!" Alistair exclaims.

"We have to help her!" Filomena says.

"How?" Alistair asks.

"Don't look at me!" says Gretel.

Filomena feels helpless as she frantically wonders how she can possibly stop this. *If only Jack were here,* she thinks.

She searches the room for him, but he's nowhere in sight. She curses to herself, knowing Beatrice could really use a hero right now. Even if they're borrowed. But Jack isn't with the group of Chessmen and he's not anywhere close. Filomena will have to save Beatrice herself.

"Wait!" Filomena cries in desperation.

Everyone turns to her, including the queen and Cinderella.

Filomena didn't think this far ahead, though. Her cheeks flush as she tries to come up with something on the spot. But she's drawing a big blank. She's never been very good under pressure. Or at lying. Or at public speaking, for that matter.

"Um . . . ," Filomena starts.

Then it hits her. She snaps her fingers in Beatrice's direction, like she recognizes her. "Wait, I know her! She's a very famous shoemaker in another kingdom. One of the very best!"

One of the Chessmen looks puzzled. "Which kingdom?" he asks.

Filomena clucks her tongue. "Oh, you know the one."

Alistair chimes in: "I know! The one called North Pasadena."

"North Pasadena? I've never heard of it," says the queen, tapping her fingers on her elbow.

"She was just going to polish the glass slippers, weren't you?" says Filomena.

Beatrice relents. "Yes."

"They need a good polish! I mean, aren't they, like, a little used? I mean, vintage is great and all, but wouldn't you rather have new things?" Gretel adds.

"I guess they are a bit dirty," says Cinderella slowly.

"You should be able to see your reflection in them!" argues Filomena.

"Okay . . ." Cinderella looks hesitant.

For a moment, it looks like they might win . . . like Beatrice will be allowed to take the glass slippers. Like Operation Stolen Slippers is a hit.

Beatrice puts the glass slippers back in her bag. "I'll polish them up right away! I'll make sure you're wearing them at midnight!"

"You do that," Cinderella says. She walks away but then turns around and narrows her eyes. "Wait a minute . . . How do you know about midnight?"

Beatrice freezes. Filomena, Gretel, and Alistair each hold their breath.

Cinderella walks right up to Beatrice and pulls off the cap covering her dark hair. "*You,*" she seethes, staring at Beatrice. The one word is so full of hatred, it makes everyone in the room stiffen.

"Me," says Beatrice.

They lock eyes, a battle of wills.

"Darling, who is this?" asks the Queen of Hearts.

"This," says Cinderella, "is one of my wicked stepsisters!"

There's gasping from the crowd. Even the queen staggers back as though slapped.

"Like I told everyone! They're wicked! She's a thief!" says Cinderella, taking back the glass slippers and pretending to be outraged. "A lying, wicked little thief!"

"A THIEF! IN THE PALACE! A DIRTY ROTTEN THIEF!" the queen howls. "CHESSMEN!"

The Chessmen surround Beatrice and grab her by the arms so she's standing alone in a sea of black-and-white-garbed guards.

Beatrice squares her shoulders and holds her head up high. "I'm no thief—you are. These slippers rightly belong to my sister. You're not going to get away with this."

Cinderella smirks. "Away with what?" she asks innocently.

Beatrice grits her teeth. "You know what."

"I don't know what you're talking about," Cinderella says, sounding bored. "And I have a party to get ready for. One that *your sister* wasn't invited to."

More Chessmen arrive, and this time Jack is with them.

After he briefly makes eye contact with Filomena, Jack sets his sights on Beatrice, who's being held against her will by the very guards he's impersonating. He marches to them. "Hey! Let go of her," Jack orders.

Confused glances land on him, and Filomena can spy his gulp from across the room. He's about to give himself away if he isn't careful. She holds her breath, knowing he needs to get a handle on his emotions. Otherwise they'll all wind up like Beatrice. And Hortense will never get her glass slippers back. Or the happily ever after that's supposed to belong to her, which also spells doom for Never After.

"We don't rough up ladies in Wonderland," Jack explains calmly. "Even if they are prisoners."

The queen seems to grow suspicious, and she aims a

questioning look at Jack. Cinderella throws a similar glance his way.

"By order of the queen herself, in a doctrine signed several years ago. Isn't that right, Your Majesty?" says Jack smoothly.

"Oh, er, yes," says the queen.

"Take her away! And take that one, too," says Cinderella, pointing to Filomena. "I bet she was in on it. They wanted to steal *my* glass slippers."

"I gave those to you for your birthday!" says the Queen of Hearts.

"You did!" says Cinderella.

"OFF WITH THEIR HEADS!" yells the Queen of Hearts.

Gretel looks as if she's about to faint.

"NO!" screams Alistair.

They turn to him.

"I mean, uh, it's hard to get blood off marble." He shrugs. "Sorry—sorry. I mean . . . carry on."

Filomena desperately hopes that she won't lose her head in all this. Or Beatrice's head, for that matter.

"Actually, the little baker is right. I have a better idea," says the queen. "Take them to the Beast!" An evil smile creeps over her lips. "He deserves a hearty meal. It is a special occasion, after all."

Two guards grab Filomena from either side and squeeze her arms. She looks over to Jack, then to Alistair, and finally, to Gretel. They look stricken.

Beatrice whispers, "I'm so sorry! This is all my fault!"

Filomena squirms against the Chessmen holding her.

But it's no use. Her strength is no match for theirs; she'll never get away. The Chessmen drag her along against her will, out of the castle and away from her friends.

And together with Beatrice, she is sent to the Beast's dungeon.

MEET THE BEAST

Once upon a time in Wonderland
There lived a terrible, disgusting Beast.
A horrid monster, an abomination,
A total eyesore to say the least.
The Beast lived alone in his dungeon
For years and years and years,
But he never let them see his tears,
And he tried to forget the kingdom's jeers.
Many in Wonderland forgot about him;
No one even knew if he was still alive.

The only sound from the dungeon
were horrible roars at a quarter to five.
The Beast is on the prowl!
Just hear him howl!
Give him something to eat!
"As long as it's not me," said the people,
"he can have a little treat."
They sent him prisoners and outcasts,
Exiles and strays,
The wrongly accused, the losers at croquet,
Hapless tourists who lost their way.
Send them to the Beast!
Let him feast!
Keep him fed and content.
As long as he's not eating us!
Leave him alone.
To rot.

PART THREE

Wherein . . .

Filomena and Beatrice are trapped in
the Beast's dungeon.

Jack, Gretel, and Alistair rescue them.

Except Beatrice and Filomena don't
want to be rescued?

CHAPTER EIGHTEEN

THE LIGHT OF CARABOSSE

Filomena and Beatrice are packed into a carriage that takes them over winding cliffside roads to a dark and desolate castle in the middle of nowhere. Once there, the guards walk them down what feels like an infinite number of stairs until finally Filomena and Beatrice are tossed into a bleak damp dungeon. The Chessmen grunt as they slam and lock the gigantic door on their way out, and the sound echoes through the darkness. The only light comes from the crack under the door.

Something wet drips from the ceiling and onto Beatrice,

who startles. "Oh! Ew!" she says, wiping her arm furiously. "This is all my fault." She sighs. "I'm so sorry I got you into this. You're just a kid."

Filomena wants to agree that Beatrice did indeed blow her cover, but she feels too sorry for Beatrice, who's obviously miserable. "Why did you come to the palace?" she asks.

"I had to do something other than just help Hori with her gown—I mean, she has lady's maids to do that. I couldn't just sit there and let Cinderella get away with it," Beatrice says. "She's my sister."

As an only child, Filomena is awed, and also a little jealous, that a person could love someone else—someone other than their parents—so much. "I understand," she tells Beatrice, even though she doesn't, not really. She would have loved a sibling, if only to have a friend to make fun of her parents with, someone who loved them just as much, but knew all their foibles.

Beatrice sniffs. "Fairies, it smells in here."

There is indeed an odor. A stench that lingers. But then again, they are trapped in a dungeon, and Filomena doesn't think dungeons are supposed to smell nice.

She's about to tell Beatrice this when they hear the most terrifying roar. It's the sound of an animal about to devour its prey—a loud thunderous bellowing that turns into a manic howl.

"It's the Beast!" Beatrice whispers. "Oh dear. That sounded really close."

"Too close!" agrees Filomena. Are they to be his dinner?

That was horrifying! What if the Beast can taste fear? What if he likes his victims extra scared before he finds and eats them? Filomena almost has a panic attack at the thought. In an effort to calm her racing thoughts, she begins to hop and shake out her arms.

The roaring echoes through the dungeon again, and for a moment, Filomena thinks the Beast is about to pounce out of the shadows and tear them both apart. But then the roars subside and it's quiet again except for the sound of their fast breathing.

"Oh dear oh dear oh dear" Beatrice is saying.

"It's okay. It'll be okay," Filomena says. "We need to stay calm." She's old enough to know that fear and anxiety are contagious. She knows this especially well from growing up with her parents; she's caught it from them plenty of times. It might be permanent at this point.

"Right, right," says Beatrice. She takes a few deep breaths. "Okay, so we have to figure out how to get out of here."

In the oppressive silence (save for steady dripping), Filomena hears Beatrice move around, her hands scratching at the dungeon's walls to try to discern how big the place is and if there's any other kind of exit.

"It's too dark," Beatrice whispers. "I can't see anything."

Filomena leans on the wall and closes her eyes; it's so dark that there's no difference from when they're open. She's trapped inside a smelly dark dungeon, and a beast of some sort is on the loose and possibly hungry. She wishes more than anything that she was safe at home right now. She wonders what her parents are doing and where they are. If they're eating takeout from the Italian place or from their favorite sushi restaurant. She's been so busy escaping from gingerbread houses and meeting wickedly fun sisters and breaking into Wonderland palaces that she hasn't had time to miss home. But now she does.

She misses them so badly, and her Pomeranian pup, too (Adelina Jefferson-Cho of North Pasadena). Heck, she even misses her betta fish (Serafina Jefferson-Cho of North Pasadena). Right now she'd trade all this adventure for a chance to stare at Serafina's fishbowl for twelve hours straight. At least that thing glows in the dark.

Glows in the dark.

"Wait a minute!" she says out loud.

"What?" Beatrice asks.

"I might come from North Pasadena, California, where nothing ever happens, but . . . I also carry the mark of the thirteenth fairy!" Filomena exclaims.

"Come again?" asks Beatrice.

"The thirteenth fairy," Filomena repeats. "I'm Filomena Jefferson-Cho of North Pasadena, but I'm also Princess Eliana of Westphalia!"

"Oh wow. You're two people?" Beatrice asks. "Cool."

"Not exactly. Well, kind of exactly," Filomena says. "Like I said, I carry the mark of the thirteenth fairy. Carabosse?

She was one of the thirteen royal fairies. She must have been your . . . grandaunt? Which makes us sort of related?"

"Oh! Aunt Carabosse, of course!" Beatrice squeals. "Granny Yvie had a lot of sisters. But they were all far apart in age. Fairies live thousands of years, you know."

"I do know."

"So what about her? She's been missing forever."

Filomena sighs. "I know. I've read all the books."

"What books?"

Filomena shakes her head. "It's too much to explain. Right now the point of this story is that I have her mark."

"Like her autograph? Do you want to sell it to *Palace Weekly*? How's that going to help us?" Beatrice is still confused.

"No! Not that kind of mark. A special magic one. It's on my forehead," Filomena explains, pointing to said forehead even though Beatrice can't see.

"And?" Beatrice sounds skeptical.

In answer, Filomena starts reciting the words her aunt Zera told her to speak in times of need. "Carabosse, Carabosse, if you're near, present the mark of the thirteenth fairy and make it clear."

"Is something supposed to happen?" Beatrice asks.

Filomena frowns. She was really hoping that would work.

Beatrice tries to help. "Maybe you have to say it twice?"

Filomena nods. She repeats the words, closing her eyes and each time saying them with more and more feeling.

"Actually," says Beatrice, "magic works in threes."

Filomena chants the words again, and even before she finishes, something miraculous happens. Beatrice watches in wonder as a luminescent mark—a tiny crescent moon surrounded by thirteen tiny stars—begins to glow on Filomena's forehead. Slowly the darkness recedes until they can finally see all around them.

"Woah!" Beatrice exclaims. "Can I?" she asks, reaching out to trace the stars.

Filomena nods. "One for each fairy," she says as Beatrice's hand grazes each of them.

"That's so cool!"

Filomena feels a warm glow inside her. She's so grateful to Zera; to Carabosse, the thirteenth fairy; and to her connection to this world and everyone she's met here. Except she wouldn't have met anyone, nor would she be locked in this dungeon, if the Weeping or the Darkening or whatever you want to call it had never occurred in Never After. Filomena wouldn't be here if someone had told the stories as they were meant to be told . . . if someone had just told the truth from the beginning.

Who's behind it all? Is it Olga of Orgdale? It has to be the ogre queen's doing, doesn't it? Filomena flashes back to their last encounter. She remembers the dark of the cavern, the glow of the lamp when Filomena's true identity was revealed, and the ogre queen's incandescent rage.

"Okay, this is good," says Beatrice, who no longer sounds

afraid. Instead she sounds hopeful. That hope may be smaller than the littlest star in Filomena's own scar—which is currently illuminating the cold empty dungeon—but it's there.

At last they have light. And so, following a path illuminated by the scar on Filomena's forehead, the two girls venture deeper into the darkness to find a way out.

CHAPTER NINETEEN

The Library

The girls wander down a dark corridor, Filomena's glowing scar lighting the way. Beatrice hooks her arm with Filomena's as they walk gingerly down the path. How long have they been down here? Where is here? How long has it been since they last heard the Beast's howls? Filomena doesn't know. But it feels like it's been hours.

Carabosse's mark emits a faint glow, allowing them to see just ahead, and finally they come upon another door. Filomena's about to try to push it open when Beatrice stops her.

"I don't know if we should go in there," she warns.

"Why not? Anywhere is better than walking around alone in the dark," replies Filomena.

"What if *it's* in there?" Beatrice shudders. "The Beast?"

Filomena shivers. She's not sure what's worse: being alone and paranoid in the dark or being possibly not alone and eaten in the light. She considers this for a moment, then puts a finger to her lips, motioning for Beatrice to hush.

Beatrice nods, and Filomena listens closely. She puts her ear to the door, listening for any noise. Any warning of any threat. Even a quiet one that may be lurking or . . . *gulp* . . . stalking.

She doesn't hear a peep. Not a lone footstep. No faint or heavy breathing. After enough time passes, Filomena feels confident that they're still very much alone and will be in the next room as well. "I think it's okay," she says. "I feel like we would've heard something by now if anyone was down here with us."

"Or any*thing*," Beatrice counters.

Filomena can hear the fear in Beatrice's tone and see the uncertain look on her face. But she knows one of them has to be brave. At least one of them . . .

Filomena doesn't like this, either. She'd much rather be at home in her favorite pajamas, cuddled up under a blanket, reading a Never After book instead of living it, trapped in some wild animal's dungeon and walking toward an ominous-looking door with no idea what lies beyond.

Beatrice, on the other hand, has no doubt that they're about to turn a corner and land straight in the mouth of a monster. First of all, Beatrice is too young to die! Second of all, "I seriously cannot afford to get eaten right now," she declares. "I have to help my sister!"

"We aren't going to get eaten, I don't think," Filomena says. It's a weak attempt to assure Beatrice—and, okay, maybe to assure herself, too. Although, after being trapped in a gingerbread house, Filomena is starting to worry that she's survived being roasted there only to be eaten alive here.

"How do you know? Beasts can be really quiet. They're hunters," says Beatrice.

Filomena frowns, but she doesn't disagree. Beatrice might have a point.

But they can't just stand there. They have to see what's inside. It could be a way out. Filomena tells Beatrice so.

Beatrice finally relents. For a moment, Filomena wishes Hortense, the fearless ogre hunter, was down here with her and not the more squeamish of the Rose sisters.

As if she's read Filomena's mind, Beatrice echoes the sentiment. "I'm sorry I'm not brave like Hori," she says sadly.

"No one's brave," Filomena replies. "Some people just act brave. Don't think about it; just do it. That's what Jack says when I ask him how he's so brave."

"Okay," says Beatrice.

"Okay," says Filomena. She tries to shake away any

morbid thoughts as she inches closer to the door. The light coming from under it is a golden hue, glowing in the dark. It dances at their feet as though beckoning them.

She reaches for the doorknob. The sound it makes as it turns is a loud, distinct *clack-clack*, which is followed by a long groan as the door creaks open.

The girls stand there in awe, staring at the sight laid out before them.

Filomena doesn't know what she expected, but it was not *this*. The door has opened to a grand light-filled library. Not just any library but a magnificent one, a soaring cathedral filled to the brim with books. Bookshelves that reach all the way up the thirty-foot ceiling line the walls, each one stuffed full of stories. Several ladders with wheels on the bottom lean against the shelves; they would enable a reader to browse freely among even the highest shelves.

The girls gasp at the sheer beauty of it all. Filomena blinks twice. It's incredible! It's a library! Her favorite kind of room in all the world! Surrounded by what she loves most, she forgets the fact that they're trapped in a dungeon with a horrible beast on the roam. She simply stares up in wonder and smiles. "Wow."

Bathed in newfound light, Filomena's scar disappears once more.

She walks around the space in a daze. It's simply superb. A dream.

Beatrice admires the utter splendor. "This is . . ." She

can't seem to finish the thought. She has no words to match the beauty surrounding them.

"I know," Filomena agrees.

As they marvel at the comfortable velvet couches and the many rolltop desks, the silence is broken by an all-too familiar sound: an awful, terrible, knee-shaking roar followed by that horrible howling.

The Beast!

The girls freeze.

"That sounds a lot closer than before!" says Filomena.

"Much closer!" Beatrice agrees.

They both duck down and hide behind a Chesterfield sofa until the sound recedes. The Beast, wherever it is, has moved on. For now.

Once Filomena's heart stops thudding in her ears, she finds the courage to creep away from the safety of the couch and toward the nearest bookshelf. She touches the leather-bound books, reading the titles on their spines. For some reason they all seem to be cookbooks. *The Definitive History of Wonderland Cuisine, The White Rabbit Entertains!,* and *Cooking with the Queen of Hearts: One Thousand and One Recipes for Love,* among many others.

Beatrice, who's also moved away from the couch, comes to read over Filomena's shoulder. "Oh, that's a great one," Beatrice tells her, motioning to the book Filomena has removed from the shelves and is paging through.

"You've read it?" asks Filomena.

"I've read a lot of these," says Beatrice, nodding as she walks up and down the rows of shelves. "Hori hunts ogres, but I mostly stay home and read."

"Me too," says Filomena.

"Really? You seem more of an ogre-hunting type. Running around with Jack Stalker and all."

"I'm really not," says Filomena, blushing.

Beatrice smiles. The library seems to have brought her back to herself. "You mentioned some books earlier. What did you call them?"

"The Never After series," Filomena tells her.

"Oh, it's about this world."

"Yes."

"But Hori and Gretel told me that you guys have all our stories wrong."

"We do—I mean, we did—until this series was published. My aunt wrote it. Carabosse." Filomena stops to think on why Carabosse told those stories, why she wanted them read and widely known. "She meant to set the record straight."

"Good for her," says Beatrice. "Hey," she adds, "am I in the stories?"

Filomena nods.

"Except we're wicked in the stories, aren't we? Hori and me."

"You're only mentioned, but yeah, I thought you guys were wicked because all the stories about you say that. I didn't realize the book actually said you were wickedly *fun*."

"And Cinderella is the heroine?"

"Yes. Everyone thinks Cinderella is innocent, that she's the victim. That's why her happily ever after is so touching, why people root for her when she marries the prince. They don't know the truth—that the prince was in love with someone else," Filomena tells Beatrice. She thinks of all the little girls who look up to Cinderella or who aspire to that life, to being swept up by a prince and rescued from misery.

Beatrice sighs. "The stories started here, as you can see. Even in our town, people think we abused Cinderella. We try to tell the truth, but no one believes it. It's so much more interesting to think that stepmothers and stepsisters are awful, right? It sells more . . . broadsheets and tabloids and village papers." Beatrice shrugs. "Do people believe the stories in your world?"

"Pretty much."

"Yeah." Beatrice sighs. "People are the same everywhere."

The two of them sink down upon the nearest couch. "Whoever Cinderella is, she's a fraud." Filomena tells Beatrice what she overheard, that Cinderella and the queen targeted Lord Rose and somehow connived to fool him into thinking Cinderella was his daughter.

"Hold on," says Beatrice. "If Cinderella isn't Lord Rose's daughter, who is she?"

"Who knows?" says Filomena. "She called the Queen of Hearts 'Mom,' didn't she?"

"That just doesn't make sense," says Beatrice. "The Queen of Hearts doesn't have a child."

"But she called her 'Mom.' I heard it, and you did, too."

"I know, it's strange," says Beatrice. "I wish my mom was alive so I could ask her. If Cinderella had cast a spell on Lord Rose, I think Mom would have noticed. She was part fairy; she could smell magic."

"There's got to be a way to fix everything," says Filomena. "To tell people the true stories so they can stop believing the lies. To expose Cinderella and get your sister's glass slippers back and secure her happily ever after."

"Right," says Beatrice, stretching and yawning. "You think of a way, and I'll just lie on this couch and nap." Then she bolts up. "But wake me if you hear that Beast again!"

Chapter Twenty

In the Lair of the Beast

Beatrice is sleeping and Filomena is reading when a thunderous roar shakes the entire library. Filomena drops her book in fright, and Beatrice wakes up with a start. They share an agonized look. The Beast! The roaring continues, and it sounds as if it's getting closer and closer.

"The door!" cries Beatrice, noticing that they left the library door open in their haste to get inside. Filomena runs over to it, slamming it shut and locking it. Slowly she backs away from the door as the roars get louder and louder and closer and closer.

The bloodcurdling howling and guttural roaring continues until it's so loud, it sounds as if that thing, whatever it is—that Beast—is right outside the door.

Filomena and Beatrice run to the opposite side of the room.

The Beast howls in frustration, slamming against the door so that it shakes on its hinges.

This is it.

That Beast is going to break inside and eat them both.

It feels as if the very earth is shaking with the Beast's savage attempt to break down the door. Thank fairies they aren't still out there in the dungeon. Filomena tries not to cry, and Beatrice grips her hands tightly. They only have each other.

But then, just as abruptly, the shaking and the roaring cease.

Heavy footsteps thunder down the hall and away.

Filomena sighs in relief. The door held. They're safe for now. Filomena's trembling—and Beatrice is, too—but she's brave enough to go near the door and listen. "I think it's gone," she whispers.

Beatrice nods, pale and frightened. "We've got to find a way out of here."

"We will," says Filomena. She doesn't know how they're

going to do that, but they must. That monster beyond the door sounded loud, angry, and hungry. And while the library door held, it won't hold forever.

Filomena didn't think she would be able to sleep after that, but when she wakes up, it must be morning. She and Beatrice had shared one of the many deep-cushioned couches in the library, each curling up on an end. Filomena supposes they could have each had their own couch, but after what happened it seemed safer to huddle together.

A quiet knock on the door wakes Beatrice, and the girls exchange a confused look. Filomena's heart is in her throat—but Chessmen wouldn't knock politely, would they? Anyone working for that stone-faced Queen of Hearts would just barge through if they were collecting prisoners. And the Beast didn't knock last night—it just tried to kick the door down.

"Hello? Hello there?" calls a soft voice.

Filomena steels her resolve and makes herself walk over to the door. Hoping she's right about this, she unlocks it and holds her breath.

A sweet-faced woman with dark brown skin and gray hair who's around the age of Filomena's mom walks inside. She wears a maid's uniform, including an apron, and is holding a breakfast tray. "Good morning!" she says cheerfully.

"Good morning," replies Filomena, relieved that the woman seems not only harmless but is also carrying pastries!

"Good morning?" echoes Beatrice, sitting up and smoothing down her dark hair. She attempts to comb it with her fingers to look vaguely presentable. Filomena tries to do the same with her unruly curls.

"There you both are," says the sweet old lady, setting down the loaded tray on the nearest table. "I was looking all over for you to see if you'd found your way to the guest quarters. But I see you've discovered the library instead."

Guest quarters?

Did she just say guest quarters?

Filomena's ears prick up just as her nose quivers at the smell of the bountiful breakfast. She spies pancakes and waffles, bacon and sausage, as well as heaping bowls of fruit and yogurt and a carafe of indigo-colored juice.

"Sorry for the delay, but the queen didn't let Master know she'd sent you here until this morning," the woman says as she readies two plates and pours drinks (hot chocolate for Filomena, and coffee for Beatrice). She folds napkins to set beside their plates and motions for them to sit at the table and eat. "You must be starving. Haven't you missed dinner?"

"Yes, but, um, who are you?" Filomena asks. She knows enough about the world by now to be suspicious of friendly people offering treats.

"Oh, I'm so sorry! It's been so long since we've had

anyone here. I'm Miss Prickett, and I'll be taking care of you girls," Miss Prickett tells them with a small curtsy.

"Filomena Jefferson-Cho of North Pasadena," Filomena replies, standing up to curtsy as well.

"Beatrice Rose," says Beatrice, doing the same.

"Of the twin Roses of Rosewood Manor!" says Miss Prickett, delighted.

"You've heard of my sister and me?"

"Why, of course I have. Your grandmother was very famous," says Miss Prickett. "She came to visit here once."

"Granny Yvie?"

"Indeed," says Miss Prickett. She wipes her hands on her apron. "A lovely lady." She smiles down at them fondly. "Please help yourselves. When I come to collect the tray, I'll show you to your rooms. The couches are comfortable for reading, but I'm sure you'd both prefer a real bed for sleeping, and a bath."

"Okay," says Filomena, who's unsure of what's happening. Last night it felt as though they were close to being mauled, or worse; today it appears they are honored guests of some manor lord?

Miss Prickett beams and leaves them to eat their breakfast.

"What is going on?" asks Filomena when the door closes.

Beatrice shrugs and reaches for a piece of bacon. "I don't know, but this looks delicious."

Filomena, who's been admiring the basket of pastries,

suddenly startles as if shocked. She flicks the piece of bacon out of Beatrice's hand; it flies across the room.

"Hey!" says Beatrice. "What was that for? There's plenty for both of us."

"Exactly!" cries Filomena. "Think about it! Why are they feeding us? I've been in a situation like this before!"

Beatrice reaches for another piece of bacon. "You have?"

"When we were trapped in the gingerbread house, that's all the witch's son did—feed us! Lots and lots of treats to fatten us up, so he could eat us!"

"Hmmm," hums Beatrice. She hasn't yet attempted another bite.

"The queen sent us to the Beast, right? And what did Miss Prickett say? Her master wasn't told until this morning. So now they're fattening us up for the kill!"

"Oh," says Beatrice. She looks glumly at the breakfast laid out in front of them. "But I'm *hungry*."

In answer, Filomena's stomach makes a roar of its own. Miss Prickett was right: They are starving. When did they last eat?

Beatrice begins heaping her plate with eggs, bacon, sausage, and croissants. "I mean, if they're fattening us up, we might as well enjoy it." She shrugs.

Filomena watches Beatrice eat for a while and then reluctantly puts a plate together as well. She can't think when she's hungry, and she needs all the energy she can muster to figure a way out of this horrible—but actually kind of nice—library. "Fine," says Filomena. "But don't say I didn't warn you."

Beatrice smiles. "The *pain au chocolat* is amazing. Maybe tomorrow they'll give us rice porridge and century eggs. That's my favorite breakfast."

Filomena wonders what her friends are doing in Wonderland. Knowing them, they're devising a plan to get Beatrice and her out of here. They better hurry. Because that Beast sounds a lot scarier and a lot stronger than the creepy candy dude who kept them caged. Even though Miss Prickett does seem so welcoming and delightful, can they truly trust anyone?

As Filomena chews a piece of fruit, she wonders why it always seems like there's someone or some*thing* that wants to eat her and her friends. Like, they're constantly two seconds away from being supper or a snack at any given moment? She's never had to worry about this before. It's so weird. Is this how gazelles feel knowing a lion is constantly tracking their every move?

But she's not a gazelle; she's a person. And she doesn't think she's delicious.

It doesn't seem normal—not at all—to always worry about being eaten. Is this really what life in Never After is like? It wasn't mentioned in the books. At least, not in the true stories. When they were still true, that is.

CHAPTER TWENTY-ONE

BE THEIR GUESTS?

As promised, Miss Prickett returns to pick up the breakfast tray and to escort them to the so-called guest quarters. They follow her out of the library to find the corridor filled with light instead of the dark and dreariness of the night before. "Oh!" says Filomena. "It looks so different."

Miss Prickett clucks her tongue. "Like I said, we weren't informed we had visitors until this morning. You girls must have been so frightened in the darkness!"

"We were," says Filomena, still mystified. This is a punishment? How is it that the formerly dark and damp and smelly dungeon is actually a clean and well-lit space? As they walk through the cavernous entrance—which is now recognizable as the first leaky-ceilinged room into which they were tossed—Miss Prickett shakes her head. "I asked Leonard to fix that the other week! Leaky pipes, old castle . . . you know. Come along now."

Beatrice and Filomena exchange another confused glance. Filomena figures it's the right time to ask about the incredibly bone-chilling roars and the howling. But Miss Prickett is walking at such a fast clip, the two of them can barely keep up. They're led through corridors and past chambers in which various staff uncover furniture, fluff pillows, and dust tables.

"It's our guests!" cries a valet. He bows as they cross his path.

Guests?

Aren't they *prisoners* of the Beast?

What is this place?

Oh. Wait.

Filomena glances at bright, bookish Beatrice. She's certainly a beauty! And here she is, trapped in a castle owned by a howling monster: a Beast!

Oh, Filomena knows how this story goes. At least, she knows the way it's told in regular fairy tales and movies, as there's no Beauty and the Beast story in the Never After books yet. Maybe because that story is *happening right now.*

"Miss Prickett?" Filomena huffs, nearly running to keep up with the fast-moving housekeeper.

"Yes, dear?"

"This is . . . this is the Beast's castle, isn't it?"

"Come again?"

"The Beast's castle?"

"The Beast?" asks Miss Prickett, who stops and looks confused. Then her face lights up. "Oh! I forget that's who he's known as to the outside world."

"Why? Who's he known as here?"

"Oh, here we call him Lord Byron," says Miss Prickett.

"But, um, can we ask about the, um . . . the roaring and the howling?"

"Oh dear, dear," says Miss Prickett. "I do wish we had been told you were coming. You must have been terrified!"

Beatrice and Filomena both nod.

"I'll tell Master to keep it down. He didn't know. Oh, he will be so embarrassed! Now come along. Here we are at last." She throws open a door and leads them into an opulent two-bedroom suite. There are roses in a crystal vase on a marble table in the anteroom and four-poster beds draped with lace curtains. There's a gold bowl filled with the most delicious-looking fruit. Filomena stayed at a fancy hotel in Paris once with her parents, and it was just like this.

She walks around dreamily. "Oh wow."

"You will be much more comfortable here," says Miss Prickett proudly. "And now, Miss Beatrice, I will show you to your rooms."

"Oh, uh, she's not staying here with me?" asks Filomena.

"Oh no. Everyone needs their privacy." Miss Prickett

purses her lips as if the thought of not having privacy is most distasteful.

"But there are two beds?"

"Our guests find they like to alternate which bed they sleep in so that they always have fresh sheets. Will that be a problem?"

"Oh no, no problem," says Filomena. "Fresh sheets it is!" But she's worried. She'll be all alone here.

"Don't worry, she'll be right next door," says Miss Prickett. And with that, she leads Beatrice down the length of the hallway to another suite of rooms, leaving Filomena alone in a room fit for a princess.

Filomena is confused. She's not scared anymore, but she's still anxious. Even though she's not being mistreated, and hopefully isn't about to be eaten, she's still trapped somewhere she's not supposed to be. And she does need to get out of here. They both do, although, if the version of the story she knows is correct, Beatrice is supposed to stay and fall in love. With the Beast, no less. Lord Byron, Miss Prickett called him.

Filomena hears the housekeeper's quick footsteps outside her door and runs to catch her. "Miss Prickett!"

"Yes, dear?"

"I was just wondering . . . when can we, uh, leave?"

"Leave?"

"Yes, you said we're guests, right? So we can leave? Guests do leave."

Miss Prickett sighs. "Oh. I'm so sorry. That's not how it works. Master will explain, of course. Not my place."

So Filomena was right: As nice as it is here, they are still trapped against their will.

"But you can get messages to Wonderland, yes? You said the queen sent a message about us being here."

"Yes, she did."

"I was a page in the palace," Filomena says, formulating a plan.

"Were you? I worked in the palace myself a long time ago."

"So, um . . . would you mind very much if I asked you to send a message?"

"A message?"

"Yes, to someone at the palace. A friend of mine. A Chessman."

Miss Prickett looks doubtful.

"Please?"

"I suppose. No one's ever asked me to do that before."

"It's really important. You know how Chessmen are. Don't want to get on their bad side."

"Oh no, heavens no!"

"It's just a short note."

Miss Prickett agrees at last. "I suppose it's all right."

"Great!" says Filomena. She runs to the bedroom side table, and sure enough, there's a pen and stationery, just like in a fancy hotel desk. Except this says *BB Castle* on the top and has a coat of arms.

Filomena taps the pen against her bottom lip, thinking of the Queen of Hearts' ring-laden fingers. She needs to choose her words carefully just in case this note should fall into the wrong hands.

She decides to keep it impersonal, simple. Vague enough not to be suspicious. She does not write *SOS* ten times in a row with countless exclamation points. She does not weep on the paper.

But she does write.

Her hand trembles as she begins to pen the message.

> *Jack,*
>
> *In accordance with our assigned duties and what we both have sworn to do, I regret to inform you that I've been removed from your watch involuntarily.*
>
> *When you report back to Vineland, please inform them that my last-known whereabouts were said to be in the Beast's castle. Exact location unknown.*
>
> *Thank you for your cooperation in this matter.*
>
> *It's been my honor to serve alongside you.*
>
> *—FJC*

Filomena tears the paper from the pad and folds it up, hoping Jack will be able to decipher her message.

She hands the note over to Miss Prickett, letting go of the paper but holding on to her faith that Jack won't let her down. "Please see that Jack—er—Chessman Rook Jackson Green gets this."

"I'll do my best."

"And, Miss Prickett? Can I ask one more question? When are we going to meet this, um, Beast—I mean, Lord Byron?"

"Oh heavens! I really am losing my mind. I forgot to tell you. Master has requested both your presences at supper."

Supper?

That's a meal, right?

Filomena fervently hopes that she and Beatrice are not on the menu.

"I'll come to collect you when the dinner bell rings. It's a big castle; I don't want you to get lost," says Miss Prickett. She leaves Filomena to her thoughts once more.

CHAPTER TWENTY-TWO

MISSING

A few hours later, Filomena's tummy is rumbling. Miss Prickett promised she would collect them for supper, but so far there's no sign of her. If the dinner bell rang, Filomena missed it. She's spent the last few hours reading and forgot the time, but now she's hungry. Where is Miss Prickett? And where's Beatrice? And more important, where's this long-promised supper? Filomena had been lost in her books; she found several interesting tomes in the library, and time had gone by without her noticing.

It's one of the main joys of reading, she reminds herself. *The grand escape.* It's something she's always loved about books: The way they can whisk you away from your own reality, bring you somewhere else. The way they can take you somewhere that feels far safer than the place you're in. In her case, the place she's trapped in—literally.

Filomena is cross with herself. This happens much too often. She gets lost in the world of the story and forgets where she is and what she's supposed to be doing. But shouldn't she have been fetched by now? And where is Beatrice? Filomena hasn't seen her since they were escorted to their separate rooms. Filomena feels a cold anxiety begin to creep into her mind.

She tries to calm her racing heart by focusing on her breathing. With a shake of her head, she tries to get rid of the oncoming panic that's about to grip her. It's fine. She's not totally alone. She has Beatrice.

Filomena decides she'll feel better if she and Beatrice wait for Miss Prickett together, so she leaves her room, walks down the hall, and knocks on Beatrice's door.

"Bea?" Filomena calls out tentatively. "It's me. Are you there?"

No response. She calls Beatrice's name again, but again no answer comes. The quiet is eerie. The hallways, which were alive with staffers in a flurry of activity not so long ago, are now deserted.

Why isn't Beatrice answering? *Maybe she's just napping,* Filomena tells herself. She reaches for the door handle, sure it's locked . . . but it opens.

Filomena steps inside Beatrice's room. It's dark, but even in the dim light, Filomena can tell it's just like hers. Lush and luxurious; a proper two-bedroom suite with an identical vase of roses on a marble table in the anteroom. "Bea? Are you in here?"

She flips the light switch and the room illuminates. She finds Beatrice's cloak and bag, but not Beatrice.

Oh my fairies, thinks Filomena. What if Beatrice was already fetched for supper?

And what if she was the main course?

Which makes Filomena . . . dessert?

Thoughts start spinning in her mind at a million miles per hour and in all different directions. She gave that note for Jack to Miss Prickett. But what if Miss Prickett didn't send it to Jack at all? What if she ripped it up? Or what if she showed it to the Queen of Hearts? The Queen of Hearts had sent them here to be *devoured.*

Filomena didn't think she put anything that bad in the note. But now she's not so sure. Clearly it was enough to get Beatrice kidnapped—or worse.

Did the unseen monster prowling the hallways finally appear from the shadows? Did the Beast not only show his face but also snatch up Beatrice with no warning? The memory of the roars and the way the horrifying sound shook the walls around them comes back to Filomena's mind. Maybe she hasn't heard the roars since then because . . . he's *eaten!*

No. No, no, no, no, no. This can't be happening! Filomena closes her eyes and puts her hand to her forehead. She cannot be the reason her friend's in trouble. The cause of Beatrice's demise. She'll never forgive herself.

There's no love story if there's no Beatrice!

Now Filomena highly doubts that message even got to Jack or that it ever will. She's out of luck. She'll be down here for eternity. Or until the Beast comes for her next.

Filomena's anxiety picks up steam again, threatening to take her down with it. Her heart beats wildly now, thrashing inside her chest. She swears it might just come out her nose or fall out of her altogether.

A frantic feeling overtakes her—there's no stopping it. In this moment, there's nothing she can do but scream.

"Bea!" she cries. "Beatrice! Where are you?!"

Filomena calls Beatrice's name over and over, running through the dark palace in search of her friend. She races down the empty corridors, hearing only her footsteps in reply.

Her screams and shouts echo back at her, ricocheting off the rock-hard surfaces; now it sounds like this place is mocking her. The empty corridors and stone walls stare back at her as though amused by her terror.

Finally Filomena wears herself out. She collapses in a heap on the floor, curling her knees into her chest. She needs water. She needs air. Sunlight. Freedom. She needs to get out of here. She needs her friends and for Beatrice to be okay. What if she's not? What if Filomena's next?

She hugs her body together, trying to comfort herself. But it's no use.

She is truly alone here. And, as though she's in her own worst nightmare, no one can hear her scream.

CHAPTER TWENTY-THREE

LORD BYRON BEASTLY

After that pity party, Filomena tells herself to get up. She can't stay curled on the floor forever. She runs to the only place she knows that feels safe: the library. There's no Beatrice there, either, but at least Filomena has books. If the Beast comes for her, maybe she can throw them at him?

She hides in the library for what feels like hours but in reality is only a few minutes. The silence is broken when she hears heavy footsteps from somewhere down the hall. Beatrice? But they're too heavy and loud to be Beatrice's light step.

The Beast!

The footsteps come closer, closer . . .

And now Filomena can hear heavy breathing as well . . .

With a start, Filomena realizes she forgot to lock the library door!

But it's too late now!

She clutches a book in her hands in case she has to use it as a weapon.

As the footsteps get closer, she backs up against a bookshelf to the right of the door. The door is slightly ajar; maybe she can remain unseen long enough to surprise the intruder.

She gulps, trying to steady her breathing. The footsteps stomp down the corridor, making the walls rumble with each step and the ground shake beneath her feet. She reaches out to hold on to a shelf, steeling herself.

She presses her mouth closed, trying to keep in a scream that's begging to come out. The footsteps get closer, closer, closer, until—

The door swings open and in walks a behemoth of a beast.

He's freaking HUGE. And so . . . furry.

But . . . but . . . he's got on a tailored velvet dress coat— emerald green with gold buttons. And elegant trousers to match. He's dressed like a complete gentleman. He even carries himself like a gentleman!

But his face! It is the face of a monster. Leonine hair and

a long canine nose and nasty drool-covered fangs. He roars, and Filomena can't help herself. She screams.

The Beast turns to her and roars again.

Filomena drops her book and screams, "DON'T EAT ME!"

The Beast immediately stops roaring. "Oh!" He steps back.

Filomena watches him through her fingers. "Oh?"

"Oh dear! I'm so sorry! I did it again, didn't I? I scared you," he says. He looks wretched, and his face—which is a little like a lion's and a little like a buffalo's and a little like a wolf's—droops in seeming despair.

But Filomena is not fooled. "Don't come any closer!" she warns, picking up the book and waving it around. "I'll use this if I have to!" she adds, wielding the book like a shield.

For a moment the Beast stares at her, and for a moment Filomena thinks this is the end. That he'll roar once more, swipe the book away, and eat her alive.

But none of that happens.

Instead, the Beast chuckles.

His shoulders start to shake, and soon he's laughing a deep belly laugh that makes the whole room quake.

She holds on to the bookshelf again so she doesn't fall. Why is he laughing?! Does he like to toy with his victims before EATING THEM?

She looks at his belly for any sign of an arm or a leg

poking through. Is Beatrice in there? Did he swallow her whole or take her in bite-sized pieces?! On second thought, Filomena doesn't want to know.

The Beast puts a giant paw over his stomach, clutching himself as he continues to laugh. "Oh, oh dear, I'm truly so sorry," he says politely. "I don't mean to laugh, but you're holding that book, and I don't know what you mean to do with it, but it says *Cooking with the Queen of Hearts.*"

Filomena looks at the front cover. The subtitle reads: *One Thousand and One Recipes for Love.* There's even a picture of the author, who looks a bit familiar, like Filomena has seen her before, but where? In any case, Filomena, too, starts to giggle.

This doesn't make sense! She's laughing, and the Beast is laughing. This shouldn't be happening. Shouldn't he be attacking her? Mauling her? Eating her?!

This is not what she expected at all.

"Forgive me," he says. "If you were about to hit me with that, please, by all means, go ahead. I deserve it."

"I'm not going to hit you," Filomena says, "as long as you don't eat me."

"I assure you, I have no intention of doing any such thing," says the Beast, continuing to confound expectations. *He's so polite!*

"Um . . . okay, then," she allows, still wary.

"Once more, I offer my apologies," he says. "I told Miss

Prickett I would fetch my guests myself, but I've really made a mess of things, haven't I?"

"What do you mean? And where's Beatrice?" Filomena demands.

"About that . . . ," he starts. He gets sheepish then. One of his mammoth arms stretches behind his head, and he rubs his furry neck. Filomena could probably see a blush tint his cheeks if they weren't covered in brown fur.

"Where is she?" Filomena cries. "Did you eat her?!"

The Beast's face twists into a look that conveys he's appalled at the idea. "What? I'd never ever—I told you, I have no intention of, ugh . . . *eating* anyone."

"Really?"

At her surprise, his expression softens. "I guess I deserve that since people will tell each other all kinds of stories if one is not there to refute them. And I suppose all the stories attest that I'm some sort of monster . . . ?"

Filomena tilts her head to the side and looks at him as if it's quite obvious what she thinks.

"The queen sends me her prisoners to punish them, but I mostly just take them in as guests. I like to keep them around for company. It gets lonely down here, if you haven't noticed," he admits. "It's nice to have people to talk to sometimes. Most of them end up staying and working for me."

It *is* lonely in the castle. Filomena agrees with him on that one, so she nods in understanding. The more he talks, the more she feels kind of . . . bad for him. It's so sad that he's here by himself all the time, waiting for the Queen of Hearts to send him prisoners so he can have company.

"So you didn't eat Beatrice?" she asks, just to confirm.

He shakes his head. "Of course not. Quite the opposite, actually. I went to fetch her for supper and . . ." He starts pacing the room. "Well, you probably know what happened next."

Filomena can just imagine. "She screamed and ran."

The Beast nodded. "I should have known. Miss Prickett did warn me that she should be the one to prepare my guests for supper, but I didn't listen." He sits down in a giant chair in front of the library's fireplace and places his big paw under his chin, resting his head on it. "I insisted on doing it myself. I wanted to greet you both."

"Where is she now?"

"I don't know. I was looking for her, although that probably scared her more. Then I found you instead."

"Well, you do roar pretty loud," Filomena says sternly.

"Oh, I'm just calling for cocktail hour."

"Cocktail hour?"

"I always roar at a quarter to five so my guests know to meet me in the drawing room for drinks and snacks," the Beast explains.

"But yesterday when the library door was locked, you roared very angrily!"

"No one told me I had new guests! I thought I'd locked it accidentally. I was very frustrated."

"You really were," agrees Filomena.

"So where do you think Beatrice went?" asks the Beast.

"I don't know," says Filomena.

"She's very pretty, isn't she?" says the Beast. "And fast on her feet."

"She is that." Filomena nods.

"I am?" calls a voice. Beatrice appears from the shadows of the bookshelves.

This time it's the Beast's turn to jump.

They see Beatrice blush as she walks toward them. "I'm so sorry. I ran away before you could explain," she tells the Beast. "That was very rude of me."

"Quite all right. I must have given you a shock," says the Beast, looking forlorn.

"Beatrice Rose," she says, introducing herself and holding out her hand.

"Byron Beastly," he says. He walks over and crouches as if to make himself as small as possible. Tentatively he takes Beatrice's hand and presses it to his lips.

"Filomena Jefferson-Cho of North Pasadena," says Filomena. "And a handshake's fine."

"Pleasure to make your acquaintances," says Byron with a smile that somehow makes him look less terrifying. He shakes Filomena's hand with his paw. "My apologies again for frightening you both out of your wits. I forget what I look like sometimes."

"And please accept *my* apologies," says Beatrice. "I should learn to let people talk before I run away."

"Would you both like to join me for supper?" he asks, and his voice, though deep, is far from a growl.

"It would be our pleasure," says Beatrice. The three of them smile at one another as if something has been settled.

Filomena thinks this Beast is not much of a beast at all, other than the whole monstrous size and covered-in-fur thing he's got going on. She's pretty sure he's not going to eat them now. "Yeah, I'm starving."

Lord Byron offers each guest an arm bent at the elbow. "Come on then. Let's go get you girls something to eat."

Filomena sighs in relief. This is so much better than being *the* thing to eat.

CHAPTER TWENTY-FOUR

BEAUTY AND THE BEAST

Filomena adjusts Byron's bow tie, making sure it looks neat and straight. When she's satisfied with her work, she stands back to look him over. He looks so handsome in his dark navy suit and baby-pink bow tie. Very dapper.

She smiles and tells him so while giving him a thumbs-up. "You look great," Filomena tells him. "I'm sure Beatrice will think so, too."

They've been guests of Beastly Castle for a few days now, and Filomena has seen how Byron looks at Beatrice and how Beatrice looks at Byron. So far it's just like how the traditional fairy tale goes—they look like they're falling in love. And so today is the big day: Byron is going to ask Beatrice to dine with him solo. Filomena has offered to take her supper in her chambers, telling him, "I'm a big fan of room service. Don't worry about me."

"You really think I can win her heart?" the Beast frets, messing with his bow tie and making it crooked.

"The thing is—and this is what my mom, who's a romance author, always tells me—a heart isn't something you can win," says Filomena, reaching up on her tippy-toes to straighten the bow tie.

"It isn't?" asks Byron, looking crestfallen.

"No, because love is something that's given freely," says Filomena.

"It is?" says Byron, still sounding doubtful.

"You've got this," says Filomena. She puts out her fist. "Bump it."

He does so with his paw.

Maybe Byron is falling in love with Beatrice because Beatrice is the first girl sent to him as punishment. Maybe Beatrice is falling in love with Byron because she's had terrible luck with guys—at least, that's what she told Filomena last night. Everyone she's met has been a jerk or turned out to be an ogre. Whatever the reason, Byron and Beatrice seem to really get along and like each other.

Even though Filomena mostly finds the idea of romance and love still so cringeworthy in general (Boys = gross! Well, except for a few. Maybe just one. Someone whose name rhymes with Mack Walker . . .), she thinks Byron is a great match for Beatrice. Especially after getting to know him. He's so kind. He'd give the shirt right off his furry back for someone. Filomena knows this firsthand because he did.

The other night, Beatrice was cold and shivering, so Byron offered her his coat. He didn't even ask if she wanted it; he just took it off and wrapped it right around her shoulders.

Now he stands in front of a gold-rimmed mirror, adjusting his suit. "Okay," he says. "I better go so I'm not late."

"Have fun!" Filomena tells him giddily. "And remember: Just be yourself."

He nods and offers a shy smile. "Thank you for your help, Filomena Jefferson-Cho of North Pasadena, California."

Filomena returns his smile. "Anything for you, Lord Byron! Good luck."

With that, Byron heaves a breath, squares his big fluffy shoulders, and walks out of the chamber.

Much later, after receiving her room service meal from Miss Prickett, Filomena is settled in bed with her latest book when there's a knock on the door. A rapturous Beatrice enters. "Are you still up?" she whispers.

"I'm up!" says Filomena. "How'd it go?"

"Amazing," says Beatrice dreamily. "He's so sweet."

"He is!" squeals Filomena, who's enjoying having something like an older sister in Beatrice. "Tell me everything!"

"Well, he really is the kindest guy I've ever met! And he's not used to being called kind, you know. Usually people just run away; they find him scary and ugly. They are so wrong!" says Beatrice.

"Well, he is very large," says Filomena.

"Tall!" says Beatrice. "He's just tall!"

"And the fangs probably don't help," adds Filomena.

"I didn't even notice," says Beatrice. "He has fangs?"

"Um, two large ones, in the front," says Filomena.

"You know he doesn't even eat meat? He's a vegetarian," says Beatrice. "Did you know?"

Filomena shakes her head.

"And he's so funny!"

Filomena doesn't think he's any funnier than Alistair, for instance, but she supposes Byron does have a sense of humor.

"And he says I'm beautiful," says Beatrice. "No one's ever said that before."

"Really?"

"I mean, no one other than my family, but that doesn't count," says Beatrice.

Filomena thinks that still counts but doesn't argue.

Beatrice holds out a rose. "He gave me this. 'A rose for a Rose,' he said." She sighs. "Everything was so romantic. He made me close my eyes, and when I opened them, we were outside, in a courtyard, in front of this fountain. There was a small table for two and wildflowers everywhere, and we had this amazing dinner in the moonlight."

"Oh, Bea, did you ask him when we can get out of here?" Filomena wants to know.

"Oh that," says Beatrice.

"Yes that."

"He can never leave this place because of his curse," she tells Filomena. "He'll die if he does."

"But what about us?"

"I think we're cursed too, we can't leave," says Beatrice.

"Oh," says Filomena. But what about Cinderella? And Hortense? And the stolen glass slippers? And her friends? She likes Byron, but she can't stay here forever. Curse or no curse.

"But you know what?" asks Beatrice dreamily. "I don't even mind. I told him I loved the entire evening, but my favorite part of it was him."

That's nice and all, thinks Filomena, but she can't stay here. She has to stop the End of the Story from happening.

CHAPTER TWENTY-FIVE

THE RESCUERS

"En garde!" Beatrice cries, swinging her saber at Byron. It's a lighter version of a slashing cavalry sword. They both have on fencing masks, gloves, and shoes as well as metallic vests and knickers. They poke and prod at each other with a friendly competitive spirit, each one laughing when they score a hit on the other.

Beatrice pokes Byron in the ribs with the end of her weapon, and he feigns injury, falling to the ground.

He rolls over onto his side, his massive size taking up a decent stretch of earth. "Please, my love, go on without me," he mocks, tossing his huge hairy head to one side. "I am grievously wounded!"

Beatrice skips over and follows suit, dropping to the ground beside him and laughing. "Hold on, did you just call me 'my love'? I mean, I know you're only teasing, but . . ."

"I'm not teasing," says Byron.

This is when Filomena turns away to give them their privacy. She can hear the two of them murmuring, and soon they're cuddling on the ground. Filomena sighs. Love stories might be interesting to those living them, but they're not to anyone else.

She turns back to see what they're doing. She frowns. Ew! Did they just mask-kiss? She can't imagine what a kiss feels like. Her dad says she can't date until she's seventy-one. She thinks that's a little on the extreme end, though.

Still, it's sort of sweet to witness the blossoming romance between Beatrice and Byron. An odd couple, to be sure. One so large and hairy, and the other so slender and slight. Beauty and the Beast for sure. But somehow they just make sense.

"Who won?" Filomena calls. The couple breaks apart.

"Oh, it's not over yet," Byron calls back, hinting that he can still win. He holds out his paw to Bea, who reaches to grab it, and helps her to her feet.

Once they right their masks, they start swinging their fencing weapons at each other again, engaging in the dance of sport.

Just as they're duking it out, a warning rings across the castle grounds.

"Stand down!" someone calls.

The voice sounds familiar to Filomena. She sits up abruptly, searching for its owner.

She sees three figures running down the hill toward them. Their arms are raised, like they have weapons—real ones. Are those Dragon's Tooth swords?

Filomena squints to make out the uninvited guests. One of them is running carefully in a dress, yelling, "Ow, ow, ow, ow!" That's a familiar voice and a familiar figure in high heels. "I swear I'll make a fur coat out of you!" the girl threatens as she nears Byron.

Oh dear. That's Gretel! And the two next to her are none other than Jack and Alistair! They've come to their rescue!

Filomena's elated!

Until she realizes—*oh no, they're about to hurt Byron!*

Filomena rushes over to the lawn then, where Beatrice and Byron have stopped their sparring. Byron holds his raised paws in the air, as Beatrice turns to see the commotion.

"Oh! You're here! Gretel! Hi!" She waves happily.

When Gretel, Jack, and Alistair approach, Jack crouches low, ready to strike, his Dragon's Tooth sword poised in the air. "Put your weapon down!" he orders Byron.

"Right now, or else!" Gretel threatens, holding up her fabric scissors.

"Yeah!" Alistair adds, swinging his . . . ladle?

Filomena reaches the group and holds her hands out, motioning for everyone to just calm down. "Wait, wait!" she says. "It's not what it looks like!"

"Filomena!" Jack yells. "You're all right?"

"We're fine!" she assures.

"Really? It looks like this beast's attacking Beatrice to me!" Jack argues, weapon still up, stance firm.

"He's not attacking me!" Beatrice cries, dropping her fencing saber. She loops her arm through Byron's and clings tight to his side. "And he's not some beast! This is Lord Byron, and I . . . I love him."

Byron seems just as surprised as the others upon hearing this. He looks at Beatrice sincerely and offers her a warm genuine smile. "I love you, too, Beatrice."

While they gaze longingly at each other, the others become more baffled.

Gretel scrunches her face in confusion, lowering her scissors. "Bea! What! You love this beast?"

"I do," Beatrice responds, squeezing Byron's arm.

But her friends still look so bewildered. They exchange glances with one another, wondering if they should believe this. It all seems so farfetched. Weren't Filomena and Beatrice sent here as prisoners? To be punished? To be . . . eaten? Hanging out in the sun and fencing sure doesn't look like torture.

"Do you think this is another one of those candy dazes?" Alistair whispers to Jack. "It doesn't look like this place is made of gingerbread, but one can't be sure until one takes a bite." He approaches a nearby brick wall, licks it, and gags. "Ugh. Rocks. Not candy."

"Nope," replies Jack, steely eyes still on Byron.

"Brainwashed, maybe?" Gretel asks, her voice low.

"We can hear you, you know," Beatrice says, putting a hand on her hip. "And I can assure you, I haven't been brainwashed. Ask me anything."

"What day is it?" Alistair tests.

Beatrice thinks it over. "You know, I'm not sure." She looks at Byron. "What day is it, babe?"

Filomena shakes her head. This is absurd. Her friends probably think Byron is in cahoots with Cinderella and the Queen of Hearts. But she already knows the whole story, and so far there doesn't seem to be anything wrong with the regular fairy tale. They just need to give Byron time to explain.

"We can trust him, you guys," Filomena insists. "I'm serious. He's a friend."

Jack finally puts his weapon down and scratches his head. "If you're sure."

"I'm sure," says Filomena. She knows what they're thinking: They came to rescue the girls, but it appears as if Beatrice doesn't want to be rescued at all.

Because the thing is, they're not very much in need of

rescue, necessarily. Filomena just needs them to understand the curse. What they need is a way out of here without putting Byron or anyone else in more danger. And there's still Hortense's story to set right and a pair of magical glass slippers to find.

CHAPTER TWENTY-SIX
THE LAST BATTLE

"You sure about this guy?" asks Jack, pulling Filomena to the side before the group reconvenes to chat in the library.

"I am," Filomena replies. "He's definitely more bark than bite. Or more fur than fang?"

Jack crosses his arms, and his vines circle his wrists—a sign that he's troubled. "The thing is, since the Darkening, you can never be sure where anyone stands these days. If he takes prisoners for the Queen of Hearts, then who knows what side he's on?"

"I don't think he has a choice in the matter," she tells Jack. "I think the prisoners are part of his curse."

Jack raises an eyebrow. "He's cursed?"

"The dude looks like an animal. That's got to be a curse, right?" jokes Filomena.

He smiles thinly. "Right."

She changes the subject. "So you got my note."

"I did," he says. "Took a while to figure out where the Beast's castle was located, but we did it."

Alistair's head pops around a bookshelf. "What are you guys whispering about over here?" he asks, coming over to snoop.

"Oh, just telling Jack about Byron's curse."

"Cor, yeah, it's a bad one," says Alistair.

"You can tell?" asks Filomena. She's impressed.

"'Course. We Barnabys know all about curses. Mostly enchanted objects like lamps. But we can always tell when someone's been bewitched. Poor guy." Alistair shrugs. "Then again, the guy can probably take an ogre in hand-to-hand combat."

Filomena notices Jack staring at Byron, who's gathering chairs around the fireplace. "What?" she asks him.

Jack shakes his head, and she notices his vines slipping down to his fingers, as if he's getting ready for battle. "He just seems . . . familiar. Like I've seen him before."

Alistair squints at Byron, who's talking animatedly to Beatrice and Gretel. "Yeah, me too. Why is that? When did we ever know a Beast? I mean . . . sorry. A Byron?"

"Byron Beastly," Jack says slowly. "It's coming to me . . ."

But before Jack can say anything more, Byron is asking everyone to sit, motioning to the circle of chairs around the fireplace. "Make yourselves comfortable, please," he tells them, ever the gracious host.

Once the group is cozily gathered by the fireplace, Byron gets a fire going. He pokes at the embers until the flames lick and lap one another, rising. Then he settles into his large chair, relaxing back with Beatrice sitting beside him.

"It's an honor to have you all," Byron says, looking humbled.

Miss Prickett enters the room. "Oh! So many lovely guests! Shall I serve tea?"

"Yes, please, if you don't mind," says Byron.

"Tea!" says Alistair. "That means cakes, right?"

Miss Prickett winks. "And scones with lemon curd, and little sandwiches. Sound all right to you?"

Alistair gives her a thumbs-up.

"Thank you for having us," replies Jack. His tone is polite, but it's clear he has reservations of his own. "Do you mind telling us, Lord Byron, how you wound up here, taking prisoners for the Queen of Hearts?"

Byron runs a paw through his mane and down over the fur on his face. "It's a long story."

"We've got time," says Jack evenly.

Beatrice pats Byron's paw. "It's okay, honey. You can tell them. These are my friends."

"Any friend of yours is a friend of mine," says Byron. "Friendship is better than fine wine."

At that, Jack's eyes glint. "What did you say?"

"Oh, it's nothing," says Byron.

"*Any friend of yours is a friend of mine. Friendship is better than fine wine,*" echoes Jack, boring holes into Byron's eyes. "A friend of mine used to say that all the time."

"A good friend?" asks Byron.

"The best," says Jack, his jaw set.

Byron sighs. "You asked me how I came to be like this."

Jack nods.

"It's a delicate subject," Byron starts, choosing his words carefully. "One that's difficult for me to express. You see, I'm . . ."

Beatrice places her hand on Byron's arm, encouraging him with a soft smile. He returns her gesture with a warm look of appreciation.

Jack leans in, and Gretel and Alistair follow suit. Even Filomena, who's heard a small portion of his story and how he wound up here all alone, is riveted. She's been wanting to know more. Ever since he mentioned that he's—

"Cursed," Byron states gravely, his eyes clouding. He stares at a gold vase on his mantel that holds a single red rose. "I suffer from a terrible, life-changing curse." He looks down. "But the worst part is, I don't know when or why or how it happened, or who cursed me."

"What?" blurts Gretel. "What do you mean you don't know?"

"I know it happened when I was young and arrogant," says Byron. "And that a witch played a part."

"That's how the story goes," says Filomena, interjecting. "You were a landed prince, and an old lady came to your castle asking for shelter, and you turned her away. But she turned out to be a witch who cursed you for being selfish. And so you're a beast until someone falls in love with you for, um, you."

"You mean he was cursed for . . . being immature?" Gretel asks, forehead crinkling as she tries to understand.

"I suppose my arrogance certainly played a role." Byron raises his furry eyebrows. "Is that the story the mortal world tells about me?"

Filomena nods. "Pretty much. But if it were true, you'd have turned back to yourself by now. Beatrice is obviously in love with you."

Byron smiles and turns to Beatrice. "Thank you, darling."

Beatrice winks. "Oh, you're just lovable."

"The curse," says Jack intently. "So is that how you came to be like this?"

Byron shook his head. "No, the tale about the old lady who turns into a witch—none of that is true. I would never turn anyone away. Why, Miss Prickett came here and I took her in without question."

"You did!" says Miss Prickett cheerfully, returning with a cartful of teatime goodies.

For a few minutes, the only sounds are of contented chewing and sipping as they avail themselves of the wonderful treats provided by Miss Prickett's kitchen. The sweet old lady points out various-flavored macarons for Alistair, helps pour tea, and passes around milk and honey.

"Oh, Miss Prickett, you're so lovely," says Alistair with a contented smile.

"Thank you, dear," says Miss Prickett, patting the top of his head before they both turn their attention back to Byron's story.

"It was a long time ago," Byron explains. "There was a battle. That's all I remember. We were fighting the ogres. I fell, and the next thing I knew, I woke up here, like this. I don't remember anything more than that. But there was a message from the Queen of Hearts. It said I had to hold her prisoners in my dungeon and that I couldn't leave here without putting my life in danger. So I've been here a very, very long time."

"We all have," agrees Miss Prickett, sighing. "We don't even remember what life was like before."

"The Queen of Hearts said this?" asks Jack. "Was she the one who cursed you?"

Byron shrinks in his chair. "I . . . I don't know . . . I can't say." His eyes fill with tears and his lower lip trembles; he looks wretched. He appears to shrink into his furry frame. "I don't remember."

Jack leans closer and closer, and his vines twitch out of his sleeves and down to his fingers. "But *I* do . . . I think . . . I think I'm starting to remember. Alistair!" Jack turns to his friend. "Do you remember? The Last Battle?"

Battle?

Alistair, who's always seemed like such a kid, suddenly looks world-weary. "Which one? There have been so many."

"The one we lost."

"Oh, righto. That one."

Filomena leans forward. She knows about this battle. The one in which the fairy tribes made their last stand against the ogre witch. When the Tree of Life began to weep for all slain.

"You may not remember me, Lord Byron, but I remember you," says Jack, his voice gaining excitement and his vines twitching every which way. "And I think Alistair does, too."

Byron starts.

Confusion spreads through the room like a curse itself, contagious and quick.

"I'm sorry?" Byron asks. A shake of his head and then: "You know me? You must be mistaken. We've never met. I'm sure of it."

"Because the curse wiped your memory and took your face," Jack tells him.

"You mean he wasn't always a big giant hairy dude?" Gretel asks. At once she covers her mouth. "Sorry! I didn't mean to be rude! It just sort of . . . slipped out." She looks to Beatrice apologetically.

"Yes," Byron says. "I wasn't always a big giant hairy dude." Then his tone lightens, amusement in his eyes. "Believe it or not, I was handsome once. But I can't fault you for observing my current appearance. It's hard to miss."

Beatrice reaches out to touch his arm again. "I think you're very handsome," she whispers.

"I'm glad you think so," Byron admits.

Beatrice sighs and turns back to the group. "What are you getting at, Jack? Who is he?"

"Lord Byron Bessley," says Jack. "At the Last Battle, you fought bravely. We were by your side when you fell. You were taken by the ogres."

"We looked for you everywhere," says Alistair.

"And all we heard was this terrible howling," says Jack, remembering.

Byron drops his teacup, spilling tea all over the hand-knit rug. "I remember," he whispers, his voice shaky. Slowly he rises to his feet, puts a paw to his forehead, and stands at attention. He salutes Jack and brings himself to his full height, looking for all intents and purposes like a nobleman instead of a beast. "I remember now. Commander of the Order of the Rose at your service, my lord."

Jack stands up and returns the salute. "Commander Bessley, it's good to see you again. Alive."

The two of them stare at each other and then hug like the old comrades they are.

"What's happening?" Gretel whispers.

"I think . . . they know each other," Filomena replies.

"Duh," says Gretel.

Filomena ruminates on everything she knows about the tragedy of the Final Battle in the Never After series. The fairies' last stand before the Darkening. Before the Weeping. The last battle for Never After. When the fairies lost to Olga and her ogres.

Thirteen fairies were born to the Fairy King and Queen.
Esmeralda, Antonia, Isabella, Philippa, Yvette, and Claudine
Died in the last battle, defending the realm.
Josefa was betrayed, Amelia was slain.
No one knows what happened to Colette and Sabine.
Beautiful Rosanna married the King.
Clever Scheherazade spun a thousand and one dreams.
And the bravest of them all, Carabosse, was the thirteenth.

Ten of the thirteen fairies are gone. Lost. Dead. How many are left? Three at most?

Now Byron is crying. Jack is crying. Filomena has never

seen Jack cry, and she wants to look away, embarrassed some-how, but Jack doesn't look at all embarrassed, and once he and Byron finish the embrace, they bring Alistair into it.

"Prince Ali Baba!" cries Byron, lifting Alistair into the air. "I thought you were dead!"

"I thought *you* were dead," says Alistair happily, patting Byron on the back.

"Queen Olga of the ogres cursed you," says Jack. "She made you forget who you are. She turned you into a beast and imprisoned you in your own castle."

"It's all Queen Olga's fault," says Filomena. "It always goes back to her."

Jack nods. "The Queen of Hearts must be working with the ogres. That means Wonderland is in peril. And if Cin-derella marries Prince Charlie, then the only free kingdoms left in Never After will be Westphalia and what's left of Vine-land."

"So how do we break this curse?" asks Alistair.

"No clue," says Byron sadly. "But we're running out of time." He motions to the vase that carries the one red rose on the mantel. "My life is tied to the rose in that vase, and only one is left. Once that rose dies, I die with it."

There is a lengthy silence as everyone contemplates the last rose in the vase. Then Filomena pipes up. She's read all twelve of the Never After books, and she realizes she knows what they have to do.

"Only fairy magic can save him now," she tells them. "It's

the only way to break a witch's curse. It says so in all the books."

"Scheherazade is in Snow Country, rallying the dwarves to our cause and looking for Colette," says Jack.

"What about Sabine?" Alistair suggests. "Last we saw her, she was in Vineland, maybe she's still there?"

"I'll go to Vineland," agrees Jack. "I haven't been home in a long time."

Byron places a paw on Jack's shoulder. "Are you sure it's safe for you? Remember Sabine's warning at the Last Battle. And we've read reports from our spies around the kingdom that the ogres encroach on Vineland's borders. They could attack again at any time."

"It's the least I can do. I have to go back," Jack tells his friend, dismissing his concern. "We need to fix this. And if the ogres are in my village, then it's best that I am there to help."

"But what about us?" asks Filomena. "Aren't we stuck here now? Bea told me we were."

"Oh! My apologies. That's a misunderstanding. You were never prisoners here. The Queen of Hearts believes everyone is eaten and punished. But, um, Miss Prickett and I, we make sure none of that happens."

"I would never leave you anyway," Beatrice says staunchly. She glances back at the one last red rose, as if willing it to remain intact.

Jack stands. "I'll leave for Vineland immediately."

"I'll go with you," Filomena replies. "You two." She turns to Alistair and Gretel. "You go back to Wonderland. Make sure you get those magical slippers from Cinderella."

So many things to do!

Curses to lift.

Slippers to steal.

Fairies to find.

Ogres to slay.

They better get to it.

Ballad of the Winter Knight

Once upon a time in Vineland
There lived a boy named Jack.
When he was born,
Thirteen fairies came to give him their blessing:
Jack be nimble, Jack be quick,
Jack jump over every candlestick!
No fire will reach him;
No part of him will burn.

Keep him safe from harm;
Keep him safe and warm.
Jack will climb mountains
And roll down hills
With nary a scratch.
He'll always find an escape hatch.
Jack of the Frost,
Summer's Son and Winter Knight.
Thirteen fairies were born to the Fairy King and Queen.
Carabosse fled to another world.
Colette is still missing.
The only ones left are Scheherazade and Sabine.
Because the others died protecting him.

Part Four

Wherein . . .

Jack's true identity is revealed.

Filomena meets another aunt.

The clock strikes midnight!

CHAPTER TWENTY-SEVEN

SWOOP, BABY, SWOOP

Filomena and Jack say one last goodbye to their friends before they leave Byron's home and set out for Vineland to see if they can find Sabine, another one of the thirteen fairies. She also happens to be Filomena's aunt. Jack had insisted on going alone—it was too dangerous for the others—but Filomena refused to let him go without her. Especially to a place that's possibly under attack by ogres! Their friends agreed.

They've already taken their leave of Byron and Beatrice, and now it's time to say farewell to Gretel and Alistair.

"You guys come back soon!" Gretel says, pulling Filomena in for a tight hug. "They'll be okay, right?" she asks, turning to Alistair, who's been pumping Jack's hand in a hearty handshake for quite a while.

"Uh . . . yeah, of course they will," replies Alistair, and finally lets go.

But Gretel picks up on his hesitation. She shoots Alistair a sharp look. "Then why the pause?"

"Yeah, Alistair," teases Filomena. "Do you think there's a chance we won't come back?"

Alistair shrugs. "Can't stand the thought of anything happening to you guys, is all." His voice cracks. "You're my best friends."

In answer, an abashed Filomena gives him another hug.

"We'll be all right," says Jack, but his face is grim, and they all know he can't wait to get going.

Gretel sighs, lifting her skirt hem and clicking her tongue—her heels are stuck in the mud. "Come on, Baker, we've got to get back to Wonderland."

"Not with those spikes on your feet," says Alistair. "Why are you wearing them in the first place? We came to rescue Filomena, not give her a makeover."

Gretel rolls her eyes. "Cinderella insisted I wear heels. She said it's because *when you look good, you feel good* and I was being *bad*." She shakes her head in annoyance. "Then she went on to say how terrible I was at my job, of course. Really,

I think she just stuck me in these because she wants me to be as miserable as she is."

Alistair laughs despite the cruelty. "She really is awful."

"She is," Gretel agrees. "Be careful or she'll try to put you in a pair of these next," she teases, gesturing down to her stilettos.

Alistair frowns. "No way! She couldn't make me put those things on for all the cheeseburgers in the land."

Gretel scoffs. "You'd be surprised what that girl can do."

"Right, so, remind me why we're going back to Wonderland? I enjoy keeping my head on my shoulders," he says a little petulantly.

"Like we have a choice. If we all go missing, she's going to know something's up. Plus I'm going to get those freaking slippers back to Hori if it's the last thing I do," Gretel declares.

"You will," agrees Filomena. "We're counting on you."

Alistair sighs. "You really think you can steal them back? Beatrice already tried, and she ended up here." He motions to the Beast's castle, where Byron and Beatrice are waving to them from the patio.

"Fair enough," says Gretel. "I won't make the mistakes she made."

"Good luck," says Filomena. She looks over at Jack, who's fidgeting with his Dragon's Tooth sword, itching to get on the move. "We'll see you guys soon."

"'Course you will," says Gretel. "Because when this is all over, I'm treating us all to a day at the spa!"

Jack is quiet as they tread through the swampy grass of Wonderland, and Filomena doesn't want to intrude on his thoughts. As much as she'd like to offer some words of comfort and solace, she simply doesn't have any. What do you say to someone who's just found out their home might be under attack? That they might lose everything and everyone close to them . . . again?

The only sounds are their shoes sinking, then popping out of the muck, which is slowing them down.

Filomena sneaks a look at Jack's profile. Since discovering what happened to his friend Byron and hearing the news about his hometown, gone is the heroic, confident Jack Stalker she knew so well. In his place stands a beaten-down boy who seems like he's already accepted defeat. She hates seeing him this way.

"Hey," Filomena says softly. "It's going to be okay."

Jack looks over to her. "You don't know that. What if we don't find Sabine, and Byron dies? What if the ogres are already in my village? How can you say anything's going to be okay?"

"It just has to be. You're Jack Stalker. If anyone can save anyone, it's you." Filomena offers a small smile.

He returns an even smaller one. "I sure hope that's true."

"It is," she assures.

As a true Nevie, Filomena has read all the books; she knows how each one ends. And every one ends with Jack Stalker saving the day in some way or another. Even during the Last Battle, it was Jack who turned the tide, saved the remaining fairies from certain slaughter, and rallied the last of the troops together before the ogres could chop down the Tree of Life. The tree weeps now, but it survived.

"I'm afraid you think too highly of me, Filomena," Jack admits.

Filomena's taken aback and stops walking for a moment. "Why would you say that?"

Jack stops, too, waiting for her. "It's the truth," he says with a shrug.

"Don't put yourself down like that," she says in total seriousness. Her face is stern. She's about to wag a finger in his face, and pure restraint alone keeps her from doing so. No one likes a nag.

"I'm not putting myself down. I'm just . . ." He shrugs once more.

"Yes, you are, and we can't have that. Never After can't afford to have you feeling this way. I believe in you, Jack—we all do. But you have to believe in yourself, too. Because in the end, that's what matters most." With the impassioned speech behind her, Filomena quickly turns away, slogging through mud as she resumes their journey.

"I just don't know if I can be the hero everyone wants me to be all the time," he admits quietly.

Filomena feels her heart ache for him. The pressure. The responsibility. She never gave it a moment's thought that the weight of it could be enormous. Especially since Jack always takes things so lightly.

"You don't have to be anyone but yourself," she tells him.

Jack stands alone for a moment, then follows her at last. They don't say anything to each other for a long time.

They continue their pace as steadily as possible, walking through the muggy swampland. "At this rate it's going to take forever to get there." Jack sighs, lifting one boot out of a particularly sticky area. He shakes the boot and mud goes flying.

Filomena ducks, narrowly avoiding getting muck all over herself.

"Oh, sorry," Jack mumbles.

But Filomena isn't too concerned about getting dirty; she's just seen something in the surrounding area. Up ahead, in the distance, there's something that looks like . . .

"Look!" She points in the direction of a path winding through the swampland. Jack follows right on her heels as they race over to it.

"Finally," Jack says in relief. "I was so sick of trying to walk through all that muck." He extends his arms. "I've never been so grateful to see dry dirt in all my life!"

"Actually, I think we've come across something even better," Filomena says, leading them off the path and into a copse of trees. "Come on!"

Jack hesitates. And then, with a certain amount of reluctance, he follows Filomena, knowing she shouldn't go wandering around the woods alone.

Then, at last, he sees what she sees.

A tree with a heart-shaped opening in its trunk.

A portal. A swoop hole. A network that can take one across Never After in a *swoosh*. Really, they should call them swoosh holes. Or maybe, like in Filomena's world, they should just call them black holes.

"To Vineland!" declares Filomena, jumping headfirst into the void.

"To Vineland!" echoes Jack.

And off they go with a *whoosh*.

Whoosh holes. That's what they should be called.

CHAPTER TWENTY-EIGHT

VINELAND IS BURNING

At first when they climb out of the tree on the other side of the void, Filomena can't open her eyes due to the smoke. It's all over the area, covering everything in a thick gray cloud. She coughs into her palm. Smoke dances around them in the wind, blurring their vision the closer they get to the flames.

Jack stands still, looking all around at the nightmare they've entered. The ogre attack has begun. The village is aflame, cottages and castles burning before them. There are people screaming; their shrill cries echo into the sky. The village folk are scattered, running about. Some are on fire and trying to put themselves out while others are frantically trying to help.

Filomena's eyes widen in shock, the terror of the scene freezing her where she stands. "We have to help them!" she cries, running to a girl who's thrashing in pain on the ground, fire snaking up her legs.

Jack unleashes the vines on his arms as he races toward the girl. He laps them against her in an attempt to put out the fire that's trying to destroy her.

Eventually he succeeds and the girl stops screaming. Her wide eyes glance up at him. "Jack Stalker?" she questions in disbelief.

"Yes, I'm here," he tells her, kneeling beside her. "Are you okay?"

She shakes her head. "This is all your fault!" she screams. "You brought them here! Get away from me!"

Jack falls back, stunned.

The girl turns her back to him, running away and disappearing into the smoke.

"Why—why did she say that?" asks Filomena, who overheard everything.

Before Jack can reply, ogres rise out of the smoke, swinging massive clubs the size of small tree trunks.

"JACK THE GIANT STALKER!" one roars. "Give him up and you will be saved!"

"I'm here!" Jack calls, looking small and human compared

to the ogres' massive heights. He runs to the middle of the clearing so they can see him.

"Jack! What are you doing?" Filomena screams.

"I have to face them!" he yells back.

"But why—why do they want you?"

Jack doesn't respond.

The ogres stomp closer and closer.

Jack just stands there.

"Jack! What are you doing? Fight them! You have to fight them!" Filomena yells. "JACK!"

But Jack just stares at the burning village, the pillaging ogres, and the fleeing villagers. He doesn't move. He doesn't call his vines. He's frozen on the spot, unmoving, with only tears running down his cheeks.

Filomena comes right next to him and pushes him so that he trips a bit, suddenly snapping him to attention. "JACK!" she screams. "DO SOMETHING!"

At last Jack begins attacking, unleashing his vines, sending them whipping over the rubble and the smoldering grass, coiling around the ogres' knees and sending them crashing to the ground.

Filomena wants to cheer but then she sees an ogre sneaking up behind him.

"Jack, look out!" She yells just in time for Jack to whip around and unleash his vines, wrapping them around the ogre's neck and squeezing.

The ogre ceases to move, and only then does Jack let go.

Just as he does, another band of ogres comes stomping toward him. One hurls a club in Jack's direction, whacking him with a heavy thump.

Filomena cries as Jack falls to the ground, eyes closed. "Jack!" She rushes to him as the ogres surround him.

Filomena scoops up the heavy weapon that knocked out her friend and begins swinging it wildly in every direction. Somehow she connects with the group of ogres, hitting them in different spots. Some grunt in pain; others laugh with amusement at the little speck below them.

"Run, you stupid girl," the largest ogre warns, baring its teeth.

But she won't be dissuaded. She won't leave Jack's side. She groans in frustration and whacks the ogre on its toes. It starts hopping on the other foot, visibly annoyed. "Just kill her already, you idiots," it barks at the others.

She's grateful they're too dumb to have figured that out by themselves . . . until they all start coming at her. Uh-oh.

She begins to back up, knowing she can't take them all at once. She's totally outnumbered. Jack might be dead. He's definitely not moving. Her friends aren't here to rescue her this time. She's on her own. With a gang of angry ogres heading straight for her.

This is it, she thinks. *This is how it ends.* She doesn't bother to think about the Never After books. It doesn't matter. The story's being rewritten as she stands there, paralyzed with fear.

The nearest ogre's club is right above Filomena's head.

It's going to crush her skull. Filomena braces for the worst. She was ready to be eaten. She was ready to be mauled. But this—this is so much worse. She cringes. All she can do is squeeze her eyes shut and hope death won't hurt too badly. Holding her head in her arms, she braces for the blow—

And hears the ogre scream just as it's about to crush her into Filomena Jefferson-Cho pulp.

She opens her eyes and sees Jack's vines wrapped around the ogre's club. He wrenches it and the ogre away from Filomena, sending the big brute crashing to the ground. Then he makes quick work of the rest of the ogres surrounding her. One by one, the vines snake around their feet and legs, crawling up and around until they're pulled down in a fury.

The earth shakes as the ogres topple, thunderbolts crashing as they misfire. Filomena heaves a sigh of relief. *He's okay. Jack is okay.*

The ogres squirm and grunt as Jack tightens his vines' grip, squeezing the life out of them.

Filomena notices a straggler stomping toward Jack, sledgehammer raised in the air and at the ready. *Oh, no, not again,* she thinks.

With a warrior's determination, she screams, wielding her club and running toward the giant. Her war cry rings out as she runs and then bludgeons the monster again and again.

At last the ogre keels over.

"Wow," says Jack, running up to her. "And I thought Gretel was scary."

"Gretel's right: That is very relaxing," says Filomena. Together they look around at all the ogres who have fallen. The smoke begins to clear. Jack saved the day once more.

Or did he?

The surviving villagers are all staring at him. "Jack Stalker," hisses one. "We warned you to stay away. Stay away forever! Haven't you done enough?" The group of villagers, each one ashy, sooty, and burned, stare at Jack and Filomena with a murderous rage that is almost more frightening than the ogres' dumb hostility.

"Hey!" says Filomena. "Jack just saved all of you!"

But Jack only hangs his head.

"Jack Stalker!" another voice calls, cutting through the murmuring. This is a different voice. A clear voice like a bell.

They turn around.

A fairy walks toward them. She has striking dark hair and beautiful bronze skin. She strides across the rubble as if her feet don't touch the ground. Her eyes are as clear as the night sky and as deep as the ocean's depths.

"Lady Sabine," Jack says, kneeling at her feet when she's near. "We have come to offer aid and to seek yours."

The fairy answers him in a voice as sad and solemn as the Weeping Tree: "Jack the Giant Stalker, Ogre Hunter, Monster Killer; Crown Prince of Vineland; Winter Knight: Blood of my blood has been shed for millennia to keep you safe. You never should have come home."

CHAPTER TWENTY-NINE

HOLDING OUT FOR A HERO

There is an awkward silence in which Jack hangs his head as low as it can go and Filomena looks between the fairy and her friend, confused. That's a whole lot of titles, as Alistair would say. What did Sabine call Jack? Crown prince of Vineland? Jack's a *prince*? And what else did Sabine call him—a winter knight? What's that? Then Filomena remembers that Byron called Jack "my lord" when they finally recognized each other. Jack is . . . Who is Jack?

Sabine finally notices that Jack isn't alone. She looks at Filomena and starts. She waves her hand, and the scar on

Filomena's forehead glows. "Is it . . . ? I see the light of Carabosse in you. Can it be?"

"It's me," says Filomena shyly.

"Eliana," whispers Sabine. "Rosanna's child. The blessed one. We thought you were dead."

"I'm not," says Filomena. "Carabosse saved me."

"And my sister?" Sabine asks hopefully.

"Carabosse is gone. I'm all that's left of her." Filomena points to the glowing scar on her forehead. With all her heart, she wishes she had known the aunt who loved her so much.

Sabine nods. Then she gathers Filomena in her arms. "I was there the day everything happened. The christening . . . I thought I'd never see you again."

"I didn't even know you existed," Filomena admits, choking back tears of her own.

Sabine releases her and looks sternly at both Jack and Filomena. "Come, we must talk. Inside. There are spies everywhere."

She leads them toward the base of the largest oak tree in the area and knocks on the trunk. A door swings open, and they follow her inside. When it seals back up again, it's like they were never there at all.

Once safe inside the tree and with comforting cups of tulip tea in hand, Jack tells Sabine that word has reached

Wonderland about the ogres at Vineland's border. "I couldn't leave Vineland to burn again."

"The ogre queen has hunted you for years. She will never rest until she has her revenge. It was dangerous to return," Sabine says sharply.

Jack grips his teacup tight. "But if I hadn't come, the villages would have been destroyed and everyone killed," he says.

"They had me. I would have protected them," says Sabine. "It is not worth risking your life. You know how important it is that you live."

"Vineland has burned on my behalf before. I am nothing to this place but a scourge," he says bitterly. "I should never have been born."

At that Sabine's expression changes; a torrent of emotions washes over her unlined yet ancient face. "I was too harsh on you earlier. I was just concerned for your welfare, and I apologize," she finally says. "If not for you, Vineland would have fallen long ago. You saved its people from the ogres who were starving them. You incurred the wrath of the ogre queen for that. But it was you who showed us that they can be defeated when you killed the ogre king."

"But we lost the battle anyway," Jack says. "So many were lost that day." He stares hard into his teacup, as if afraid to meet Sabine's eyes.

"But we haven't lost the war, Jack. Not yet. Remember that. As long as there is a fairy alive in Never After, there is hope."

"Who are you?" Filomena asks Jack, her voice full of

wonder. She's read all twelve books in the series, and she thinks she knows but isn't sure. Not completely. So she turns to Sabine. "Who is he?"

"He is a gift from the fairies to this land. A hero," says Sabine with a smile. "A child blessed to lead the way. Like you."

Filomena feels a warmth all over, because she was right about Jack.

"I'm not a hero," Jack whispers.

Filomena looks at her friend. *This again?* Didn't they already go over this on the way here? "Excuse me?" she asks, putting her hands on her hips. "You're not a hero? The guy who literally came out of nowhere to save us from being roasted by the witch's son? The guy who single-handedly took down all the ogres out there?"

"You helped." He smiles.

She dismisses it. "I don't know about you, but in my books—and I have read all *twelve* of them—you *are* a hero. No, mister, you are *the* hero. And you know what else? You're my hero." There. She said it. Even though it made her face as red as a tomato, she said it. She didn't mean to blurt it out, but she didn't want to see Jack so dejected again. And everything she said was true. He is her hero.

Jack raises his eyes from his teacup and looks at Filomena. "I'm your hero?" he echoes.

"Well, um, yeah, I guess?" she says, like it's not a big deal.

They stare at each other for a while until, suddenly, they both begin laughing.

Sabine, confused, laughs with them. The sound of their laughter fills the tree with an unexpected joy.

"Why are we laughing?" asks Jack.

"Because if we didn't laugh, we would cry," says Filomena.

"You're pretty cool yourself when you get all fairy warrior," Jack says with an elbow to her ribs. "Not going to lie: It's kind of nice knowing someone has my back, too."

"Oh. Yeah. That's cool," Filomena says. "I got you."

"I see that," Jack says, with the biggest grin she's ever seen on his face.

"Don't get used to it, though," teases Filomena, grinning back.

Soon they're both blushing once more.

Jack turns away and coughs. Then he turns back to Sabine. "But I'm also here because I have a friend in trouble, and only a fairy can help us."

"Oh?" Sabine raises an eyebrow.

"Remember the Last Battle at the Tree of Life? When Lord Byron Bessley fell and the ogres took him? The ogre witch—Queen Olga—cursed Byron. She turned him into a beast and trapped him in his castle. He can never leave," Jack tells her.

"Oh dear! Poor Byron!" Sabine cries. "He was such a handsome young man! So very brave! Is that what happened to him?"

"Yes. We need to lift the curse and turn him back into himself. And his life, such as it is, was tied to a vase of roses, and only one remains. If it dies while he is still a Beast, then he'll die with it."

"There's only one spell that can undo a Beastly curse," says Sabine. "It's not going to be easy." She looks around for a feather pen and then writes down a few instructions on a piece of parchment, which she hands to Jack.

He reads it. "Okay."

Filomena tries to peek over his shoulder, but Jack folds it away before she can read the words.

"Okay?" echoes Sabine.

"Yeah," he says. "I'll do it."

The fairy looks at Jack with troubled eyes. "I cannot stop you. But think before you agree to this. Byron would never want you to provide such a sacrifice."

"He's my friend," says Jack. "I'll do anything for him."

Sabine nods. "You will have to."

Chapter Thirty

The Royal Ball

"And as for you, Princess Eliana, child of Rosanna who carries the light of Carabosse, also known as Filomena Jefferson-Cho of North Pasadena, California: You know what you must do, don't you?" Sabine asks.

"I'm starting to get the feeling . . . ," says Filomena.

"As I understand it, my sister wrote twelve books about our world. But the thirteenth is unwritten. You must tell the tales true and finish the story to undo all of Olga's evil deeds and tell the truth of Never After. Only in this way shall we finally have victory over the darkness. The truth shall shine over their lies, and our story will continue," Sabine says, her eyes glittering in the dim light. "This cannot be The End."

"I promise I will," says Filomena. "I'll tell the story."

"Now go," says Sabine. "The clock nears midnight, and there's still a story to be told."

"The royal ball!" cries Filomena. "We've got to hurry back."

Filomena and Jack return to the palace as a page and a guard once more and look for their friends. When they reach the kitchen, they find all the chefs and bakers hard at work preparing for the royal feast. Filomena motions to Jack to wait and pops her head around the doorway. "Psst," she whispers, trying to get Alistair's attention.

Alistair is very clearly struggling with one recipe in particular, since it appears as though all the ingredients have wound up on his clothes. So much for his baker's uniform being white. Filomena tries to get his attention again, this time by randomly shouting, "Is that a cheeseburger over there?"

Alistair drops his mixer and peers from side to side. "Did someone say cheeseburger?" he asks no one in particular.

The rest of the kitchen staff ignore Alistair, but he knows what he heard. Or he's pretty sure, anyway, as he glances around the room. Filomena waves her arms to try to get his attention.

"Filomena!" he cries, and rushes over. "You're alive!"

The other cooks look up, curious about the sudden commotion in the kitchen. "Is that a page?" someone asks.

Filomena palms her forehead. So much for staying undercover and unnoticed. She puts a finger to her lips and shushes him. "We're alive! Jack's here, too!" she whispers.

Alistair yelps and then freezes when he realizes all eyes in the kitchen are on him. He removes his baker's toque and wipes his forehead. "Oh, would you look at that! It's time for my break!" he announces, then leaves the room.

When he meets Filomena and Jack in the hallway, the three share a quick hug before Jack steers them away from the crowded area and toward an alcove where they can talk privately.

"You guys are okay! You're back!" says Alistair, who can't contain his excitement. "What happened?"

"Jack saved his village—again," Filomena tells him. "And, um, did you know he's a prince?"

Alistair looks at Jack before answering. "Um, yeah . . ."

"Is *everyone* a prince?" Filomena demands, remembering that Alistair has a title, too.

"Well, um . . . I mean . . . you're a princess, too," reminds Alistair.

"Oh, right," says Filomena, who's conveniently forgotten.

"Jack is the prince of Vineland, but more importantly, he's the Winter Knight," Alistair explains. "Long ago there were two fairy courts: the Summer Court and the Winter Court.

The Winter Court was slain by the ogre tribes. Jack is the last of the Winter Court's line, so when he was born, the thirteen fairies of the Summer Court blessed him as their hero. Jack of the Frost. Jack the Giant Stalker. Crown prince of Vineland. Blah blah blah."

"Right," says Filomena. "And in the books the Winter Knight is hidden from the ogres for his safety."

"Exactly," says Alistair.

Jack looks increasingly uncomfortable at this discussion of his provenance and background. "Okay, well, now that you know, can we focus on the mission? What's been happening? Was Gretel able to steal back the magic shoes?"

"Slippers," corrects Filomena. "Magic slippers."

"Technically they're mules," says Alistair, "since they don't have backs on the heel." He shrugs at the incredulous looks on their faces; Filomena's face in particular seems to say, *Who cares about fashion at a time like this?* He shrugs again. "What? You guys were gone. I've been spending a lot of time with Gretel."

"How is Gretel?" asks Filomena.

As if in answer, they hear a piercing shriek ring throughout the castle. "PRETTIER!" screams a voice from the direction of Cinderella's room. "MAKE THIS DRESS PRETTIER, YOU MORON!"

The three of them wince.

"Nothing will make her prettier with that kind of attitude," Filomena observes.

"Anyway, about the glass slippers?" asks Jack.

"Cinderella's got them under lock and key." Alistair sighs. "But at least Hori's received her invitation. She'll be at the royal ball tonight."

"Maybe Prince Charlie will still choose her to be his bride," Filomena says hopefully.

"Maybe," says Alistair.

Jack shakes his head.

Filomena bites her thumb and thinks deeply. They're supposed to steal back the slippers for Hortense, but the glass slippers are magic, a gift of the fairies. If Filomena has learned anything from reading about Never After and from living here, it's that fairy gifts are trickier than they seem on the surface.

"Maybe Cinderella's *supposed* to wear them," she says thoughtfully.

"She's certainly planning to," says Alistair.

A few hours later, Filomena, Jack, Gretel, and Alistair are gathered in an empty hallway upstairs. Filomena wears a bonnet low across her forehead; she's hoping the Queen of Hearts won't recognize her as the page who was sent away with Beatrice to the Beast's castle. Meanwhile, Gretel is fretting about having failed to steal back the glass slippers. "I tried everything, but she sleeps with them under her pillow," Gretel tells them. "The other night I almost managed to pull them out from under her, but they're sharp, and I almost poked her with them, and she almost woke up, so I left them. And I'm sorry about her dress, too."

"What happened to her dress?" Filomena asks.

"I made it gorgeous." Gretel sighs. "She looks divine in it. If she doesn't open her mouth, Prince Charlie might just fall for her. She's going to look incredible tonight."

"Oh," says Filomena.

"Like I said, I'm sorry," says Gretel.

"You couldn't help it. It's what you do." Filomena puts an arm around Gretel's shoulders to comfort her. "You're very talented."

"Maybe we can trip her?" asks Alistair. "And the slippers will fall off her feet?"

"Maybe," says Filomena.

Jack merely shakes his head. He's been quiet since their return from Vineland, as if the fate of the world is resting on his shoulders. Filomena can't blame him; it's kind of the truth.

A bell chimes in the distance, and the footmen make a big show of opening the palace doors. The royal fanfare plays, and the court steward announces that the party has formally begun. "The Queen of Hearts welcomes all to the royal ball for Prince Charlemagne of Eastphalia," he proclaims.

"What are we going to do?" Gretel frets, tapping her foot nervously.

"We're going to wait and see what happens and be ready to fight," says Jack, a hand on the pommel of his Dragon's Tooth sword.

"You think it will come to that? Some kind of battle?" asks Gretel.

Jack nods. "I can feel it."

"We'll be ready," says Alistair, who's traded in his dirty baker's whites for a server's uniform.

They follow Jack down the steps to the ballroom. Jack takes his place with another guard just inside, by the door. Alistair moves to the buffet line, standing behind a random dessert concoction of his own making, which looks inedible even to him. Gretel and Filomena shimmy their way into the crowd, trying to blend in as party guests.

"Princess Charlotte of Southphalia," announces the steward as a raven-haired beauty enters the room.

More guests are announced. Everyone who is anyone in Never After is here, from Dorothy the Great and Powerful of Oz to Lord Peter and Lady Wendy of Neverland.

After all the guests are arrived and announced, the royal fanfare plays again, and this time the orchestra launches into "God Save the Queen of Hearts." The Queen of Hearts enters the room wearing a striking black-and-white-checkered dress dotted with her signature red hearts. The queen looks indulgently at her crowded ballroom and takes to the dais. "Welcome, welcome, all. Thank you so much for joining us. May I present our honored guest, Prince Charlemagne of Eastphalia!"

Prince Charlie enters the room. He's a rather mild-looking guy in a stiff uniform decorated with many medals and sashes. There's nothing terribly exciting about him aside from the fact that he's a prince. Filomena steals a look at Jack in his Chessman regalia. She thinks he's much more handsome and princely.

Prince Charlie looks abashed as he bows to the queen. "Er, um, thanks, all, for coming." He waves gingerly to the crowd.

"Prince Charlemagne will be making a royal announcement tonight, won't you, Prince?" declares the Queen of Hearts with a smile. She looks as if she could eat him right up.

"Uh, yeah, I guess so," says Prince Charlie, who looks like he has no idea why he's at this event or what he's supposed to do. He keeps craning his neck to scan for someone in the crowd.

"I bet he's looking for Hori," whispers Gretel.

"Totes," says Filomena.

"Where is she?" hisses Gretel.

"I sent her the invite. She'll be here," says Filomena, crossing her fingers for luck. "Alistair said she received it."

The royal fanfare blares again, and this time the orchestra plays a popular love song. A dazzling creature enters the room in a dress the color of the brightest blue sky. Cinderella is the image of utmost loveliness. Her golden hair is piled upon her head with peekaboo tendrils wisping down. Her blue eyes shine like sapphires, and on her feet are the most delicate glass slippers. They catch the light and refract its rays.

"Prince Charlemagne," the Queen of Hearts says proudly, "may I introduce you to my daughter, Cinderella."

The prince bows deeply, and Cinderella affects the most flirtatious curtsy. Gretel curses underneath her breath.

"Let the dancing begin!" announces the royal steward.

"But where's Hori?" Filomena whispers. She catches Alistair's eye across the room.

Where's Hori? he mouths.

I don't know, she mouths back.

"She'd better be here," growls Gretel, "or she'll lose her chance for sure. That dress and those shoes are definitely casting some sort of spell."

They look to the front of the room, where Cinderella is talking animatedly to the prince. He doesn't look as if he's *not* enjoying it.

Then the doors to the ballroom open once more, and a girl steps through the doorway. "Look! It's Hori!" whispers Filomena. "At last!"

"Oh, she looks lovely!" Gretel sighs. "I'm so glad I had time to work on her dress before we left for Wonderland. It was my aunt's."

Hortense enters the room looking beautiful but nervous in a traditional dress from her family. It's a *hanbok* with a tight gold-colored bodice and flowing sleeves. A black satin sash is cinched around an empire waist that flows out into a crimson skirt. The fabric floats like the airiest balloon. Hortense's black hair is pulled up and away from her face, and she looks delicate and precious.

Hortense hands her invitation to the royal steward, her hand shaking a little as she does so.

"My apologies, we have one more guest. Presenting Lady Hortense Marie Rose of Rosewood Manor!" the steward announces.

There is a murmur in the crowd, but most comments are in appreciation of Hortense's beauty. Heads turn as she glides into the room.

"Hortense Rose!" shrieks an all-too-familiar voice.

The spell is broken. Heads whip from the back of the room to the front. Cinderella is starting to look purple with rage, the color clashing against the blue hue of her dress.

"Guards!" calls Cinderella. "There's an intru—"

But before she can finish the sentence, another voice rings out loud and clear. "Hori! There you are!"

It's Prince Charming—Prince Charlie to the rescue—striding across the ballroom, his eyes trained only on Hortense. He looks no longer sleepy and mild-mannered but alert and filled with purpose, as if the very sight of Hortense has animated his entire being, and maybe it has. Maybe he was just a nice guy, but now? With Hortense in the room, he's more than that. Maybe he's actually worthy of all this attention.

The prince reaches Hortense's side and bows deeply. "Lady Hortense!" he yelps, as if he can't quite believe it.

"Prince Charlie!" Hortense cries back, as if she can't quite believe it, either. They're staring at each other so intensely, it's as if they are the only two people in the room.

Filomena and Gretel inch forward so they can hear what the couple are saying. They clutch each other to keep from swooning. It's just so romantic. Better than any fairy tale.

"You made it!" Charlie says with his widest grin of the night. "I've been worried sick! When I didn't see your RSVP, I thought maybe the queen didn't send you an invite, so I asked my people to find out where you were, but no one knew."

Hortense's smile lights up the entire room. She, too, is changed by his presence. She's softer and more vulnerable, less brusque somehow. "I'm here now," she murmurs, and offers her hand.

"You're here now," echoes Charlie. His eyes do not leave her face even as he kisses the back of her hand.

"Ahem." Cinderella clears her throat, appearing behind him. "I'm here, too."

But no one pays her even an ounce of attention.

CHAPTER THIRTY-ONE

MIDNIGHT

"I'm sorry to interrupt," says Cinderella, speaking through gritted teeth and sounding not the least bit apologetic. "But I believe I have this dance." She flashes her dance card, which clearly has Prince Charlie's name written all over it for every dance.

Prince Charlie looks dumbfounded at this news. "Oh. Gee . . . but . . ."

Before he can protest, Cinderella has wormed her way between him and Hortense and is leading him away.

Hortense stands to the side, and Filomena and Gretel come up to her. "You okay?" whispers Gretel.

"Yeah, I am," says Hortense. "She can have this dance, for propriety's sake. But you know what? She won't have him." Her eyes flash with love. "He loves me. I know he does."

"Everyone can see it," agrees Filomena. "He's totally smitten."

"Except, um, guys?" says Alistair, who's sidled up to them from his position on the buffet line. "Weren't we supposed to steal back the glass slippers?"

"Well, it's kind of hard since she's still wearing them," Gretel points out.

Alistair does some pointing of his own and motions to the clock. "Well, just in case anyone cares, it's almost midnight."

Filomena wasn't sure what she thought would happen when the clock struck midnight and Cinderella was still dancing with Prince Charlie. But it certainly wasn't what happened next.

One moment Prince Charlie and Cinderella are dancing all over the ballroom, with the Queen of Hearts looking down at them with smug approval from her throne on the dais. From afar, they look like the couple they could have been, if they'd been in love and if everything was going the way the traditional fairy tale is told. Except, if one looks close, one might notice Cinderella has Charlie's hand gripped so tight that he couldn't go anywhere, and Prince Charlie is visibly sweating and looking over his shoulder to see where Hortense has gone.

Then the clock begins to strike midnight.

Bong . . .

Bong . . .

The orchestra continues to play the waltz . . . *Bong . . . Bong . . .*

"Oh!" Cinderella shrieks.

Bong . . .

"What is it?" asks Prince Charlie.

"Fiddlesticks!" Cinderella curses.

Bong . . .

Cinderella looks down at her feet in horror—they are somehow expanding, and then the glass slipper on her right foot flies off with an audible *pop*. The slipper flies through the air; Filomena dives to catch it.

Cinderella stumbles in Charlie's arms.

"Are you all right?" he asks.

Bong . . .

"Uh . . ." Cinderella grunts, tripping over herself as her feet continue to grow in size. She looks down and screams a scream so shrill, all the champagne glasses in the vicinity break.

Bong . . .

Another *pop*—the other slipper flies off Cinderella's left foot and hurtles through the air.

Bong . . .

Without missing a sip of her mocktail, Gretel catches it. Filomena and Gretel look at each other and high-five. They've got them! They've got the slippers back!

Bong . . .

And that's when Filomena and the rest of the guests notice what's happened to Cinderella's feet. Her feet! They're . . . so large! That's why the glass slippers flew off—because they can't fit anymore! Cinderella's feet are humongous! The size of gravy boats! And not only are they large; they're scaly and hairy and covered with bulbous warts!

And that's not all. Because as for the rest of her . . .

Bong . . .

Prince Charlie gasps.

The crowd screams.

"WHAT ARE YOU STARING AT?" Cinderella growls, her high, shrill voice replaced by a guttural snarl as the clock strikes its final chime.

Bong!

Midnight!

They're magic shoes, Gretel had explained early on their journey. *These glass slippers . . . reveal and greatly enhance the true beauty of the wearer.* Thus they have revealed the truth about Cinderella: Her ugly, grotesque personality matches an ugly and grotesque physical form.

Whispers begin to spread, becoming louder and louder

the more hideous Cinderella becomes. Surprisingly, no one's run out of the room yet, except maybe to grab a snack. "This is pure entertainment," says a lady by the buffet. "It's amazing what makeup can cover, right?"

Her friend chuckles in response, then covers her mouth like she shouldn't have laughed. "Oh wow, hurts to look at her," the girl says. "Literally pains my eyes."

Cinderella is hobbling along the marble floor. Her dress ripped at the bodice and the waist as she expanded in size. Hairy, bulging arms appear underneath the puffed sleeves of the ruined dress.

Prince Charlie takes more than five steps back. "What on earth?!" he yells.

Cinderella screams again, and this time it's a howl of rage. Her breath blows through the room and extinguishes candle flames as the long wail continues. As a result, the lighting dims; the ballroom darkens. Cinderella gets uglier and uglier.

The crowd is appalled—and also amused. The guests begin to laugh.

Filomena and Gretel share a shocked glance, both stunned into silence at the scene and unsure what to do next. They each hold a glass slipper. They're not quite sure this is funny.

"Will you look at that!" Gretel breathes. A giant wart is growing on the tip of Cinderella's big round snout of a nose, and even her hands are ten times the size of a human's; they look like bloated gloves.

"Is she—?" Filomena starts to ask, but she's interrupted by laughter that turns into screams.

She is.

"CINDERELLA'S AN OGRE!"

CHAPTER THIRTY-TWO

Like Mother, like Daughter? Part Two

Screams ring out and panic rises as the crowd finally recognizes Cinderella for what she has become. Guests start running about the ballroom, trying to find an exit. Bodies collide, sending glasses and plates of food flying. Chessmen rush in, the guards trying to keep the peace as best they can. But there's so much chaos that they can only raise their weapons on reflex, not having any idea what's going on. Or . . . who the enemy is.

Frantic shouts and screams surround them. "We have to get out of here!" someone yells. "Now!" another urges, voice high with panic. "OGRE!" screams another. "THERE'S AN OGRE IN THE PALACE!"

Filomena and Gretel pocket the glass slippers and go look for their friends. They run into countless people—a butler covered in sauce, a handmaiden drenched in drink.

"Filomena!" Alistair calls from across the room. The buffet line is all but destroyed, the silver serving dishes knocked over and spilled. Alistair is currently slipping into a mound of noodles and unable to find his footing. He seems to sink farther the more he tries to escape.

Filomena and Gretel race over to him, and Jack appears moments later.

The three friends take Alistair's hand and tug him loose from the mound of noodles wrapped around his legs.

In the middle of the ballroom, Cinderella's transformation is complete. The beautiful girl is no more, and in her place is a marauding beast. A marauding beast that is screaming for her—

"MOTHER!"

All at once the chaos and the screams die down, replaced with an eerie silence. The Queen of Hearts steps from her throne. No one screams; no one cries. There's no yelling or shouting.

Filomena glances up. She can see why everyone has fallen silent. The queen, before everyone's very eyes, has morphed into another queen. The Queen of Hearts is none other than the witch queen, the ogre queen, Never After's nemesis, the curse of the boglands—Queen Olga herself.

Like the rest of the guests in the ballroom, Filomena's too panicked to move, too terrified to make a sound. She can feel her fright all the way in her throat.

Queen Olga of Orgdale is back. Beautiful and terrible, her golden locks flying and her eyes like braziers. This is the witch queen who cursed a kingdom, who sent the fairy tribes into hiding, who rules almost all of Never After. Who planned to marry her daughter to a prince of one of the last free kingdoms. With Wonderland and Eastphalia under her reign, and Westphalia and Vineland battered and in ruins, Olga's power would be unshakable.

Filomena shrinks toward the ground, trying to remain unseen. Her friends are crouched around her. "Wait," orders Jack, a hand on his blade. "Wait till I say go. Then we attack."

The three of them nod. He made sure they are ready for this. This is what they are prepared to do.

Meanwhile, with each step she takes toward Cinderella, Olga further transforms into the oily, bulbous ogre she truly is. Her looming presence fills the room with utter malice.

Queen Olga stands proud beside her daughter. "My beauty!" she hisses in a voice like snakes and sandpaper. She kisses Cinderella on her pus-filled forehead.

"What happened to our real queen?" asks a brave soul. "What happened to the real Queen of Hearts?"

Olga laughs—a sound so terrible, it strikes despair into all who hear it. "What do you think happened? I ATE HER HEART!"

The crowd screams again. Filomena flinches and squeezes her eyes shut as if to leave this nightmare. She grasps the hilt of her Dragon's Tooth sword.

"Wait," cautions Jack. "Wait."

Olga surveys the room, her eyes running over the crowd and the impressive number of people. A wicked smile begins to grow on her lips. "That's right. I ate your precious Queen of Hearts. But I'm still hungry! And—how about that? Dinner is served."

She snaps her fingers. Each ballroom door shuts and locks, trapping everyone inside.

"Just our luck," mutters Jack.

"Why," groans Alistair, "are we always in *danger*?"

"Yeah, we'll have to discuss this later in the group chat," says Gretel.

Filomena agrees. Why the obsession with cannibalism? From the gingerbread house to the Beast's castle, it seems Filomena's always worrying about being eaten. And this time she and her friends aren't the only ones on the menu.

The Charge of the Thirteen Tribes

Half a league, half a league,
Half a league onward,
Defending the Tree of Life
Rode the thirteen tribes of the Summer Court.
Ogres to the left of them;
Ogres to the right of them.
Dragon's Teeth met ogre's hammer.
Winter Knight with Summer glamour.

Spells cast and thunderbolts crashed.

Stormed at with wrath and club.

Defending the Tree of Life

From witchcraft, malice, and strife.

Thirteen fairies were born to the Summer Court's Fairy King
and Queen.

Esmeralda, Antonia, Isabella, Philippa, Yvette, and Claudine.

Six fought bravely in the battle but fell at the last stand.

Lost, too, was Lord Byron Bessley, Jack's first in command.

From east to west, from north to south,

The ogres' march was never in doubt.

Westphalia cursed to sleep, Vineland burned,

While the Tree of Life weeps and Wonderland sinks.

All hope rests on the few who remain—

While the ogres hunt Scheherazade, Colette, and Sabine in vain.

The Darkening is upon the land; there's no changing the past.

Who shall rise to save this world at last?

PART FIVE

Wherein . . .

The Queen of Hearts is victorious.

Four Hearts Beat as Two.

Everyone lives happily ever after.

Or do they?

CHAPTER THIRTY-THREE

ATTACK OF THE LIVING OGRES

The possibility of being eaten alive is suddenly so much greater than ever before. Filomena takes comfort in the fact that, if this is how it ends, at least she's surrounded by her friends. "Come on, say the word, Jack," says Gretel, fabric scissors in one hand and her Dragon's Tooth sword in the other. "Let's get these witches."

Filomena unsheathes her sword as well, and Alistair does the same.

Hortense and Charlie run over to the group. "I left my bow and arrows at the inn," says Hortense. "I'm so annoyed!"

"Here," says Gretel, handing her cousin a glass slipper. "I mean, they're pointy." Filomena hands Hortense the other. Hortense smiles and holds the shoes out like daggers.

"Those are cool. Dragon's Tooth?" asks Charlie, admiring the group's impressive array of weapons. "Mine is mostly decorative," he laments, drawing his sword, which came with the uniform.

"All right," says Jack. "You guys take Cinderella. I'll face Olga."

"Not alone," says Filomena. "We'll do it together. I've got your back, remember?"

Jack smiles and doesn't argue.

"Um, guys? I think the time is now," says Gretel as Olga stomps down into the crowd and plucks her first victim.

The ogre queen has a hapless guest in the palm of her hand and is about to pop them into her mouth when she's inconveniently interrupted. She looks down to see Filomena stab her foot with a kind of small but very pointy sword. Olga's face shifts from mildly amused to not amused at all. "OUCH!" she shrieks, dropping the unlucky (or lucky) guest. "STOP THAT!"

Then she notices who is doing the stabbing. "It's *you!*"

Filomena looks up and doesn't back down. "It's me!" She'd hoped Olga wouldn't recognize her immediately—

she's grown a little taller since their last encounter in the cave, and her hair isn't quite as unruly. But no such luck.

Alistair, who's right behind her, chuckles nervously. "I guess she's still miffed about the whole lamp thing."

Filomena isn't laughing. She keeps her face straight and her eyes pinned on Olga. "Let them go," she says. "Leave these people alone!" Her voice is calm but firm. She tries not to falter under the queen's threatening stare.

"You already got your wish," Olga spits, her tone reeking of venom and vengeance. "Genie's not here to help you this time. Besides, it's my turn now."

"Nope," says Jack, who's shooting vines out of his hands. "Actually, I'm pretty sure you had your turn at the Last Battle. And you know what? I think the tide is turning. I think your turn is over."

And with a pull of his wrists, he sends the ogre witch flailing.

On the other side of the ballroom, Hortense, Charlie, and Gretel aren't having as much luck with Cinderella. The ogre princess is plucking guests out of the crowd and tossing them into her mouth like crunchy little morsels. And now she has a certain delicacy in her hands.

Gretel.

"I always thought you were too skinny to eat," says Cinderella with a smirk. "My brother was right in fattening you up!"

"Your brother? That creepy candy dude was your brother?!" Gretel squirms in Cinderella's grasp. "Good riddance!"

"Oh, he's fine." Cinderella yawns. "We got him out of there. He just has a tan now, like Mom."

"Hansel and I pushed your mom into the oven!" Gretel exclaims. "I saw it with my own eyes."

"And we got her out of there, too!" says Cinderella gleefully. "Don't you guys get it by now? Ogres always win!"

"Not in that dress, you don't!" says Gretel. "Look what you did to my beautiful creation!"

Cinderella scowls. "Actually, I thought it was kind of last season, to be honest."

"Oh, you filthy . . . ," Gretel rants.

"SHUT UP!" Cinderella screams right in Gretel's face, sending her hair flying.

Gretel wipes the ogre spittle from her cheek. She promised she'd treat herself when this was all over, but this is *so* not the kind of blowout she'd had in mind. She sticks her Dragon's Tooth sword into Cinderella's thumb and, using her other hand, stabs her with the fabric scissors.

"Owwww!" Cinderella yowls in pain and drops Gretel.

The ogre queen isn't having much luck getting rid of Filomena, Jack, and Alistair. Her attention is focused on Jack now. "I know you," she says, her voice full of venom and loathing.

"The Vineland twerp who killed my husband. The so-called hero. Why don't you run away like you did last time?"

Olga sees the looks on Filomena's and Alistair's faces and laughs. "Oh yes, your hero ran away, tail between his legs. He left the fairies to die and his friend to the ogres. He let his village burn. Some hero!"

Jack steps back, pain etched all over his face. He's shaking.

"He didn't have a choice!" Alistair yells, defending his friend. "He doesn't have to justify his actions to you!"

The ogre queen stomps closer and closer, and Filomena feels small, smaller than she's ever felt before.

"How many died because of you, Jack Stalker? Some Winter Knight you are. You don't deserve to live," Olga sneers, opening her cavernous mouth. "But I think I'll eat your friends first so you can watch them die." She reaches for Alistair with one hand and for Filomena with the other.

But before the ogre queen can grasp either, vines shoot out of Jack's hands and around her wrists and ankles, wrapping and trapping her where she stands.

"I may not deserve the gifts I was given," says Jack, "but I will do my best to live up to them!"

And just like that, the ogre queen is caught once more. Filomena heaves a sigh of relief.

Meanwhile, Cinderella has given up on eating Gretel. She now looms over Charlie, laughing a wild and bone-shaking laugh. "If you won't marry me, Prince, I'll have you any-way! I'm ready for dessert!" She cackles as she bends down, intending to pick him up and toss him down her gullet.

"Not so fast!" screams Hortense. With absolute precision, she throws both glass slippers at Cinderella. The shoes pin the ogre's hairy wrists to the wall before she can pick up and eat Charlie.

Charlie looks agape at the horrible ogress who was just seconds away from chomping his head.

"May I," asks Jack, appearing just when he's needed to wrap his vines around Cinderella's wrists—as he did her mother. He pulls the glass slippers from where they're stuck in the wall and hands them to Filomena, who hands them to Charlie.

Even as the fighting rages around them, Charlie knows what he wants to do. He accepts them and walks up to Hortense. He kneels before her and holds out the glass slip-pers. "Hortense Marie Rose, will you marry me?" he proposes.

"I thought you'd never ask," says Hortense, picking up her skirts and slipping her dainty feet into the glass slippers.

Charlie beams at Hortense. Hortense beams at Charlie.

Cinderella screams in rage. But it's too late. Hortense Rose will be queen of Eastphalia, not Cinderella.

CHAPTER THIRTY-FOUR

THE QUEEN OF HEARTS

Cinderella finally stops howling as she squirms against the vines that hold her tight. "Mother, help me!" Queen Olga stomps over to Cinderella's side, vines flapping from her wrists and ankles. "Just pull against them," she instructs her daughter. "They won't hold you for long."

Olga turns to Hortense and Charlie. "You may have stolen my daughter's happily ever after, but you'll never get to live it. None of you are leaving this place! Enough of this nonsense! Chessmen!" she orders.

"Hold on," says a new voice. A calm and reasonable voice.

A familiar voice. A voice Filomena has heard before. "Just a moment now, please."

"Yes?" Olga sniffs, turning to see who had spoken.

Filomena holds her breath and looks questioningly at Jack, who shakes his head. He doesn't know what's going on, either. Gretel is nursing a headache and Alistair is licking his wounds. But they're all riveted by the voice.

Miss Prickett appears out of the shadows. She's still wearing her maid's uniform. "It's been a long time since I've been to a party. We're not invited much anymore. And I was mostly looking for my friend Filomena, as we need her back at the castle. But once I got here, you know what's strange? I'm starting to remember things."

Queen Olga harrumphs. "Oh shush, you silly old lady."

"Like, this place . . . this was *my* palace." Miss Prickett marvels, walking around the ballroom. She stands taller than Filomena has ever seen her, no longer hunched over breakfast trays and tea service. Her back is straight, and her eyes sparkle with amusement and delight.

Olga steps back, outrage all over her purple-pocked face. *"Your palace?"*

"You've forgotten, haven't you? You've forgotten who I am," says Miss Prickett, removing her apron and her maid's cap. In a plain black dress, she's somehow impossibly elegant. *Why has no one ever noticed how impossibly lovely she is?* wonders Filomena. It's as if she's seeing Miss Prickett for the first time.

"Who are you?" demands the ogre queen.

"Why, Olga. Don't you remember? I'm the Queen of Hearts. The real one."

"You are! That's why you look so familiar," cries Filomena. "Your picture—it was on the back of the cookbook—*Cooking with the Queen of Hearts!*"

Miss Prickett looks at Filomena with a smile. "One of my many cookbooks. Try *Breakfast Bites with the Queen of Hearts*—that's my favorite."

"Enough!" screeches Olga. "Enough about breakfast. Get this imposter out of here! You can't be the Queen of Hearts; I *ate* her heart! She's dead!"

"I surely am not," says the Queen of Hearts with a chuckle. "I am very much alive. I just forgot who I was for a while."

"Chessmen! Seize her!" Olga commands. "CHESSMEN! NOW!"

Yet the Chessmen remain still. It's as if everyone in the ballroom is under a spell, but a good one this time, like a veil has been lifted from their eyes.

"Yes, I remember now. At the Last Battle, our side fought bravely, but so many of us were slain, so many of my friends who fought valiantly for this land we love. You took my son hostage and placed a curse on him," says Miss Prickett. "You turned him into a Beast."

She walks straight up to Olga so that the two of them are seeing each other eye to eye. The ogre queen shrinks away in distaste, as if trying to duck from the truth in Miss Prickett's words.

But Miss Prickett is relentless. "We lost, so you took my memory and my crown and my beautiful Wonderland and turned it into a hideous swamp. And the stories they tell about me now—that I'm horrible and obsessed with croquet, and that I scream 'Off with their heads!' at every provocation! Those stories about the Queen of Hearts aren't about me; they're about *you*."

"Oh, well," says Olga, looking bored. "Stories become truth. Lies become truth." She snickers. "That's how the world works!"

"Huh," says Miss Prickett. "I guess so. Chessmen," she says, pointing at Olga, "off with her head!"

CHAPTER THIRTY-FIVE

THE SACRIFICE

The Chessmen surround the ogre queen, but alas— Olga is more slippery and the slipperiest slipper. She takes her ogre daughter, Cinderella, and together they disappear in the clap of an Ogre's Wrath.

"You might have your castle and your precious Wonderland back, Alice Prickett," Olga booms from the ether. "But I'll find Sabine! And Scheherazade can't hide from me forever. Neither can Colette. Only three fairies are left, and when none live, Never After WILL BE MINE!"

With a terrible explosion of black smoke, the voice recedes.

"Oh thank goodness!" says Miss Prickett, shuddering. "I don't think I'd like to have seen her head chopped off, actually. Too gory." She turns to the crowd. "Ladies and gentlemen, it's wonderful to be back, but I'm afraid I have a pressing emergency to attend. Is Filomena Jefferson-Cho here?"

"I'm here!" says Filomena, raising her hand.

"You must come back to Byron's castle with me," says Miss Prickett.

"Is everything all right?" asks Hortense. "How is my sister?"

"Beatrice is quite all right," says Miss Prickett. "But Byron is at death's door. There is but one petal on the rose left."

"I know how to save him and lift the curse," Jack tells her. "We will go at once."

Filomena, Jack, Alistair, and Gretel head out with Miss Prickett, leaving Hortense and Charlie to clean up the mess made by the ogres. Back at the Beast's castle, they follow Miss Prickett to a small room off the kitchen, to a cot where they find Byron shivering under a blanket. He looks terrible; his fur is matted, and there are sores all over his body.

Beatrice is by his side, weeping. "I don't think he's going to make it!"

Miss Prickett puts a hand on Byron's chest. "Hold on, my son," she tells him.

Jack joins her next to the bed. "To break the curse, one must sacrifice their heart," he tells them. "That's what Sabine instructed." He removes his sword and holds it above his chest, his face determined and brave. "It's me the ogres want. What happened to Byron is my fault. I will give my heart for his."

"Jack! No!" says Filomena, and Gretel and Alistair gasp.

"Oh, my boy," says Miss Prickett, coming between Jack and Byron. "There's no need for that."

"What's going on?" groans Byron, his eyelids fluttering.

"Hush, my dear," says Miss Prickett. "Everything will be all right."

Byron startles. "Miss . . . Prick—hold on . . . Why do I remember now . . . Mom? Mom! What are you doing?" he stammers, attempting to sit up.

"Rest!" cries Beatrice, helping him lie back down. "Miss Prickett—I mean, Your Majesty, what are you . . . ?"

Miss Prickett looks at them with a benevolent smile. "All will be well, my dears. Now, Jack, darling, will you please hand me that lovely little blade you have there?"

Jack hesitates.

"Don't worry, sweetheart. You'll have it back soon enough," she says.

"Here you go, ma'am," he says, offering it to her with a bow.

"Thanks, dear," says Miss Prickett. She takes Jack's Dragon's Tooth sword in her hands and, without further ado, plunges the blade into her own chest.

The girls scream. Alistair yelps.

Jack runs to grab back his blade, but it's too late. "No!" he yells. "It was supposed to be me!"

They all watch in grief and horror as blood from Miss Prickett's heart seeps down onto Byron's chest. She falls to the floor, dead.

But then, something amazing happens. Byron's fur fades, and his wolf nose shrinks. His fangs recede. His body returns to human size beneath the blanket. When the transformation is over, the Beast is gone. In his place is a very, very, very handsome man. He has dark brown skin and deep black eyes, and his curly hair is cropped close to his head. His massive chest is muscled and defined in a way that harks back to classical statues of antiquity.

"Oh! Hi there," says Beatrice a little shyly. "You're almost too much to look at."

Byron smiles. "I hope you like me this way, too."

"I'll have to get used to it," says Beatrice honestly. "I kind of liked the Beast."

"He's still here," Byron promises with a flirtatious growl. Then he notices the strange, sad look on Beatrice's face. "What?"

"Honey, your mom . . . she . . ."

"Mom! Can you believe that was Miss Prickett? How could we have forgotten who we were to each other?" Byron asks, scrambling to sit up.

"Honey . . . ," Beatrice tries again. She points to the slumped figure on the ground next to the bed.

Only then does Byron notice that Miss Prickett's lying in a pool of blood. "Oh my fairies! Mom! Mom! What have you done?"

Filomena and Gretel have tears in their eyes. "She gave her heart for you," says Gretel. Filomena wipes the tears on her cheek, thinking of her own mother and missing her.

Byron falls down to the floor and holds Miss Prickett's limp body in his arms. His tears fall. "No, Mom, no. We just found each other . . ." He sobs into his mother's neck.

Then . . . magic.

Miss Prickett's wound closes. The blood draws away. She opens her eyes. "Oh, Byron, dear. There's your face! I've missed it so! You look just like your father," she says, patting his cheek.

"Mom!" says Byron. "You're alive! And I'm me again!"

"But . . . you gave your heart," says Beatrice.

"*One* of my hearts," says Miss Prickett with a warm smile. She truly is so lovely and kind. "Now enough of that, Son," she chastises. "Nothing to cry about here."

Mother and son hug each other fiercely. Miss Prickett pats Byron's back. "All is well, just like I said."

They release each other from the embrace, and Byron gestures toward Beatrice. "Mom, I want you to meet my fiancée," he says.

"Oh!" says Beatrice. "Are you asking me to marry you?"

Byron blushes. "Will you?"

"Yes." Beatrice smiles. "You know, you were a Beast, but you're also the first guy who didn't turn out to be an ogre."

"Welcome to the family," says Miss Prickett, pulling Beatrice in for a hug.

"Thanks, Miss Prickett . . . I mean, Your Majesty," says Beatrice.

"'Mom' will do just fine," says Miss Prickett with a wink.

Beatrice helps Byron out of bed and escorts him to his bedroom so he can change for dinner. Miss Prickett tidies her skirt. "I did make a big mess, didn't I?" She tuts. "I hope I can get the bloodstains out of this dress."

"I've got a great stain solution," says Gretel. "I'll share it with you."

"So Queen Olga wasn't lying after all—she *did* eat your heart," Filomena says thoughtfully.

"*One* of my hearts," Miss Prickett corrects once more.

"How many do you have?" wonders Alistair just as Jack kicks his shin.

"It's perfectly fine to ask. But a lady never tells," says the Queen of Hearts with a mysterious smile. "Now come on, who wants some breakfast bites? They're good at any time of day."

CHAPTER THIRTY-SIX

HERE COME THE BRIDES

The day of the weddings is a day not many in Never After will soon forget. It's the most perfect of perfect days, with the sun shining bright and all the courts of Wonderland and Eastphalia out in their finest regalia. It's as if a fairy godmother waved her wand and brought Wonderland back to life. The palace has been restored to its former splendor; its people are no longer harried and anxious but proud and productive. Filomena, Jack, Alistair, and Gretel are no longer undercover; they are honored guests at the double wedding.

Like the twins they are, Hortense and Beatrice insisted on sharing their wedding day, even though, as Hortense reminds everyone, they aren't identical but *fraternal* twins and look alike merely because they're sisters (duh).

Gretel has been working day and night on her cousins' wedding dresses. Hortense opted for a silky white slip, while Beatrice is going with a traditional cupcake-style ball gown, including a tight bodice, a long flowing skirt, and a veil.

The girls are gathered in the brides' suite at the palace. Hortense stands in front of a full-length mirror, fretting at the straps of her dress. Her long, straight black hair falls like satin across her bare shoulders and arms. She looks like a wood nymph, especially with the crown of flowers on her forehead.

"What's the matter?" asks Filomena. She holds two bouquets: one of red roses, the other pink.

"I don't know. I've just waited so long for this day. I want everything to be perfect."

"It will be," Filomena reassures her with a smile, "because I'm going to write it that way."

Hortense exhales. "Okay." She puts her hands on her hips and nods at her reflection. "Let's make those trolls at the *Palace Inquirer* who called me 'Hopeless Hori' eat their words."

Beatrice's head pops out from behind the dressing screen on the opposite side of the room. "Ready?" she asks with a shy smile.

The girls nod eagerly. Beatrice steps out from behind the screen, and Filomena and Hortense both gasp, their breaths hitching. Hortense's nerves appear to finally dissipate at the sight of her sister.

Beatrice has styled her hair in an elegant chignon. A thin strand of blood-red rubies around her neck is her only jewelry—"A gift from the Queen of Hearts," she tells them. Her dress is a confection of lace and embroidery with a tight corset and voluminous layers of the lightest tulle.

"You look radiant!" Hortense says, tears filling her eyes as she rushes over to admire her sister's dress. She takes Beatrice's hand and twirls her around, smiling the entire time. The tears threaten to fall.

Upon noticing the glossy look in her sister's eyes, Beatrice reaches out to wipe away a tear. "Hey, no crying today, remember?"

"Yeah," Gretel agrees. "No crying. That makeup took me hours!" she teases. "But seriously, you both look amazing." She lowers to the floor, fluffing Beatrice's petticoat and checking to make sure no more adjustments are needed to the hem of Hortense's dress. Once satisfied, she hops back to her feet. "I'm so happy for you two!" she tells them.

Hortense and Beatrice each hug and kiss Gretel in turn. Afterward, Hortense turns to the younger girls and wags a finger. "You guys are next!" She laughs.

Gretel scoffs. "Um, we're underage? And I have no intention of ever getting married."

"Really?" asks Beatrice, taking her bouquet from Filomena.

"Totally. I plan to be married to my career," says Gretel cheerfully. "What's next for me is a mani-pedi!" She holds out her hands as evidence. "Look at these! They're like claws!"

Gretel's still shaking her head and the other girls are laughing when a knock sounds on the door. "Come in," Beatrice calls.

The chamber door swings open, and Alistair's head pops in.

"Hey, guys," he says, peeking inside. "Five minutes till the ceremony starts." He's wearing a gray-pinstriped morning suit with a jaunty top hat and boutonniere. He whistles. "Looking good, ladies."

Hortense and Beatrice beam at Alistair. "Thanks," they chorus. They've grown used to this lately. Both brides, both sisters, both getting married on the same day. It's easier to have just one conversation together rather than two apart.

"Not so bad yourself." Filomena smiles at Alistair, who proudly pulls on his lapels to show his appreciation.

Hortense takes a deep breath and faces her sister. They squeeze each other's hands. "Ready to do this?"

Beatrice twinkles back at her, nodding. "Do you like Byron? I mean, we've known Charlie for ages, so he's always been like a brother to me. But you only just met my guy."

In answer, Hortense squeezes her sister's hand tighter. "I already love him like a brother. He's wonderful. And he's so lucky."

"I only wish Mom and Dad were alive to see this day," says Beatrice.

Hortense blinks away her tears. "Me too."

"Oh! I almost forgot," says Gretel. "Dad sent something through the portal." She leaves the room and comes back with a box. She opens the parcel and shows them what's inside: another pair of magical glass slippers, exactly like the original. "He says he should have made two pairs in the beginning since his sister had two daughters."

Beatrice reverently takes them out of the box. "For me?"

Hortense claps her hands in delight. "Now we really match!" Her own glass slippers shine on her feet; they're no worse for wear despite being used as projectile weapons.

Another knock at the door. This time it's Jack. "Um, I think it's starting," he warns. "People are a little restless out there. The Caterpillar keeps threatening to turn into a butterfly." Like Alistair, Jack wears a formal morning suit with a jaunty top hat. He tips it to Filomena. "You look nice."

"So do you." She smiles and tries not to blush this time.

Gretel, Filomena, Jack, and Alistair leave the brides and look for seats in the courtyard. A few minutes later, the royal musicians play the familiar strains of "Here Comes the Bride" as Hortense and Beatrice walk down the aisle hand in hand, carrying their matching bouquets and wearing their matching glass slippers. ("Glass *mules*," whispers Alistair.)

At an arbor of flowers stand the grooms. Byron looks the pinnacle of health in his commander's uniform, all square shoulders and newly shaven face. Charlie, eyes crinkling in the sun, looks spiffy in his princely regalia. Both wait for their soon-to-be wives.

The Queen of Hearts stands between them with a warm, benevolent smile for the two couples, as well as for all who journeyed to see them wed. "Today is indeed a happy day," the queen declares. "Today is a day when two hearts beat as one. Or as the case may be, when four hearts become two."

Alistair pulls on his collar. "Oof, this is itchy." He leans over to whisper, "Do you think there's candy at the reception? I've got a taste for it again."

"Shh!" Filomena elbows him. "They're about to say 'I do'!"

"Who is?" replies Jack, leaning forward.

"Both of them!" says Gretel with a laugh.

As if on cue, Beatrice and Hortense say "I do" at the exact same time and then kiss their husbands—a little too long and deep, if one can be perfectly honest.

Jack, Alistair, Filomena, and Gretel each frown in their seats and whisper "Ew!" at the exact same time while the rest of the audience claps.

CHAPTER THIRTY-SEVEN
GIFTS OF THE FAIRIES

After the weddings, Beatrice and Byron take off to Bali (at Gretel's suggestion and with instructions on how to find the portal) while Hortense and Charlie stay local—well, sort of. Charlie is so taken with Jack's Dragon's Tooth blade, he proclaims, that what he wants most of all—save for his new blushing bride—is that very item.

So his wife, who is likewise keenly interested in adding a few Dragon's Claw arrows to her quiver, decides they should honeymoon with a little trip to the Deep, where they can pay the dragons a visit and procure more of this weaponry.

"Tell Darius I sent you," Jack adds with a wink. "And brush up on your riddles!"

At last it is time to go back. Back to North Pasadena, where nothing ever happens; back home to Mum and Dad, who are no doubt on the edge of anxiety, waiting for their precious daughter. Jack assures Filomena that time works differently in her world; when she returns, it will be as if she went to dinner and came back just a few hours later.

In her room in the palace, Filomena finishes scribbling notes for her book. She has to finish what Carabosse started: She has to tell the tales true. As she writes their adventures, she rereads a line in the Prophecy about the fairies' gifts. Aladdin's Lamp was one, and so were the Stolen Slippers. But when Filomena asked Sabine about Jack's real identity, what did her aunt call him? *A gift of the fairies . . . Like you.*

Thirteen blessings the fairies gave;
All the gifts that ogres crave.

So the two of them—she and Jack, that meant they were part of the fairies' gifts, too. That's why the ogres hunted them. Why Queen Olga poisoned Filomena's mother, Queen Rosanna, and married King Vladimir. And why Jack's village was burned down.

The ogres want to bring about the End of the Story. No

more Never After. No more fairies. No more fairy tales. Or at least, they want the mortal world to know all the wrong versions of the story, so that the truth disappears from memory and only the lies live on. Well. She won't let that happen. She'll write the Thirteenth Book. She'll keep the real fairy tales alive.

Filomena shudders as she packs her notebook into her backpack full of books, wondering if she'll ever feel safe knowing what she knows now. She knocks on Gretel's door to find her friend bouncing up and down on her suitcase in an attempt to close it while bickering with Alistair, who's helping to zip it.

"No, a hamburger has NO cheese," argues Gretel, straining as she pushes down the lid of her suitcase. "That's why it's called a hamburger and not a cheeseburger."

"So a hamburger only has ham? That doesn't make any sense," Alistair retorts. He's out of breath from pulling the zipper.

Gretel sighs loudly in exasperation, but at least she's finished packing.

"Come on, you guys, we can show Alistair the difference when we get back to the mortal world," says Filomena.

They find Jack waiting patiently in the hallway. He leads them to the throne room, where Miss Prickett is waiting to say goodbye to her guests.

"I hope you come visit again soon," says Miss Prickett, who's packed them all box lunches.

The four are promising they will when a breathless page with a look of horror on his young face enters the room. "Your Majesty! We just received a message from Snow Country!"

"Yes?"

"It's from Scheherazade. She's found Colette, but they are under attack. Queen Olga has learned of their location, and they call for aid."

"Zera! She's in trouble!" says Filomena.

Jack springs to action and motions for the message so he can read it himself. The page hands it over. "This has Zera's mark on it," Jack says. "It's real."

"I have a feeling that our spa day is going to have to wait," Gretel laments.

"Cheeseburgers, too." Alistair sighs. "No rest for the weary, is there?"

Miss Prickett thanks the messenger and turns to the group. "We have just begun to reclaim Wonderland. I cannot spare any Chessmen right now, I'm so sorry."

"It's safer if we four go alone," says Jack. "We can move quickly without being detected."

"I guess that means I should store my luggage," Gretel says to no one in particular.

"Not me. I'm bringing my books," says Filomena, shouldering her backpack. She has her headlamp, her safety whistle, her Dragon's Tooth sword, and her notebook. She's ready for whatever comes next. She'd love to go home, see her mom and dad, and tell them she's okay. But time works differently here; she comforts herself by thinking how, in her parents' reality, she hasn't been gone all that long.

"Snow Country then," says Alistair. "Cold this time of year, isn't it?"

"We'll need parkas," Gretel realizes. "I hope I packed my puffer."

"Is this helpful?" asks Filomena, retrieving a book from her collection and showing them a map of Never After that's printed on the first two pages.

Jack studies it. "There's a shortcut through Northphalia that'll take us right where we need to go."

Filomena puts the book away. Together with her friends, Filomena leaves Wonderland for another hair-raising, ogre-packed adventure. Maybe this time she won't have as much fear of being eaten alive, but she highly doubts it. Perhaps she is very tasty.

ACKNOWLEDGMENTS

A big wave of a wand of thanks to all the sorcerers who made this book happen: my amazing editors and friends Jen Besser and Kate Meltzer, and the entire Macmillan team: Kayla Overbey, Linda Minton, Allison Verost, Molly Ellis, Mariel Dawson, Beth Clark, Aurora Parlagreco, Veronica Mang, Melissa Zar, Teresa Ferraiolo, Mary Van Akin, Olivia Oleck, Kenya Baker, Brittany Pearlman, Jennifer Healey, and Allene Cassagnol. I hope one day to meet you all in person and not just on our Zoom screens.

Thank you always to my agents and friends Richard Abate and Martha Stevens at 3Arts, and Ellen Goldsmith-Vein at Gotham Group. Thank you to all my family and friends. Thank you to all my loyal readers. Thank you to Mike and Mattie—everything is for you.